Return of the Sphinx

LAURENTIAN LIBRARY 10

 Macmillan of Canada / Toronto

Return of the Sphinx

Hugh MacLennan

Copyright © 1967 HUGH MACLENNAN

All rights reserved. The use of any part of this
publication reproduced, transmitted in any form
or by any means, electronic, mechanical,
photocopying, recording, or otherwise, or stored
in a retrieval system, without the prior consent
of the publisher is an infringement of
copyright law.

ISBN 0-7705-0255-5

First published by Macmillan of Canada 1967
First published in the Laurentian Library 1971
Reprinted 1971, 1972

The lines (adapted slightly) from "Where Have
All the Flowers Gone?" by Peter Seeger,
on page 58, are used with permission
(Copyright © 1961 by Fall River Music, Inc.).
All rights reserved.

Printed in Canada
for The Macmillan Company of Canada Limited
70 Bond Street, Toronto

Francescae Alinae Carissimae

Book One

ONE

THE LAND defied everyone's idea of what a land ought to be; just the land by being where it was, what it was and how it was. A month and a half ago people had been saying that another cold cycle had established itself, for seven inches of snow had fallen on the tenth of May; after that came weeks of cold rains and now, suddenly, this.

It was a Saturday afternoon hotter than Singapore and almost as humid. The atmosphere was a golden soup with the sun afloat in it and Gabriel Fleury had played golf at a club on the verge of the city. He was not a good golfer—he preferred winter to summer on account of the skiing, at which he was very good—but it was the only summer game he knew and physical exercise was the one permanent security in his life. Without it he felt disagreeable to himself. He felt a lovely release on the relatively few occasions when a good ball soared away; he liked the fresh grass of the fairways and the coolness of copses when he hunted for lost balls and best of all he liked the sensations afterwards: relaxed muscles, a sense of being easy with things.

On this afternoon they gave up after nine holes on account of the heat, and the other three of the foursome went to their showers immediately. Gabriel sat alone in the shade of the club veranda and gazed out over fairways deep-green from the long rains of June. The changed air of the last three days had created a different kind of country; if it lasted like this for a year it might even create a different culture. The heavy aspect of the trees in this unusual light, the velvet shadows over the alluvial land near the river, reminded him of France in deep summer and his mind ached a little and not without pleasure. Several miles away the city sweltered like a kiln, but here the soft air and subtle light imparted to the entire landscape a European formality that called his memory home.

He had been sitting there with his thoughts for more than half an hour before Tarnley appeared, dropped into the empty chair beside him and made some philosophical comments on the climate. A climate with such violent changes ought to produce a violently dramatic people, he said; it was strange that it hadn't done so.

"Give it a little more time," Gabriel said and Tarnley shot him an appraising glance.

Gabriel had never met Herbert Tarnley before that afternoon, though he had heard of him often enough. In a country where rich men had been flourishing like flowers and weeds in a well-manured garden, Tarnley had become a minor legend. In his appearance he was no typical North American businessman. He looked a little like an English statesman of the Edwardian period with a face sceptical, civilized and sure of itself. He wore his authority as unobtrusively as he wore his clothes and, though older than any of the other three men in the foursome that day, he had been the best and steadiest player. Though Gabriel had noted that no man could own a pair of eyes like Tarnley's without having earned them, the man did not seem any ordinary user and destroyer of people like most of the tycoons he had met.

Gabriel took out his cigarettes, offered the package and was refused with a wry smile.

"I gave those things up long ago," Tarnley said. "I let them bully me out of them. If I didn't feel better without smoking I'd be ashamed of myself. These days you can't pick up a newspaper without being told by some scientist

2

that whatever you're doing is going to kill you." He smiled wryly again. "And I can remember a day in 1917 when I told myself that if I was alive a week from then I'd have lived forever!"

"If I may say so, you don't look old enough for the 1914 war."

"I was old enough. Indeed I was old enough for it." Tarnley had a strange smile. "To be perfectly frank with you, the second installment didn't even interest me once I knew we were going to win it. It was in the first one that it all started. I mean when it *all* started. I suppose you were in the second one?"

"After a fashion."

While Gabriel smoked they talked of minor things until Tarnley glanced at his watch, remarked that it was five o'clock and asked if Gabriel would mind driving him back to the city when he left the club.

"Jack drove me out and I've only just discovered it's his anniversary. He and his wife had been planning a quiet dinner out here and they hadn't expected me. I suddenly decided I'd better come to Montreal to look things over for myself. I've been here more than half the week. But if it's a trouble to you, don't bother. I can call a taxi."

"It would be a pleasure," Gabriel said, and rose and went to his shower.

While the water splashed over him he wondered idly what this strange rich man wanted of him, his instinct saying that he wanted more than a drive back to his hotel. He left the shower feeling a little cooler and soon he and Tarnley were in the Saturday-afternoon traffic returning to the city. Tarnley began talking of France with the tenderness of a connoisseur of old furniture and glass, without a trace of sentimentality, and Gabriel warmed to him. Tenderness of this sort went so rarely with the kind of ability Tarnley must have. Finally he heard Tarnley asking why he had emigrated and remarking that so few Frenchmen ever did.

Gabriel smiled. "As you said yourself, it all began in the 1914 war."

"But you must have been a baby then."

"My father died of his wounds a little while after the war ended. My mother came from Ireland and after his death she took me with her to Dublin and for a time we lived with her family. It was toward the end of the Irish troubles and in spite of being Irish nationalists they sent me to an English public school for a while."

"I guessed that much from your accent, of course. But Jack told me you did your university work in France."

"Yes, I did."

After a moment of silence Tarnley asked, "Are you a brother of Armand de Fleury, by any chance?"

"For heaven's sake! He's my second cousin. Where did you run across him?"

"I've known him for years. One of my hobbies is riding, and that explains it. The last time he was over here he was my guest for a few days. You know, when I first saw you I thought for a moment you were Armand himself. The resemblance is amazing. You could pass for twins."

"That, I'm afraid, is all too possible."

For in Gabriel's family so many distant cousins had married each other over the years that they all looked somewhat alike. Gabriel had a theory that the concentration of genes had never given the outsiders a chance; he also had a theory that his family was like the Catholic Church: a united front to all heretics, but on the inside a maze of variations, of loves and guilts and broken hearts all held together by the bond of a common loyalty which was a kind of fate. There was so much love-hunger in his family, so much greed for the love of others of their own blood, so much doubt in each individual of his worthiness or ability to win it, so much difficulty in understanding that outsiders were also real people like themselves. Those who were secure in love were exploited by those who were insecure in it, these latter seeking authority within the family and usually getting it, so that Gabriel, his sense of flesh being their sense of flesh, he slowly acquiring an understanding of what motivated them while none of the others ever did, had come to the conclusion that all the politics of the world originated in the nurseries of large families like his own or in the despair of outsiders who craved to belong to such groups and didn't: thence were translated into public life, but the origin always the same, the process the same, love-hunger growing imperceptibly into hunger for power.

"There's no question in my mind," Tarnley was saying, "that your cousin is one of the three greatest riders alive. I love watching him. That man commanding a horse—it's as though his body is a part of the animal with his brain ruling the whole combination and loving it. When I see him like that he's one of the proudest sights I've ever looked at."

Gabriel laughed. "You make me envious of him. You know, Mr. Tarnley, Armand was the only one of the whole lot of us who was ever able to turn the family curse into a way of earning a living. And I doubt if the others have ever forgiven him for doing it."

The de Fleurys—Gabriel had dropped the *de* from his name when he crossed the Atlantic—were of the *petite noblesse* of the French provinces. Their first remembered ancestor had been honored on the battlefield by Henri IV and had previously been a small land-holder in the far southwest. Before the King's death he had been granted land in Dauphiné where his descendants had remained ever since. During and after the Revolution they had been consistently on the wrong side of politics and had lost most of their property, and for this failure they had compensated by increasing their pride. The pride of the un-appreciated, Gabriel believed, was the strongest and most self-destructive emotion anyone could nourish.

Regardless of their financial condition his family had never changed its ways. Scraping and saving, often going cold in the winters, they had sent their sons to Saint-Cyr

5

or Brienne, from which the young men graduated to offer their lives in the service of government after government they had been educated to detest and despise. They were still doing it. Last summer on a visit home Gabriel had learned that one of his many cousins had been killed in Viet Nam and that still another had disappeared in Algeria. His own father had been a colonel in the Chasseurs Alpins and in memory Gabriel was apt to confuse him with a Spanish gentleman painted by Velázquez; eyes baffled but undaunted, an expression dignified by tragedy. It had been universally assumed that the character of Colonel de Fleury had been a noble one. An aunt of Gabriel, unmarried as so many of his aunts were, had told him on the day of his father's funeral that he was going to grow up to become his father's double. The little boy had been terrified by the idea. Yet, so far as physical appearances went, his aunt had been right. He had inherited the colonel's wiry physique and reticent mouth, the dark hair so stiff he could wear it only *en brosse* and wished this were not so because he disliked the crew-cut so much. But he had not inherited his father's eyes or his father's expressions, at least not as he remembered them. He felt half-guilty, sometimes, because he had not, just as he also suspected that there must be something lacking in his character because he had abandoned his family and gone to live in the New World.

Tarnley was speaking again: "I understand that Alan Ainslie's a close friend of yours."

So this was it! Gabriel forgot about his father and became alert.

"We flew together in the war," he said casually. "I mean, we were in the same *équipage*. He was my pilot. He was my squadron leader too, as a matter of fact. I did some navigating for him for a time. We bought it, finally. We ended the war in the same prison camp."

"After that you must feel closer than brothers."

"I don't know. I have myriads of cousins, but I have no brothers. I was an only son."

6

"Ainslie's an exceptional man," Tarnley said thoughtfully. "In the early days of the war I saw quite a lot of him. That was when he was with External and we had all those arrangements with the Americans. In those days he had quite a way with him. I don't know how to put it—he was unusual. I mean, he never made any effort to be unusual, but that's how he was. I took quite a fancy to him. I've always liked men who insist on being themselves, if you know what I mean. Suddenly I found he was in the Air Force. Did he ever tell you how he worked it? He was classified, of course, and they didn't want to let him go. So what did he do? He went to C.D. and C.D. got him in. C.D. told me that himself, and he wasn't even in C.D.'s department. C.D. was a rare judge of men, God rest him. He told me personally he worked that for Ainslie even though Ainslie was technically over-age for active operations."

Gabriel smiled. "He was the best pilot on our base. He had the reflexes of a boy of nineteen."

"I haven't seen him since the war. How seriously was he wounded?"

"At first it looked pretty desperate, but he came out of it very well finally. He has a glass eye but you don't notice it. There's a skin graft on the left side of his face and he limps slightly, but he wasn't hit in the spine or the head."

The city was thickening around them as they drove in. They were running through one of the new, mass-produced suburbs of red-brick apartment blocks, all of them identical, that had mushroomed around the city since the war and turned so many real-estate operators into millionaires. The rise of the mountain was visible ahead and when they climbed the crest of Côte Saint-Luc they saw the wide expanse of southeastern Montreal pouring down the slope of the mountain and in the distance the St. Lawrence blue-gray under the heat-haze.

"Ainslie was in the news again today," Tarnley said quietly, but in a changed tone that Gabriel took note of.

"I heard it on the car radio on the way out to the club."

"Since he's been in the government he's been in the news pretty often. That department of his attracts it."

"It was about that riot here yesterday."

"I was afraid that was going to land on his doorstep." Tarnley gave a rueful laugh. "It seems that it didn't exactly land on it. He seems to have invited it in. He asked the ringleaders to confer with him in Ottawa this morning and afterwards they all met the press."

Gabriel made no comment on this and it was not until they stopped at a traffic light that Tarnley spoke again.

"You know, Gabriel—do you mind me calling you Gabriel?—things are getting out of hand in this country you chose to live in. I'd like to talk to you a little about it, but before I begin—are you *du côté français,* as they say in this city?"

"I'm not *du côté* anything. I just live here and earn a living."

"But the French Canadians must talk more frankly to you than they'd ever talk to someone like me."

"Yes, they do. But that doesn't make me any kind of authority on what's happening here. Talk?" He shrugged his shoulders. "Man is a talking animal. People can talk themselves into anything."

Then Tarnley asked him the anticipated question. "What I really want, of course, is your opinion of this so-called revolution here."

"Perhaps I'd better ask you first what your own particular interest is."

"That's fair enough. I've got some very valuable business in this province. It's no secret, God knows. For quite a while I've been reading these things in the newspapers, but to be frank with you it's only in the last week that I've begun to take them seriously. After the last few days I've spent in this city, I've begun to ask myself whether I shouldn't move my business out of here."

This statement was of course a question, but Gabriel,

who had heard it often before from businessmen from the outside, did not even try to answer it.

"Of course it may be nothing but politics," Tarnley went on. "If that's all it is—" He shrugged slightly. "But I have a feeling that this time it goes deeper. Would you agree?"

"On the whole, yes, I would."

"It's all very peculiar. I know quite a few French Canadians and I like them. I always have. They can't accuse me of not speaking their language, either. But they're too suspicious. Their priests teach them to complain from the cradle against the rest of us. Whatever goes wrong here, they're taught to blame it on us. Sometimes I think if we turned the whole country over to them they'd complain because we hadn't left them with anything more to complain about." Tarnley went on in the tone of a puzzled man thinking aloud to himself. "You see, in the past this French-English thing was never personal. In the old days, whenever I came to Montreal, I used to look up one of their politicians whose stock-in-trade was French-Canadian nationalism, but that never made the slightest difference between us. I always considered him a good friend and I knew he felt the same about me. But now it seems different. This time it seems to be personal. I'm beginning to think they really hate us now, and honestly I can't understand why they do. Am I right?"

"Maybe I could answer you if I knew what real hatred is."

"My men here aren't stupid," Tarnley went on, "but none of them can tell me anything definite. One of them's an Englishman—very experienced. He speaks reasonable French and up to now he's always liked the French better than the Canadian English. That's why I picked him for the job." Tarnley's forehead wrinkled. "Well, this Englishman's spent a lot of time in Kenya and he told me only yesterday that the old queer sensation he used to have in Africa was coming back to him. He told me he felt as though an invisible curtain had

9

suddenly been drawn. On the surface everything calm and normal, but now—nobody's told him this, mark you—now he tells me he has the feeling that the French Canadians have all made up their minds about something. He feels he's being quietly watched. Well, Gabriel—how does that strike you?"

Gabriel smiled slightly. "It strikes me that your Englishman's a very intelligent Englishman."

"He told me something else. I remember his exact words—'Mr. Tarnley,' he said, 'I haven't got a single shred of proof, but I can't help believing that this country's on the point of breaking up.' So, Gabriel—is he being sensational or is he on the right track?"

"How would I know? Nothing here ever seems to turn out the way it does in other countries."

Everyone Gabriel met from the English-speaking provinces sooner or later asked him questions like these and he would have answered them directly if he could. But he really did not know. One day he was sure of one thing, the day following of its direct opposite. The French Canadians were very different from the French of France and over against them was the Anglo-Saxon attitude which looked on life as a series of problems to be solved by intelligent management. Religion and their own peculiar history had made the French Canadians a people capable of tragedy—yes, and of the dignity of tragedy. Everyone knew of their previous isolation and how it had built into them a kind of tribal endurance. But now they were no longer isolated in their spirits, and the young generation was finding itself lost and excited in a new world. But it was more than this, much more. What was happening here—or rather what he dreaded was going to happen—seemed to him a part of the mysterious emotion which was sweeping the world and causing crowds to break the windows of American embassies in country after country.

"I saw that riot with my own eyes," Tarnley said. "They staged it right underneath our windows and interrupted a board meeting. I tell you, Gabriel, it was something entirely new in this country. It wasn't a strike. It didn't seem to be in favor of anything in particular. It was nothing more than an explosion of mass emotion so far as I could see. First of all, they burned Moses Bulstrode in effigy. Well, that wouldn't have cost me any sleep. Sometimes I've wanted to do more than burn him in effigy myself. But after that they tore down the flag and burned that too. I watched their faces and rubbed my eyes. I wondered for a moment if I'd bought the wrong plane ticket and landed in Indonesia by mistake. But what really shook me was the attitude of the police. They did nothing to stop it. I even saw a few of them laughing." Tarnley paused a moment. "So naturally, after that I want to know who's behind it. If the police behave that way, it's more than students and leather jackets. Do you know?"

"Not only do I not know, but I don't know anyone who does."

"You can't even guess?"

"Mr. Tarnley, has anyone really succeeded in explaining the French Revolution—I mean, when you add Napoleon onto it?"

Tarnley gave him another appraising glance and nodded affirmatively.

"So that's how you see it? Yes—I get the point. Certainly all this talk of independence makes no sense when they run the whole province and a good deal of the federal government as well. Politically they're as independent as you and me right now. One of my men is sure they'll soon be taking to guns and bombs—what do you think of that?"

"I try not to. When I came over here I thought I was going to be rid of those things forever."

"It doesn't make any sense."

"Mr. Tarnley, do you really expect things to make sense?"

Tarnley laughed and Gabriel slowed down for a traffic light and came to a full stop.

"Your friend Ainslie," Tarnley said, "has been right pretty often about Quebec. I mean in a general way, of course. You still see him, I suppose? What does he really think these days? I'm not talking about what he says in public. He's been saying that for years and now it's his job to keep on saying it, but what does he really think at the present moment?"

"I haven't seen Alan for months and I've been asking myself the same question."

"Then let me ask you another one—what about the Church in this?"

Gabriel shook his head. "Three-quarters of those rioters you saw yesterday don't give a damn what the Church thinks of anything. The old control is gone."

A cloud shaped like Australia was bulging over the mountain and the sun darkened. The traffic light changed and the car rolled on. A flurry of wind upset the leaves and their undersides flashed pale gray, but it was still hot and in the distance he could see sunlight glittering on the chrome and glass of the new skyscrapers in the center of the city. Now they were driving past the stone and brick houses recently described by a nationalist politician as *les châteaux des riches Anglais*. High trees shaded the roofs, the gardens were bright with flowers and sprayers were curtseying to each other on the lawns. Gabriel was an architect by profession; his work had made him fairly familiar with the patterns of land-holding in Montreal, and the legend that this district was an Anglo-Saxon fortress seemed to him about as substantial as Hitler's claim that the Germans are a pure race. All kinds of people lived here besides rich Anglo-Saxons: rich Jews, rich immigrants from Europe, rich French Canadians, even a few not-so-rich doctors and dentists and college professors.

Tarnley appeared to change the subject. "By the way, have you ever met Moses Bulstrode?"

"Not off a television screen."

Tarnley shook his head. "I'm sorry for Ainslie. I really

12

am. Of course, the old Prime Minister is a tragedy. Personally, I never did believe he'd be successful when he finally took office, but—well, look at what's happened! Bulstrode had been sitting on the back benches since the mind of man runneth not to the contrary. That riding of his up in the Ontario bush has returned him automatically for more than thirty years, and the Old Gentleman, when finally he got to power, decided to reward Bulstrode's loyalty. For loyal Bulstrode is—professionally so. And patriotic he is—professionally so. And honest he is—and here let me tell you he's so honest he doesn't even include the tips in his expense accounts. I know that for a fact. But the Old Gentleman has never been the same since that gall-bladder operation a year ago and that was one of those little things that can have such strange results. Bulstrode always admired the P.M. He's a curious, solitary type, Bulstrode is, and the fact that he talks so much only proves that he's much more solitary than people think. He's one of those lonely men who read a lot and carry on dialogues in their own minds. The P.M. was one of the few men in Ottawa who ever invited Bulstrode to his home, and the moment the P.M. was off the danger list Bulstrode haunted the hospital. I don't think he did it for any ulterior purpose at all. I think he just liked the old man. But when he got out, the Old Gentleman told people that Bulstrode was the most underrated man in this country. He said he pulled him through by sheer moral force, and ever since then Bulstrode's been his man Friday. At the moment a number of key departments are virtually funnelled through Bulstrode to the Prime Minister and your friend Ainslie's department is one of them. Of course, the effect of all this sudden power on Bulstrode might have been predicted. I wish Ainslie'd never run for office. He'd have done better if he'd stayed with that magazine of his."

"How could he, when it failed?"

"I know," said Tarnley. "Like the rest of them, it had no chance against the American competition and control of the advertising market. But surely Ainslie could have found something better after that than politics?"

"Alan's had a pretty difficult year."

"Who hasn't?"

"Evidently you don't know he lost his wife?"

Tarnley was surprised. "No, I didn't know that. It must have happened when I was in Japan. She must have been a reasonably young woman. What was it—cancer?"

"It was a completely senseless street accident. A truck broke its brakes on a hill and went out of control and she never had a chance."

Gabriel did not add that he had been with her when the accident occurred and that it was a miracle that he himself had not been killed at the same time. Tarnley let a few moments pass before he said, "I always heard they were very fond of each other. I suppose she was the explanation of his politics?"

Gabriel shook his head. "Everyone thinks that because she was a French Canadian, but there's nothing in it. I suppose Constance had the same general ideas about the country he has. Why shouldn't she? They're the only ones that ever made any sense to me. But she never felt them the way Alan does. When people call him a Canadian nationalist, he squirms. Political nationalism is the last thing he'd ever go out for. He has a curious mystique about the country. He really loves it. If this makes any sense to you, he reminds me sometimes of William Butler Yeats. My mother's family knew Yeats in Dublin and when I was living with them he came to my uncle's house several times. When Alan was trying to make up his mind about whether or not to run in that by-election, I reminded him of what the Irish did to Yeats after they'd squeezed out of him all they wanted. I don't think he even heard me, Mr. Tarnley. And if he had heard me, I don't think it would have made the slightest difference to his decision."

They were silent for several blocks and when Tarnley next spoke it was to change the subject completely.

"How did you ever find yourself in the same aircraft with Ainslie in the war? I'd have expected you to have been with the Free French."

"That's a long story and not very interesting. I was never with De Gaulle's people at any time. When France fell I was on the other side of the world."

Gabriel paused; he disliked talking about himself, but he wanted to get the conversation away from Alan Ainslie. He did not know enough about Tarnley to feel safe in talking about Alan.

"You see," he went on, "I got my architect's diploma in 1939. Like everyone else I took it for granted the war would begin any moment, and like everyone else I couldn't really believe that it would. You know how it was then. One knew, and at the same time one behaved as though one didn't. I'd finally graduated. I had no money and I had to get a job and the only one I could find was with an oil company that shipped me out to Saigon. Out there it was the same thing all over again. After France fell we all knew the jig was up, but we kept right on making the familiar motions. My job was superintending gangs of coolies setting up pre-fab storage tanks made in America, but when the Jap transports appeared in Camranh Bay I decided to get out. To cut a long story short, I reached Australia and joined the Air Force and from there I was sent to western Canada to train."

When the light halted them at the intersection of Côte des Neiges a covey of black-robed nuns with little white faces peering out of their wimples rustled across in front of them. The nuns were immediately followed by a trio of girls with slovenly hair and the lower halves of their bodies enclosed in skin-tight stretchies, one pink, one magenta, one yellow, and the buttocks of the one in magenta quivered like jello in a mold.

"You know," Tarnley said, his voice suddenly solid, "I've been mulling over what you said about the Church losing its control here. Do you really believe that?"

Gabriel glanced at the firm profile, at Tarnley living in secret behind those pale-blue eyes of his.

"Whenever I drive about in this province," Tarnley continued, "and see all these churches and seminaries and institutions, I can't help asking myself a businessman's question—how much does the capital investment in all that come to? Of course, nobody will ever know. No outsider can even ask what goes on behind all those gray-stone walls and he wouldn't be told anything if he did. Three centuries of confessions and prayers and contributions." He eyed Gabriel quizzically. "Can anyone in his senses expect all that to abdicate? And why should it? The Church has at least two things in common with international business—it carries no flag and it's everywhere on earth." Tarnley gave a short laugh. "The socialists are always cursing international business. Every nationalist politician gets his start by fighting it. But what difference does that make? It goes on no matter what laws they pass. It goes on for the simple reason that it adapts itself to human nature and no country on earth can do without it. These politicians!" He paused a moment. "I'm not a Catholic. I'm not much of anything. But I'd a hundred times sooner take my chances with a Church that's lasted two thousand years than with any of these politicians in the welfare-state racket." The pale-blue eyes narrowed. "Control doesn't have to be direct, you know. In anything that counts these days it never is. Even the controllers are controlled by the things they control. I am myself, and I've never pretended otherwise. Control isn't necessarily lost just because some bright young men with some not-so-new political ideas take it into their heads that a voice from a bishop's palace can be ignored and they can laugh at their priests over their beer without the heavens falling on top of them—if you follow what's in my mind, Gabriel."

Gabriel looked at him and thought, Yes, you didn't acquire those eyes without earning them.

The light changed and they crossed into McGregor and began passing the consulates. The Stars and Stripes hung limply from a staff over the portico of the largest of them, and as they passed by Tarnley nodded in its direction.

"I suppose you know they demonstrated here as well as downtown?"

"If so, it wasn't the first time. The Americans must be used to that by now."

Tarnley smiled. "They'll never get used to it. They're not like the British were. As the saying goes, they long to be loved. But in any case I'm afraid they'd take a grave view—I think that's the diplomatic phrase—of one of our ministers endorsing an insult to their flag."

"Come, Mr. Tarnley—Alan never did that."

Tarnley was still smiling. "The Americans are very sensitive about things like that. Those students certainly insulted their flag yesterday, and this morning Ainslie gave their ringleaders a most cordial reception in Ottawa. He said—at least according to the news he said it—that ever since the war Canadian businessmen have been getting quietly rich by quietly selling out this country's future for capital gains to American interests." Seeing Gabriel's expression, Tarnley smiled even more widely. "I know. I know. It's the truth and the truth hurts. That's why no politician should ever descend to it. And what's anti-Americanism anyway? One of those things hard to describe, isn't it? Like heresy used to be? Of course Ainslie is only a simple Canadian patriot, but can you tell me how anyone can be that these days—at least if he's in public life—without being anti-American? It astounds me that he never seems to have thought about it. The others do, though. The others up there in Ottawa never forget it for a moment. Gabriel, I fear that your friend is too naïve for the profession of politics."

They turned down into Simpson, descended the hill, turned left into Sherbrooke, and several blocks away Gabriel caught sight of the flags over the marquee of the Ritz, where Tarnley was staying. He drove on, at last feeling irritated by Tarnley, and when he stopped the car in front of the hotel he turned directly to him and examined his face without speaking. Tarnley looked right back at him.

"If I thought Ainslie had a chance," he said, "I'd back him myself."

"A chance in what?"

"In the long run."

"I don't follow you."

Tarnley smiled. "Are you sure you don't?"

"Mr. Tarnley, a country seems to me a good deal more than an economic system. Don't forget I'm a Frenchman. You can't ever persuade me that what happened to France during and since the French Revolution can be explained by economics. If you want the real reason why Alan Ainslie's in politics, I can tell you. He's terrified that unless English Canada wakes up pretty soon, things in this country will drift into civil war."

"Oh, come off of it, Gabriel. If a civil war ever started here—and I'll believe *that* only when I see it—it would be stopped inside forty-eight hours."

"And if the Marines marched up Dorchester Street, do you think that would end the situation that had brought them there?"

"That," said Tarnley so shortly it was like closing the lid of a box, "is the nub of the whole thing. If it ever came to that, this country wouldn't be fit for a dog to live in."

"Well?"

"Listen, Gabriel—I don't enjoy saying things like this but I can't help being a realist. Things can happen quietly as they've been happening for years without people noticing, or they can happen noisily as they do in South America, and with the same results. This country is too big to be left alone, it has too small a population to talk back and it has too many of its own citizens all too eager to sell. What I say is, let's be thankful that our friends south of the border are still willing to pay. But at the same time let's remember that people who invest billions of dollars don't intend to lose them, and they don't intend to take orders from two-by-four governments about how they run their affairs. Even Moses Bulstrode knows that—though he'd never admit it."

People were languidly parading the sidewalks and as Gabriel's eye fell on some girls in beach clothes he found it hard to remember that only six weeks ago at least some of them had been in furs.

Tarnley was laughing. "You see, Gabriel—Bulstrode wants to be Prime Minister."

"But surely that's impossible!"

"Of course it's impossible, but he doesn't know it. If this were 1900 I'd say he might have had a chance. No— he'll never make it, but he's going to try. Do you know, Gabriel—a politician can be as honest as God, but if he's a real politician—If a country had only twenty-four hours to live, and everyone knew it, there'd be politicians fighting each other to be President or Prime Minister for those last twenty-four hours. And some of them would be honest." Tarnley laughed again. "The point of all this is to point out that Bulstrode won't upset any applecarts— not unless he does it by accident, which is always possible with a man like him."

Gabriel was silent; he was wondering what all this was about. He decided to ask Tarnley.

"Mr. Tarnley, would you do me a favor? Would you tell me what our conversation is really about? I mean, the part of it connected with Alan Ainslie?"

"I don't like to see a civilized man—how shall I put it?—eroded by second- and third-raters."

"Only that?"

"Ainslie's what you French call *chevalier*. He just can't understand for what low stakes most people are eager and thankful to play. Of course, people respect him. The best people in English Canada have a bad conscience about the French and so they should. Ainslie at the moment is listened to by people like them. But when the pinch comes, will they be willing to be pinched? Tell me—am I right in believing that he's trying to use French-Canadian nationalism as a lever to make English Canada do something before it's too late?"

"Yes, I think that's about right."

"Meantime, of course, some of their nationalists are using *him* to soften up the rest of us for the final kill. But they're even more naïve than he is. They're completely out of their league."

"Mr. Tarnley, what do you really mean by all this?"

"Have you ever heard of any patriotic movement ever getting anywhere unless it rested on a solid foundation of greed and was in a position of power to cash in? Sincere? Of course they are. But not many of them want to die poor. I know what their idea is—declare Quebec an independent state and then nationalize the industry. If they could get away with that program they'd be sitting pretty. But I don't have to tell you that the industry doesn't belong to them and that if they ever tried anything like that the Americans would call it communism. Don't ask me to tell you precisely what the Americans would do with Quebec if anything like that happened here but it's my guess that Quebec would find herself an appendage on the Latin American desk of the State Department —and would have the same kind of future that every other banana republic has."

Gabriel sat in gloomy silence.

"So if you have any influence on Ainslie, I'd appreciate it if you'd tell him what I've just said and suggest that he accept reality."

A light seemed to snap on in Gabriel's brain. "I've just thought of a line I read in Freud once. You may be familiar with it—'the meager satisfaction a man can extract from reality leaves him starving.' "

Then Gabriel saw something that astounded him: a tremor passed through Tarnley's firm features as though whoever it was who lived behind them had just been kicked in the groin.

"So Freud said that, did he? He seems to have said so many intelligent things that don't help."

Tarnley got out of the car and looked up at the sky. The Australia-shaped cloud was now directly over their heads and a few heavy raindrops fell out of it, making splashes on the pavement that looked like squashed starfish. The doorman, seeing Tarnley standing there and recognizing him, came forward and Tarnley pointed to his bag of clubs in the back seat of the car. After the man had lifted them out, Tarnley leaned in through the open door, his forehead furrowed and his whole manner so changed that Gabriel had an idea that a man who had been hiding inside of a locked house had suddenly come to the window and was looking out.

"I have a son who makes remarks like that last one of yours," he said. "I married late in life and he's quite young. Do you meet many young people? Do you understand them?"

Gabriel was so startled by the change in Tarnley he could think of nothing to say.

"This boy of mine wants to be an artist, needless to say. The last time I was in Montreal—he's living here now—I went to see him and I met Ainslie's daughter there. She was the only decent person of the lot. The rest of them all needed baths." Tarnley's face had become diffuse. "Would there be the least chance of you dining with me tonight? I wish you would. My boy might listen to you. He admires Europeans and you might have some influence on him."

Gabriel thanked him but pleaded another engagement. Tarnley continued.

"I suppose I've given employment, directly or indirectly, to nearly a hundred thousand people. But do you know what my son calls me? He calls me a fink. I always assumed a fink was some kind of strike-breaker in the United States, but apparently the word seems something different now. Do you understand the kind of language they're using? To me it sounds like some kind of private code." Tarnley kept rushing on. "I'd like nothing better than for my boy to be an artist if he had the talent. I own a pretty fair collection myself, but what's the use?

I could tell myself that he didn't have it, but just to make sure, I had three of my men—all of them separately, mind you—I had them buy pictures from him. He didn't know they were my men, of course. They're the only pictures the poor boy's ever sold. Later I found out I'd made a serious mistake. All I'd done was to give him encouragement and now when I try to talk some sense to him, he throws those three pictures he sold into my face. I had them turned over to experts for assessment and the verdict was unanimous. He has no talent whatever. He's wasting his life."

"Can you be so sure he is?"

"Oh yes, I can be sure. My boy wants desperately to succeed."

Tarnley's face congealed, the hidden man disappeared from the window, he shook hands perfunctorily and Gabriel watched his broad back and muscular neck disappear through the revolving door of the hotel. Then he set the Citroën in motion and drove to the garage where he stored it. The attendant was an ardent nationalist and as he lovingly took over the wheel he leaned out and asked Gabriel how long it would be before *les Anglais* put up the tariff and drove all these good French cars out of the Canadian market.

"Do *les Anglais* make the other cars?" Gabriel asked drily, and left him.

He walked down to the corner to buy an evening paper, thankful to be alone. He saw a flurry of wind pick up some dust and whirl it, but the funnel collapsed almost immediately. The light grew dramatically stronger as it does after an eclipse and he saw the Australia-shaped cloud, its underside the color of a bruise, drifting off down the St. Lawrence valley. The sun was clear of it and crashed with a hard, naphtha glare against the new high-rises and the glittering chrome and glass of the skyscrapers of the central city. The weather report at the top of the paper promised that it would stay hot and humid the rest of the weekend. He walked slowly home.

TWO

GABRIEL'S ROOMS were deliciously cool after the streets because they were on the ground floor of an old house with thick stone walls. The sun struck into them only for a few hours in the mornings. He took a shower and changed into the lightest tropical suit he owned and went out through the high French doors of his living room into a small garden at the back. It was fragrant and very still. The surrounding walls of neighboring buildings guarded it from the city's noise, which throbbed, but throbbed like the sea on a distant beach.

Gabriel had lived in this house continuously for ten years, the longest time he had lived in any single place except the old family house in Dauphiné. He was resigned to the knowledge that he could not expect to do so much longer, for this house was surely doomed. It had no more chance of survival than Latin and Greek as serious subjects in a modern university. The land it was built on was growing in value every month and any year now the big iron ball would begin to swing and bombard its stuccoed walls into fragments. For a few hours after the assault, the interior wallpapers, the designs which had meant something to a variety of people who had lived here, would be exposed to the stares of passers-by like the tattered undergarments of a proud, poor gentlewoman picked up after a street accident; then the rubble of what had been a home for four generations would be trucked away to be used as fill for another project and in its place would rise another lofty oblong homogenized out of steel, concrete and glass, financed by European, American or new-adventurer money and housing the business machines of another American-controlled corporation. Meanwhile the house rested a souvenir of the age of coziness when the Good Old Queen was still on her throne and the English of Montreal had believed their position in the city would last forever.

After half an hour with the flowers, Gabriel went inside, poured himself a gin and tonic, put a disc on the gramophone and settled down with the evening paper.

He found the story about Alan Ainslie on page three and read it carefully. Alan had said what Tarnley had reported him as saying, but there was a good deal more he had said that was more important than this. He did not sound stupid or confused in this account and Gabriel had the feeling that the reporter who had written it had liked and respected him. Then he shrugged and asked what good it could do. It was too much for the English at the moment and probably it was not enough for the French. The picture of Alan with the four students interested him more than the story of what Alan had said.

His old friend, the man who once had saved his life; the man of another country who was the only real friend he had ever had. As he had said to Tarnley, it was months since he had seen Alan Ainslie. He still looked young for his age, but he looked older than a year ago and strained, tense and tired. While Constance was alive a native optimism, or perhaps only that driving force that worked like an engine inside of him (and often worked against parts of his nature that wanted to work oppositely), had masked an underlying sadness Gabriel did not understand; he only knew it was there and had probably been there for many years. The mask was off the sadness now, at least in this picture, and it was naked. Gabriel smiled with rueful affection and again he remembered Tarnley. "What kind of a world would you be able to buy your way into, Mr. Tarnley, if there were no men in it like this one you call naïve?" And aloud he said to the image in the picture, "You impulsive man! By all the laws of probability you ought to have been dead long ago. Me too, for that matter." What would a picture of Alan look like if it showed the other side of the face with the sightless glass eye and the stiff, shiny skin-graft grown onto it by the German doctor in the hospital where the police took him after they hauled him out of the burning building into which the people had thrown him when he floated down to them through the tracers out of the sky? Alan never referred to that night any more. Neither did Gabriel.

In the prison camp after Alan was released from the hospital he and Gabriel had come to know one another and had uttered things that normally two men like them would never have said. Gabriel told Alan of his English wife and said their marriage had been a mistake, simply sex and an incompatibility so fundamental he dreaded returning to her after the war was over. Alan said quite simply, one night after dark when they were speaking in whispers while the others slept, that Constance had been his salvation. "Without her I'd have cracked up long ago. It was wicked of me to have gone to the war and left her. Why did I do it? Why do I do so many of these things I do?"

Also he had spoken of Canada in a homesick way full of a curious mixture of longing and depreciation. He wanted it to be so much more than it was. Apparently he had been all over the vast land. He spoke about the thousands of empty lakes in the north and the sense of infinity that lies in a hush over the deltas of huge northern rivers, the deltas swarming with millions of wild fowl, of prairie sloughs ringing with bird songs after the snow melts in the spring, and he wondered if the people would ever become worthy of a land like that. He told Gabriel about one of his early training flights in the west. It was winter and he had flown east against the direction of the sun, and after sunset the plane was in a limbo between day and night. Ahead was night, but behind the plane the western sky was a deep, dense band of orange-red between the purple of the upper darkness and the whiteness of the snow-covered earth, the scene below as empty as the frozen Arctic Ocean, the prairie a sea of snow stained faintly orange from the band of light in the west. Then suddenly, majestically, there appeared a many-pointed, star-shaped brooch in the sea of snow, all of it bronze-gold and shining, and it was the city of Winnipeg. The plane flew on; the city passed below in slow motion; the star-shaped brooch of the city receded into the west as though it were moving and the plane were still, and then there was nothing underneath the aircraft but scattered pin-pricks of light. "Farmers milking their cows in barns. Housewives in their kitchens. Soon there was nothing at all."

That same night in the prison camp in Germany he talked about the son who had been born after he had gone away. He talked of him wonderingly as though he could not really believe that he had a son.

How to assess a man like this? As Gabriel saw Ainslie, he was too many-sided to be absolutely solid in anything. Almost a writer, but never a professional one. An apparently brilliant career in External Affairs thrown away because he had suddenly believed there was more urgent work outside of it. An excellent editor, yet all the time he was running the magazine he had known that the American stranglehold on advertising revenues in his own country was sure, ultimately, to starve it out of existence. To Gabriel, he seemed to love this huge, mostly unknown country as some people love the idea of growth in a child, and in this respect Gabriel believed he was much closer to what the politicians called "the people" than any of the professional politicians could ever be. He wondered if Alan understood the real difference between his love of the country and theirs—that they loved it mainly for the opportunities it gave them to practice their trade.

Gabriel finished his drink, hesitated about another but did not take it. He put the decanter away, took his glass out to the kitchen and rinsed it, turned off the record-player and left the house to eat his dinner in a small restaurant nearby. Liquor was not much good to him any more.

THREE

HAZE OF a summer twilight hot and heavy; remnants of a sunset smoldering behind Mount Royal but the city purplish and unnaturally livid; streets all-but-empty caverns charged with hot, humid air contaminated by carbon monoxide; a sports car with two crew-cut boys and two girls roaring up the curve of the street with screaming tires and the girls' pony tails flying out like pennons. History was a pursuer, a slow but inexorable pursuer moving heavily from continent to continent. Out of France before Hitler, out of Saigon before the Japanese, out of the youthful Australia through the youthful Canada into an England fighting for nothing more than her life, then back in Canada again, and was history once more on the point of hunting him down? The heat and the humidity, even the hour of the day, took his mind back to the evening when he had been shipwrecked outside the Malacca Strait and he and the retired English colonel, who had boarded the ship at Singapore less than two days earlier, were talking together as though they had known one another for years, both of them leaning against the railing while they watched the twilight deepen over a glassy sea.

"Odd to think it's all over," the colonel was saying. "Very difficult to believe, actually. Your chaps packing up in Indo-China now, ours in the F.M.S. tomorrow. India'll be the next to go. But she's not gone yet and I've made arrangements for one more pig-sticking party up country before the Monkeys come in and the curtain falls for good. Why don't you join me?"

Gabriel told him he'd never done any pig-sticking.

"I've always said you Frenchmen never quite understood how to enjoy your colonies. I suppose you went for tiger. I did too, at first, but after my first pig, never again. A hundred-weight and a half of wild pig, when he breaks"—the colonel sighed. "It's a damned shame, really. The Huns, the Ruskies, the Yanks and the Monkeys, they'll never enjoy their colonies. They'll upset and ruin the natives—mark my words you're going to live to see them do it. The Ruskies'll turn them into factory hands and the Yanks'll have them all drinking Coca-Cola. They'll never even bother to learn how to enjoy a colony."

The colonel had a bristly white moustache and white hair, protuberant front teeth and an expression of rare sweetness in a face so florid he reminded Gabriel of a badger dipped in tomato juice. He was almost too perfectly cast to be real and Gabriel, thinking of his father, felt very tender toward the old man. This English colonel was still boyish at seventy; his own father, the French colonel, had probably ceased being boyish at ten. Yet both of them could shake hands in heaven if there was one.

"Has it ever occurred to you," the colonel asked him, "that everything on this blasted ship is just a little too exaggerated to be true?"

"The first time I saw her in Saigon I was almost afraid to board her. She looks like something out of a Conrad novel."

"Never read Conrad but I dare say you're right. This captain now—I'll wager you half a guinea that when he left Belgium the police were after him."

Gabriel agreed that this might well be true. The captain shaved only when he felt like it, he smelled sourly of opium and he punctuated the day by unnecessary announcements delivered from the bridge by megaphone. The decks and even the companionways of the ancient vessel were jammed with Europeans who had been in the East so long they could imagine themselves living nowhere else. They had come to the end of the meaning in their lives and they knew it—they could even read it in each other's faces—but they all assured each other they would come back to their plantations and businesses when the troubles blew over. The ship was bound for Calcutta and Gabriel told the colonel that as soon as he got there he intended to enlist in the R.A.F. if they would take him.

"They'll take you all right," the colonel said gloomily. "Those Raf types will take anyone they can get these days. It's going to be their war, I'm afraid." The colonel perked up a little. "I've not entirely given up hope of getting into it myself, you know. I know India jolly well and don't you believe all this you hear about them lying down if the Monkeys come in. If the Monkeys come in, the Indians are going to fight them."

They never reached Calcutta. The captain had been jittery ever since leaving Saigon. "He's afraid the Monkeys are going to take away his pipe," the colonel explained. And when he sighted the ugly silhouette of a Japanese heavy cruiser against the sunset he changed course and ran for cover behind some small islands on his port bow. "Bloody fool!" was the colonel's comment on this. "The worst possible thing to do. Never turn tail to a tiger, a fighting pig or a native." In the shallow water behind the nearest island the ship ran over a submerged rock which slit her bottom as neatly as a fisherman's knife guts a codfish. The captain then lost his head entirely and announced over his megaphone that he was putting back to Singapore for repairs. They foundered at midnight out of sight of any kind of land and the ship went down so levelly that the boats floated off the deck by themselves, the crew cutting the ropes with axes because all but one of the davits were locked fast in rust. Afterwards they rested the night on an ocean velvet-soft, gently undulant and profound with the luminosity of millions of stars. All responsibility was gone. Without a single thing left to which he could sensibly attach his loyalty, with nothing he could even imagine himself doing to help anyone or anything, Gabriel felt a mysterious peace. Odors of spice trees drifted to them across the water and he almost fell asleep. The bodies of graceful girls floated through his mind and were pleasant to contemplate because he knew now that he would never meet any of them. He was back-to-back with the colonel, half-dozing with his hand trailing overside in a milk-warm sea, when he heard the colonel's voice.

"I'd take my hand out of the water if I were you."

"But it's very comfortable in the water."

"Make a recce over the side, my boy."

Gabriel did so and stared into the slit eyes of a tiger shark that was nuzzling the boards of the lifeboat.

The next day a Dutch steamer picked them up and took them slowly to Australia, where Gabriel still found himself when the Japanese struck Pearl Harbor.

All this had happened years ago, but on this tropical night in Montreal the memory of it seemed more real than his present life. He kept passing people fanning themselves with folded newspapers, the people sitting on doorsteps which only two months ago had been crusted with snow and ice. The humid heat had brought out trillions of insects that swarmed and incinerated themselves in death-dances about the hot glass of the street lamps so that the coverings of all the lights were like quivering brown mats. The new skyscrapers on Dorchester Street were alight and the searchlights on the top of the most ambitious among them revolved over the city like the spokes of a turning wheel three miles in diameter. A thin-buttocked boy in jeans and a fat-buttocked girl in leotards embraced each other frantically in the entrance to a closed office building and soon he was passing the long stone wall enclosing the gray-stone edifice of Le Grand Séminaire des Messieurs de Saint-Sulpice and he saw in the lighted frames of the windows the black outlines of the heads and shoulders of student priests staring out into the tropic night. His suit was damp when he reached home so he undressed and showered for the fourth time that day, put on freshly laundered pajamas and settled into his usual chair with a book.

It had been such a long time, it had been such a flash of time, that nothing real seemed to have happened since 1945. Here he sat. The peak in Dauphiné which one of his aunts, the mad one, had told him was the dying Negro Warrior, the huge Negro Warrior who had turned into a cliff above the valley where they lived, with his shoulders propped against the sunsets looking down on everyone who had ever been there—on Caesar's legions marching to Geneva through the land of the Allobroges, on Napoleon riding north for his last gamble, on the *maquis* who had come down out of the high valley behind the Negro to blow up the German lorries in 1943—that Negro Warrior who would still be there after the bombs were dropped and the memories extinguished forever. Gabriel heard the noise of insects mating in the garden, the heavy slither under the jungle fronds of a hamadryad hunting rats in the night; he smelled the fragrance of the white nicotianas which had opened wide in the dark, and then the doorbell, sudden and fierce as a dentist's drill, brought him up with a jerk and he rushed to the cupboard and put on a light cotton dressing gown over his pajamas. He opened the door and Chantal Ainslie stood there.

FOUR

"GABRIEL, please forgive me for breaking in on you like this. I know I should have telephoned first." Noting him in dressing gown and pajamas, she added, "Were you just going to bed?"

His heart gave a flip of joy and he said, "Chantal, how lovely to see you! And how sweet of you to think of coming at all! I've just been sitting here half-asleep from boredom, hoping for a miracle."

She laid a small handbag on a table near the door, gave a touch to her hair and extended her cheek for him to kiss. "How could I have known there wouldn't be somebody else here before me?" she said.

"Well, now you know there isn't."

"I've been worried about you, Gabriel. You're never seen out with anyone any more. I've heard you're living like a dormouse."

He turned on another light but she asked him to shut it off, saying that the room seemed cooler in semi-darkness. She moved lightly about and came to rest beside a high, dark armoire where he kept his china and liquor, and passed her hand over wood satin-smooth from the polishing of three centuries of human hands.

"How I crave this old furniture of yours, Gabriel!"

"Too many memories about it, Chantal. Sometimes I wish I'd left it in France."

She went to the open door and stood breathing in the fragrance of the flowers.

"Are those little white stars out there nicotianas?"

"My landlady says she planted them specially for me because they're night flowers and I'm only here at night."

"She sounds a lovely person for a landlady."

"She is. Now, what would you like to drink?"

"I'd adore a gin and tonic if you have one. I almost never drink after dinner, but this is a very strange night."

As he got out the bottles and glasses he said, "I met a man this afternoon who very much admires you. His name's Tarnley."

"How old was he?"

"Closer to seventy than sixty, I'd guess, though he doesn't look it."

"That must have been the father," she said without interest.

"He told me you're a friend of his son."

"I haven't seen Guy for months. He's a nice boy in an ineffectual way." She turned to him. "Did you ever see that old play *Outward Bound*? That's how I feel in all this queer heat. The city's very strange suddenly. It reminds me of a puritan when the bottom falls out of his character and all those polypy things that are inside of puritans come crawling out for a Mardi Gras. I'm not exaggerating, Gabriel. I just saw a naked Negro."

"You shouldn't go to those places alone, Chantal."

"He wasn't in one of those places. He was right on a corner of Sherbrooke Street. He wasn't entirely naked, of course, but he was certainly stripped to the waist and he was holding his shirt in his hand, just standing there. He was covered with tattoos and he was glistening all over in the lights as though he'd oiled himself."

"He sounds like a snake-handler in the circus—if you didn't just imagine him."

"I certainly did *not* imagine him. He was too obscenely huge for anyone to imagine him. There was a funny jungle smell about him too, I thought."

"How do you know what a jungle smells like?"

Gabriel prepared the drinks and she sat on the edge of his largest chair, a throne of a thing from the days when chairs were intended to denote gradations in rank. She told him his drink was *à point* and began talking in French without even noticing that she had switched her languages. He went to an easier chair and watched her pass a slender hand over hair which most people called blonde but which he thought of as French-blonde because its basic chestnut was highlighted with pale-silver in a way he associated with girls of northern France. Her mother's hair had been ebony against a very white, soft skin. Chantal was not as handsome as her mother had been; her mouth was wide and her nose was somewhat snubbed, but she moved with her mother's grace and was so supple she seemed double-jointed. She could be as practical and clear-headed as most French girls—at the moment she was running a small art gallery for somebody else—but there were times when the Celtic feyness she had from her father, or at least the Celtic unease in life (for her father never seemed fey to Gabriel), came to the surface and this seemed to be how she was now. Gabriel loved the straight line of her back when she sat. Her mother had taught her that.

"Do tell me something I have to know, Gabriel. Do you feel any older than the first time we met?"

"Years older."

"You don't look it, you know. You were thirty then, weren't you?"

"That would be about right. Why?"

"Because it's just occurred to me that at last I've caught up with you. For all practical purposes you and I are the same age now. I don't know what it is about my generation, but ever since I was eighteen the boys of my own age have seemed like children to me. As for the ones younger than them—" Her face changed sharply. "By the way, have you seen anything of Daniel lately?"

He shook his head. "He's been on my mind for months.

I've been intending to ask him to lunch, but something always seems to turn up at the last moment the way it does in this city, and the few times I called your house there was no answer."

"I'm not surprised at that. Nobody's ever home any more."

The world which only a few minutes ago had seemed like the dream of a tired man now was alive for him again. He really did adore this daughter of his best friend and there was an understanding between them so natural he thought it must be instinctive. Even as a very little girl, as a child, she had given him the feeling that she knew everything about him that mattered to himself even though, so far as the facts were concerned, she knew virtually nothing. They could sit together for long periods without talking, or with one of them talking and the other only half-listening. Now as she spoke of various small things his mind wandered off while his soul was totally conscious of her. He began wondering about time and how deceptive it was. For him it had passed in such a blur since the war that it did not seem to be passing at all. For Chantal, in those years, every two months must have been the equivalent of twelve months with him.

"You know, Gabriel, when you went back to France last summer I was sure you were going to stay. It was in your mind to stay, wasn't it?"

"If it was, it went out of my mind after my first day home."

It was on the second day home that he had begun meeting relations and old friends and at first they had all shocked him, they had seemed so old and scarred by their lives. He heard them saying the same old things and realized that in spite of the war they had been doing the same old things. But after half an hour with them it was as though they had not changed at all; as though the age-marks, the experience-marks, on their faces had dissolved like the later writings on a palimpsest after acid has been applied to it and he was seeing them much as they had looked twenty or thirty years ago. Very strange. Also, to Gabriel, sad.

"Have I said anything to depress you, Gabriel?"

"No, of course not."

"You looked as if you'd gone away from me somewhere."

He smiled. "Well, now I'm back again."

As indeed he was, for Chantal was offering him the opposite experience to the one in France. He had first seen her as a flaxen child turning somersaults on her bed the night her father had introduced him into the family, and now he realized that this earlier image had only now been corrected. He had continually thought of her as younger than she was. Now he realized that if, in his Air Force days, he had known the Chantal who was seated on that seventeenth-century chair, he would have thought her older than twenty-five.

"Why haven't you come to see me, Gabriel? Since Dad went to Ottawa I've only seen you twice, and that's been ages. You used to be almost a fixture in our lives. I've missed you terribly."

He was touched, and murmured something conventional.

"For a while I supposed it was because you had met somebody, then people told me you're never seen out at all. Don't you know any women, Gabriel?"

He smiled. "Let's say I have the occasional acquaintance."

"Yes," she said and glanced away. "And is anything more lonely-making?"

"It's hard to believe that someone like you is lonely. Are you really, Chantal?"

"I don't know what's happened to me. When I was little I always longed to grow up. It was heaven when I was young at the lake. The French people who lived around there—you remember the Provenchers, the farmers and carpenters who looked after our cottage? There were literally dozens of them. I remember old Grandfather Provencher with his pipe on a night when there was one of those fabulous Laurentian sunsets and he was looking at it and I came up and sat on the log beside him. After a while he said, *'Le bon Dieu nous aime, ce soir!'* Then he was silent for nearly a minute and he tapped out his pipe and said, *'Mais il n'aime pas Marial, pour sûr. Jamais Marial à c't'heure.'* It used to be such fun in those days just after Dad came back from the war. I used to feel like a worm coming out of its hole in the morning with the dew all over the grass. We were all so happy then, and Dad used to take Daniel and me out fishing before sunrise and when we came back we could smell the bacon in the frying pan even before the canoe touched the shore. It was when we went to New York that everything changed. Suddenly Dad had no time for his family any more. With Daniel it was hopeless. He loathed New York the first time he saw it and, even though he was a kid, he was able to see something there. I remember him saying, 'If this is right, then all the rest of us might just as well kill ourselves!' Maman and Dad decided then and there to send him home and that's why he went to the seminary. I didn't like the life there myself, but I never let on because the U.N. meant so much to Dad. For a while it was almost like a religion to him—you know how he is about things like that. He did well there—I know he did. But to me it was all so unreal. Those grown-up men with their diplomatic faces acting as solemn as priests while the ones they worked for kept on making more and more bombs." She looked directly at him. "This exquisitely honest world has been giving Dad's idealism quite a postgraduate course, hasn't it? Have you seen him lately?"

"Not in three months. I was in Ottawa three months ago and we had lunch together."

"How did he seem to you, Gabriel?"

"That's hard to say. Your father's never seemed to me a simple man. This is something entirely new for him and

40

I don't suppose he knows his way around in it yet. But he's always had an enormous capital of energy to draw from. Don't I know it!"

"And how long is that going to last the way he's drawing on it? This sounds funny I know, coming from me, but I wish he had a religion he could go to. You know how fond he is of saying that he believes in God but won't go to church? That's no help to him, you know. If I believed in God and saw what He's let humanity in for, I'd hate Him. The man I really envy is Grandfather. *Un très bon catholique de la vieille roche.* Eighty years old, a huge family and for a good deal of his life mistresses on the side. He never pretended otherwise and in that family it wouldn't have done him any good if he'd tried. Guess where I found him the last time I was in Quebec? Down on his knees, roaring like a bear with his great-grandchildren."

Gabriel smiled. "Did you know he had the reputation of being one of the toughest judges on the Superior Court?"

"Is that really true?"

"I didn't say a bad judge—he knew his law better than any of them. I just said a tough judge. About ten years ago, when he was still on the bench, he had to sentence a man to hang. I happened to meet him at that time and it was a case everyone was talking about so I asked him if having to sentence that man troubled him. He looked at me as if he couldn't understand what I meant. 'I ate a good dinner that night,' he said. But a few years ago, just before he retired, I met him again and he was just plain cantankerous. 'I like it on the bench,' he said. 'I hate the idea of retirement. My mind is just as good as it ever was, but I've decided to retire, and do you know why? Because I had to sentence a twenty-four-year-old man to death last week and afterwards—even though I had no discretion in it—I suddenly realized that I didn't care what happened to him. I've only got a few years

41

left myself, you see. So in the long run, what's the difference between you and me? I mean the prisoner and me. You'll have a quick end and I'll probably have a miserable one from cancer." Gabriel realized that she had ceased listening and his voice softened. "Chantal dear—whatever it is with you tonight, do you want to talk about it?"

She looked away. "It's Dad, of course. Why didn't you stop him from doing it?"

"From going into the government?" He shook his head. "Nobody could have stopped him from doing that last year."

"He just dove in the way he dove into the war and that magazine of his. He's not so young as he was and he doesn't seem to know it. Only a part of Dad ever grew up, you know."

"That's what I've always envied in him."

"But that quality in him is going to be murdered where he is now. That old father of his—he gave Dad the idea that his life ought to be some kind of Pilgrim's Progress to some kind of City of God and what did Dad turn *that* into? His City of God is this greedy country that rewards every bastard who milks it, and breaks the heart of everyone who loves it. Every time I hear the word 'Canada' mentioned these days I feel like screaming. We used to be sensible, but look at us now. Quebec's behaving like a woman in the menopause and the rest of them—"

He made a gesture of impatience. "Don't, Chantal. All you Canadians depreciate everything about this country. Every country that ever amounted to anything half-murders the people who serve it. Look at France if you want an example. Do you know what your father said to me once in prison camp? He said it very shyly. I'll never forget the expression of his face when he said it. He said, 'Gabriel, I know you'll find it hard to believe this, but I'm as sure of it as I'm sitting here. That funny country I come from, if she can accept her own nature and live with it, is going to become priceless to mankind.' And then he said, 'Maybe even a quarter as priceless as France has been, in time.' "

Chantal looked at him, bit her lip and looked away, and to change the subject Gabriel, remembering his conversation with Tarnley, asked her if she had ever met Moses Bulstrode.

"I met him once." She turned back to him. "And I wish sophisticated people would stop laughing at him. I'm not in the habit of being scared by men, I can tell you, but I was scared by Moses Bulstrode. I wish I knew why. He was as charming as he knows how to be—fatherly, ponderously so, five platitudes a minute followed by a corny joke. But that man has a will of granite. People keep asking me how Dad ever let himself get involved with him. Well, he hadn't any choice in the matter. The P.M. let him down flat. And now quite a few of Dad's old friends nod their heads and tell each other that Alan Ainslie was always a poor judge of character."

Again trying to turn the subject, Gabriel said, "You said something about being in Quebec a while ago—how was all the family?"

"Well, it was a funeral—one of *those* funerals. Great-Aunt Chlotilde finally died and they were all there. I was so fond of her. She never married, but she was lovely to Daniel and me when Dad was overseas and Maman was doing all that war work. You know, Gabriel, I'd forgotten all the people I'm related to and how lop-sided it is. Absolutely nobody on Dad's side of the fence, but so many on Maman's side they almost filled the church. There were two judges besides Grandfather and there must have been at least a dozen lawyers. Notaries galore. Uncle Jacques was made a senator while we were in New York and he was there. I hadn't seen him since I was a child, but he was bigger and more florid than ever. Uncle Lucien had just returned from his hospital in Colombia and even Uncle Paul had reappeared. He's supposed to be one of the more formidable Jesuits. God only knows how many females rustling around. I suppose they all think I'm terrible because I don't go to church any more and I'm perfectly sure that some of them say among themselves that Dad corrupted Maman so far as religion is concerned, but in a funny way they all seem to like him. Do big families scare you, Gabriel?"

"One big family certainly did."

"Was yours like mine? I mean, nobody in my family ever listens to a word anyone else in the family says. They just talk *at* one another. They can say horrid things too, but they don't think anyone ought to mind. Aunt Louise was there with her long nose and she looked really stricken. She adored Great-aunt but, do you know, when I was a little girl I remember hearing her whispering to Maman in that horrid little way she has that Great-aunt reminded her of the smell inside a confessional box? Uncle Jacques never could stand Aunt Louise. *He* used to say that that sister of his found it harder to pass a confessional box without going in than a drunk when he reached a tavern. Incredibly, Maman seemed to get along perfectly with all of them."

"Your mother was rare."

"I came away from them all—I don't know how to put it. It was as if I didn't know where I was any more. It must be because there are so many of them. They seem to think of themselves—I mean they think of themselves without actually *thinking*—as though they were eternity. As though no matter what happened there'd always be people of their blood alive somewhere. Dad thinks he understands Quebec but I wonder if he possibly can. It's like understanding something that understands itself without actually doing it. You know my Uncle Ephrem, don't you?"

"Isn't he the one who was in the army and won the D.S.O.?"

"He's still in the army. Well, I wonder what Dad would have made of *this* one? When this separatist thing began

44

and Dad was so worried about it, I heard Uncle Ephrem say to him—I mean, I was there and I heard it with my own ears—I heard him say, 'Listen, Alan, have you been here all this time without learning a thing? This separatist nonsense is just plain nothing. I don't even bother reading about it.'" She paused. "Gabriel, that was less than three years ago, but can you guess what Uncle Ephrem said to me last week? He said it with relish too. 'This is a good thing, this movement. It's the first thing that's ever made *les Anglais* squirm.' But I tell you, Gabriel, that if the Queen visited Quebec tomorrow, Uncle Ephrem would probably be in command of the guard of honor, and if he wasn't he'd be furiously angry."

Chantal got up and stood looking out the door. "How lovely the garden smells when it's damp like this!" She stood in silence for several minutes before returning to her chair. "I'm scared, Gabriel."

"Anything particular or just scared like everyone else?"

"I could have wrung the necks of those brats Dad interviewed this morning. Their self-importance is out of this world. One of them told a newspaper there was no doubt about Dad's sincerity but he was pretty naïve just the same. So of course the newspapers give a child of twenty the right to sit in judgment over a man like my father."

She went on: "It's months since I've seen him. You know those queer black moods when he disappears into himself? He's living in the hotel up there for the time being and of course it's costing him more than he can afford. He used to have a very comfortable bed-sitting room in an old house, but three nights ago when I talked to him over the phone he said he had to get out for a fortnight because they're making renovations in the house and he had no choice except to go to the hotel. I hope he's not drinking too much. Three nights ago when I talked to him his voice sounded slurred, but he may only have been tired. I'd planned something quiet and different for him here and he promised to come. Some of his old friends to dinner—including you, of course—but I didn't dare ask anybody until I knew his plans. Then that riot happened and sure enough—Dad phoned to say he'd have to spend the weekend in Ottawa. Why did he do it, Gabriel, why? Why did he invite those boys up there and treat them as equals and give them all that publicity? He must be losing his judgment."

Gabriel shrugged. "I'm not so sure that he is. It's not what I'd have done in his position, but then I'd never have been in his position in the first place. But he may have been right about it. He's always had a way with young people. You should have seen him with the young boys in the Air Force."

"This is a very different kind of young people, Gabriel. Forgive me for saying this, but you don't know very much about them yourself."

Gabriel picked up a pipe from the table beside him and when he lit it the match's flare puffed up and down on the walls.

"Dad's always been apt to lose his judgment when he's overtired, and the hours he keeps up there are awful. Besides that, he's been making speeches. He's just back from a tour of the west and out there all the newspapers were on top of him. Their reporters cross-examined him like a prisoner in the dock. They seemed to think he was a salesman for Quebec, or something, when all he's trying to do is hold the country together, or at least prevent it from throwing itself away. Everything is getting so ugly and naked." She stopped, then blurted out, "Gabriel, something absolutely awful has happened."

He waited with eyebrows raised and furrows on his forehead.

"Daniel was in that riot yesterday," she said.

At first he did not take in the meaning of what she said.

"I told you," she repeated, *"Daniel was in that riot yesterday."*

He stared at her with his mouth open.

"My little brother Daniel," she said. "For the third time I'm telling you—my little brother Daniel was in that riot yesterday. He was one of the planners of it. He told me so himself."

Gabriel Fleury liked to flatter himself that nothing could really surprise him, but now his mouth fell open and stayed open and he stared at her with his pipe in his hand.

"Daniel told me it will get them on the front page of every newspaper in Canada and in the middle pages of most of them in the States. He even expects it will get into *France-Soir*."

"That's an ambition, I must say." Gabriel put his pipe stem between his teeth and bit down on it. "Look, I just can't believe this. You must be wrong about something."

She smiled rather wildly.

"All right, you're not wrong. But are you telling me you only knew this about Daniel yesterday?"

"That's right. Only yesterday."

"Does your father know?"

"I don't see how he can, but he soon enough will. Something else about Daniel that's incredible. He's got a job on the French-language television network. He's had it for two weeks. I hardly ever look at the idiot box and he could have been on it for months without me knowing. He's become very secretive, Gabriel. He always was, I suppose. Somebody met me on the street and congratulated me on him, and two days ago I watched his second performance. It's a youth program and he's the moderator. Very, very modern—Youth summons Age to the bar of TV justice. It's caught on so well he told me he's going to drop out of college for the duration."

"For the duration of what?"

"The independence movement, of course. They've even set a schedule for it—1967, of all the years in the calendar!"

47

"Oh, my God!" Gabriel said.

"We had an awful scene last night. When he told me about the riot and his part in it, I no more believed him than you did. I suppose people in a family are the very last to know what's really going on. I can see now that Daniel's always been a little odd. Underneath, he's never liked me, really. When Dad and Maman and I were in New York and he was in the seminary he went through a religious phase and Aunt Louise was simply delighted. She was sure he was going to be a priest. I'm not certain if even Maman could really handle him. I mean, not underneath. Just before she was killed he was getting awfully strained with her and he used to say some pretty terrible things to her. I suppose I should have paid attention but all he did was make me impatient because he was such a child. Of course I knew he'd lost his religion along with most of the rest of them his age and I was frankly relieved. I certainly never wanted to see him a priest. Well, after that, one thing must have led to another. Over at the university they talk politics day and night and a few politicians on the make have begun holding meetings with them and of course that makes them all feel gloriously important. Anyway, when he told me about being part of that riot I was so horrified I think I screamed. And do you know what he said to me then? He told me Dad had spoiled me for years and that the time of people like me was up. These were his exact words—'You're one of those society bitches who can't tell the difference between freedom and the freedom to fornicate anyone you like.' His exact words, Gabriel, his exact words."

"I hope you slapped his face."

"I wish I had, but I just stared at him."

"Didn't you say anything about the position this might put his father into?"

"Of course I did, and that was the worst of all. Can anything on God's earth be more priggish than a young boy who thinks he's noble? He told me he was really doing all this to save Dad from himself. He has Dad all figured out. According to him, Dad is a saint and saints are used by politicians and crooks to soften the masses."

Gabriel got to his feet. "So that's where the wind blows!"

"What do you mean?"

"That sort of talk sounds so excruciatingly reminiscent of students in the '30s that I could—Listen, Chantal, you can't expect me to believe you had no hint of all this before last night?"

"I suppose I was stupid, but I honestly didn't. It may be all my fault. The plain truth is that Daniel's bored me for years. All those students babble day and night about separatism, but they're such children they—"

"Do you think there's a possibility he's got a girl in trouble?"

"What could that have to do with it?"

Gabriel shrugged. "In my day it drove more than one righteous young man into the arms of the communist party."

She frowned and shook her head. "Daniel's never gone much with girls. That pure look of his could be real, you know. Well—no, perhaps he's changing a little. About a fortnight ago he came home with some girl he'd met at the university. I couldn't stand her. She comes from France by her accent. No—as a matter of fact I remember her telling me she was born in Morocco—French family, of course. She's living here with her mother somewhere. Come to think of it, she's exactly the kind of sullen, female intellectual a pure-minded innocent like Daniel would fall for. Maybe she's behind all this. She easily could be. Some of these *colons* who've come here since De Gaulle cracked down on them have been having quite an influence in the New Quebec."

Gabriel was hunched forward with his elbows on his knees and his jaw in his cupped hands, his abrupt forehead corrugated with wrinkles under the widow's peak of his stiff, dark hair, his face looking lean and nut-brown in the dim light.

"Talk," he muttered. "It's always been the same. People can talk themselves into anything. Why? Because if they don't, they're bored."

He got to his feet and went to the door. The faint white dots of the nicotianas were visible in the dark and he heard the city's voice. It had doubled its volume since he had come here to live. It was growing into a megalopolis that pressed on you and harried you and tired your nerves.

"Gabriel," he heard Chantal saying behind him, "please come and sit beside me. If I don't touch a human being I think I'll go around the bend."

Things are falling apart, he thought, but he came over. The center cannot hold, he thought, but he put his arm about her shoulders. She nestled against him, she kissed him softly on the cheek and kissed him again, and he felt tense and uneasy and at the same time the feeling came over him that this was exquisite. He had forgotten how exquisite a young girl could be.

"Would you be shocked if I said I wished you'd make love to me?" she said.

He drew back. "Come, Chantal!"

"Don't go away from me. I won't say that again, Gabriel."

Again he put his arm about her. "It was your mother's death, of course. I mean with Daniel. It must have been that. Even the senselessness of how it happened."

"I know. If I live to be ninety I'll never get over the total and absolute senselessness of it. Tell me something, Gabriel—was ours really a happy family?"

"If it wasn't, I never knew one that was."

"Now I'm beginning to wonder if we weren't fooling ourselves all the time. I remember some expressions on Dad's face and I wonder. But if there's one thing I'm sure of, he adored Maman. She was everything on earth to him. She'll always seem something of a miracle to me. She was one of those women who can love a man—I mean passionately love him—and the same time stand apart and be herself completely."

"She was very rare."

Chantal smiled. "Remember the time you said she could see through people's motives better than any Paris landlady you ever met?"

"She could too."

Chantal chuckled. "Once in New York at one of those dinners, I remember sitting beside an ambassador. One of the smaller Latin countries, I remember. He couldn't take his eyes off Maman but at the same time he had his eyes on me too. He whispered to me, 'No wonder your country's getting a reputation for diplomacy when its envoys have consorts like your *Madame Mère*.' She's made me feel terribly inadequate, you know. Besides all that, you had only to look at her to know how wonderfully she must have made love. I never thought about anything like that when I was a child, but later on I did. I think she was one of those women who can have affairs with other men—I mean if they need them—without it in the least interfering with how they feel about the men they really love. To me that's the perfect fidelity. One time some woman came to her—this was in New York too and this woman was an American—and she told Maman she was having an affair and was feeling nearly desperate with guilt. I just happened to come in from another room and overheard the tail end of the conversation. They didn't even know I was there. Anyway, this is what I heard Maman say—'People don't feel half as guilty for the things they do as for the things they want to do and don't.' She made everything seem so simple because I think everything, no matter what, seemed simple to her. And then that ghastly thing had to happen to her!"

"Please, Chantal—talk about anything you like but not about that."

"I'm sorry. I'd forgotten you were there and saw it. Were you in love with her too?"

"No."

"Of course, being you, you wouldn't let yourself be. But other men were."

"Were they?"

"But you did love her, just the same?"

"The Greeks had three different words for love. It's typical of the English that they have only one."

She lay against his shoulder for a long time without talking and slowly he grew relaxed, slowly he began to feel that this was natural.

"Dad and she were such lovers," she said finally. "Afterwards it used to show all over them. I thought it was lovely, but more than once I noticed Daniel watching them like a fox watching his shadow."

"You were only imagining that."

"I wasn't imagining it at all. There was a frightful Jansenist confessor in that seminary he went to and what that kind of a man can do to a sensitive boy—did Dad have any other women besides Maman, do you think?"

He answered her sharply. "Don't ask me questions like that. And if you take my advice, don't ask yourself them, either."

"But did he? I must know."

"Why must you know?"

"Isn't it obvious?"

"Not to me."

"Not even overseas all that time?"

"No, I don't think so."

Another long silence and a feeling of danger increasing in Gabriel, and with it a sensation that the frames were melting off his pictures.

"I wish you'd told me he had," she said. "I really mean that. It's what's so terrible for him now. He needs girls now. Oh, not women who'd compete inside of him with Maman—that would be awful—but girls who'd like him and, well—you know what I mean."

He disengaged himself and went to the open door again. Where have you been all the day? he thought. Where have

52

you been all these years while the child you thought you knew was growing into a woman like this? Ah, Chantal—Chantal dear—when and where did the garden gates first clang shut on you? A wave of tenderness came over him and he felt a stranger to his own idea of himself. The night had become very loud in his ears as though a switch had been turned inside of his head and, hearing the throb of the insects outside, he remembered the deep, monotonous roar of the Asian jungle at night.

Then she was beside him saying. "Are we allowed to go out into that garden of yours?"

"Of course we are. Why didn't you suggest it before?"

"And forget all these hateful things?"

The little white eyes of the nicotianas powdered the dark about their feet, mingled their scent with the climbing roses in their first bloom and when he looked up into the gap between the buildings the hazed stars seemed set in a frame.

"Why did you really leave France, Gabriel?"

"I've told you."

"It must have been much more than that family you told me about. You could have got away from them without getting away from France itself. You could have gone to Paris. You could have gone to all sorts of places."

"You weren't in France just after the war. I was in France just after both wars."

"If you'd been there under the occupation, what would you have done?"

"Collaborated, probably."

"I don't believe you."

"Anyway, I didn't have to make that choice."

"What will you do if things explode over here?"

"Try to ignore them." He pointed up to the stars framed in the square of sky between the lines of the neighboring roofs. "This reminds me of something. One night when I was sixteen I walked alone in Avignon and the idea came to me that the stars look different when you see them from a walled city. It was spring, I remember, and the shrubs were all in flower and it was too enchanting to sleep. I walked out the gate finally and went across the Grande Route to the grass beside the river, and I sat there for hours. It was near the old bridge." He paused. "Well, Avignon is still there. It's still there in spite of everything."

She turned with a swirl and stood on tiptoe, her body leaped against his and her warm, wide mouth came against his and opened; he kissed her back and they clung and he knew it could never be the same for them again.

After a moment he quietly disengaged himself and said, "Your father is the best friend I ever had, Chantal."

"Gabriel, please! Oh, Gabriel, please!"

In the not-quite-total darkness of the garden they looked at one another and took hands, and each felt the other tremble.

"Don't ever misunderstand like that," she whispered, "or think you have to remind me of things I know."

He left her and went inside, dropped into a chair and closed his eyes, feeling that he was everywhere he had ever been and seeing people he had known for years in various times and places, all of them set in a vast fresco, all of them stirring and moving in harmony in their several directions. A long time passed. Then with a rustle she was on the floor with her cheek against his knee; he dropped his hand to her hair and caressed it; she took his hand and pressed its palm against her lips and the sweetness of her nearly overpowered him. If I say no to her now, I will be saying yes to my own death, and then he heard her say, "Dad told me once I wasn't to ask you questions about your wife."

"And now you're asking them? Well, if you'd asked me before, I'd have told you."

"Did you love her?"

"For a time I must have thought I did."

Barbara's image leaped into his mind, at once absurd and sensual. Chantal was so close, her head against his knee, the sense of her body in all of his nerves, and the physical contact was reminding him of Barbara years ago and making him desire her again. It was bizarre.

"Was she exciting to you?" Chantal asked.

"She was a graduate of the London School of Economics and her father was a well-known left-wing professor. When I met her she was in the WAAF, if you know what they were."

"But surely she was more exciting than that?"

"She was a born student," Gabriel said. "She studied to be best at everything she did. She got books about love-making and studied them just as she studied everything else. She learned to make love from a book."

"That sounds absolutely disgusting. I don't believe it."

"She believed in a planned society. She believed we'd all reach paradise if only people learned the right way to do it."

"And that was how she made love?"

Gabriel tweaked her ear. "I told you, she was a very good student in everything she did."

"You're not being serious with me. You're joking."

"The truth makes excellent jokes sometimes. I'm sorry, I'm not being fair to her. We simply didn't know each other. We hadn't any real time together. Lots of men in the war expected it would be the other fellow who'd be killed, but with me it was the opposite. I was *sure* I was going to be killed. I was sure of it from the first time I enlisted in the Air Force. I have a marvelous talent for being wrong about everything."

"Do you often think of her now?"

"The dreadful thing is that months can pass without her even entering my mind. I tell you, that is really a dreadful thing."

"Is she still in England?"

"So far as I know she still is. After me, she married a banker much older than herself and the last I heard she had five children."

She was smiling at him tenderly. She looked up; she rose; with the suppleness of the double-jointed she slid onto his knees and kissed him with open lips so that he felt a gasp inside of himself and then her father's face rose between them like a wall, Alan Ainslie's face the first time the two men met.

In 1943 the age-gap between them had been much more marked than it was now, when it hardly seemed to exist. In 1943 Gabriel was barely out of his youth; not so much timid (this at last he understood, though he had not understood it then) as empathetic and therefore diffident with others and more terrified by the war than most of them were. Ainslie was then in his thirties; he was already a veteran of some twenty-five missions and to young Gabriel he had seemed a confident, almost a senior, commander. The rest of the crew were boys, but ten years of disciplined work in External Affairs had printed on Alan Ainslie's face the signs of proved authority which other men recognize instinctively. Gabriel knew nothing of Canadians then and had thought of them vaguely as a rougher version of Americans. Alan's manners had taken him aback for, without his even being aware of it, they had verged on courtliness. Gabriel had been posted to this crew because all of the aviators except Alan were French Canadians and the previous navigator was in hospital with a ruptured appendix. The moment Alan saw the *France* shoulder-flash he addressed Gabriel in excellent French with an accent Gabriel could not place, and when Gabriel answered him in his public-school English he switched back into English immediately. "One's apt to be nervous the first time out. Speaking for myself I was scared to death. But tonight is nothing but a milk run. I think you're going to enjoy it."

Gabriel almost did enjoy it; it was the only operation he didn't actually hate. In the half-light of dawn flying home over the North Sea with little Joe Lacombe telling bawdy stories over the inter-com, Joe sitting behind his tail guns all alone back there chattering in what seemed to Gabriel at the time the most barbarous French he had ever heard, a French so barbarous he told himself it was impossible for French ever to be turned into this—and then he remembered that in Brittany Joe Lacombe would have no trouble at all—Gabriel Fleury at that moment felt himself immortal and would have embraced the gay little French Canadian if he had been able to reach him. It had been an easy operation so far as enemy action was concerned, but there had been heavy crosswinds and he had been the one responsible for getting them over their target on time, and the others in the crew went out of their way to be complimentary. "It looks like we got ourselves a navigator, boys," said Lacombe from the tail of the aircraft. "It looks like we got ourselves a navigator that can navigate us right up Hitler's arse." And Alan Ainslie, gloved hands gripping the controls, had winked at Gabriel who had come up with another course-direction and said into the mouthpiece, "If that's what he's going to do to us, let's throw him overboard right away."

The next afternoon Alan invited Gabriel into his quarters and after they had talked a while, he showed him photographs of his family. One was of a tiny male baby only a few months old whom Alan said he had never seen; the other was of an enchanting girl-child who looked to be about six. Now the being that child had become was in his arms and it was hard to believe it.

"Your father was marvelous in the war," he said to her. "When I first saw him I thought he was a natural officer, but he wasn't that at all once I knew him better. He didn't have the instinct for it. That's why he was never even made a wing-commander in spite of his record."

"You and Dad always come back to the war, don't you? Often I think you're sorry it ended."

"At least we believed in heaven then. We called it peace."

"Where have all the husbands gone?" She crooned the song to him. "Long time passing. Where have all the husbands gone? Long time ago. Where have all the husbands gone? They're gone soldiers, every one. Oh, when will they ever learn? Oh, when will they ever learn?"

With an effort of will he disengaged himself from her and again went to the open door. Behind him he heard her crooning another verse of her song and he did not know whether he felt frightened, horrified or merely ridiculous. When he turned to her and their eyes met, her face was wide open to him.

"Gabriel dear, please don't turn me away tonight. If you do, I won't go home to that empty place, you know. If I must leave you, I think I'll go down to one of the railway stations where there are lights and people."

Is this emotional blackmail? he wondered. Or am I simply out of tune with what's happened in the world? He glanced at his watch and saw it was nearly midnight, but in this city no European bells tolled the hour out of the past's continuum. Instead he heard the wail of a police-car siren.

"Chantal, I'm too old for you and that's final. For heaven's sake, why can't you like men your own age?"

She looked at him helplessly, but his back was still toward her. "Because all the ones I've ever met are children."

He turned and she was still crouched on the floor and her eyes were looking at him as though saying she knew that his words were no more than the routine gestures of a gentleman.

"Why?" he demanded. "Why can't you? You and me—it's not right. You know it isn't."

She gave a little shrug. "I had hopes a little while ago. He's a nice enough boy. Good-looking and sensitive and full of all the things he wants to do and knows he can't. But what can a girl do with a man who's likely to break down and weep after he's made love to her? He's the

58

son of that Tarnley man you said you met this afternoon."

Gabriel felt a flick of pain and anger and was humiliated to realize that he was jealous.

"Poor Guy," she was saying, "he's like so many of them. He hasn't a chance. His father had it all laid out for him on the line. They all had it all laid out for him on the line. None of them ever gave him a chance."

"None of whom ever gave him a chance?"

"They. Just 'they.' "

His legs felt as if they were made of uranium.

"Chantal, I'm tired out. Stay if you want to, but I've got to go to bed. There's a bed made up in the spare room and you'll find pajamas in the drawer of the dresser there. They'll be too big for you, but at least they're pajamas. You'll even find a toothbrush in the room next to it."

"All right, Gabriel dear."

Fifteen minutes later she presented herself to him to say good-night, tiny in pajamas so big for her that she had to hold them up to keep from tripping.

"These smell of lavender," she said. "Did you know they do?"

"You'd better go back and turn off the light and go to sleep."

But for him, half an hour later, sleep was a continent away and his eyes were open in the dark and his nerves were so tight that his whole body felt encased in a straitjacket. That uncontrollable memory of his—that awful memory of his. Now he was walking up Guy Street beside Constance and the thing was coming at them down the slope of Côte des Neiges and people were staring or running. It was a double-zero coming down the hill with broken brakes—actually a truck with a trailer. Traffic was crossing normally from east to west and from west to east and this thing smashed through the double lines and automobiles burst up and to right and left as it came through them, the truck now detached from its trailer, an automobile impaled on its radiator. It was the trailer that did the important work. It went wild—no control but its own momentum, it began to lurch and it went over on the two wheels of the left side and came straight at them, snaking and falling over as it came. There was no place to go because they were up against the wall of a building and when it reached them it went all the way over and came down. He tried to shield Constance but something knocked him over and the thing smashed down flat on the sidewalk a few inches from his face while he lay on his side with his back pressed by reflex against the wall. Lying there he saw the engine part of the apparatus running wild down the hill, smashing into one car after another, and he crawled to his feet with blood all over him which he realized was not his own. He saw Constance's body without a head. What had been her head was under the trailer and was still joined to her shoulders. She had not been decapitated; her head had merely been squashed flat. Five minutes earlier the two of them had met by chance on the corner below and she had suggested that he join her for coffee in the little restaurant here. Two more steps and they would have been inside its door.

It took police and workmen more than two hours to hoist the truck upright and get what was left of Constance's head clear of its oppressor. Gabriel had stayed there. The trailer with its load was too heavy to move and it took more than an hour for the workmen and police to empty it. The load consisted of tons of processed cheese in cartons, and his mind was sufficiently detached to observe that this processed cheese had been scientifically and internationally processed to look cheesier than real cheese. Several dozen cartons had broken open and their contents were spread on the pavement glistening in the sun with whatever it is that holds processed cheese together and makes it glisten.

It was only after the ambulance carried her off that Gabriel left the scene to tell Alan about it. Alan was in his office a quarter of a mile away winding up the affairs of his magazine. He guessed what had happened the moment he saw Gabriel's face and bloodstained clothes, and his face went green before it clamped shut in the expression Gabriel had seen on it that night over the German city when Alan sat in the flames, holding the plane up while the rest of them bailed out.

People still talked about the senselessness of that accident; Gabriel did himself. But what was so senseless about it, after all? Mathematical odds were surely available to cover that sort of thing. Before each weekend the press published the mathematical prognosis for fatalities on the road and they were always right to within a few decimal points. If not me, why not you? It was all entered into the book of human statistics now. Whenever he saw a jetliner hovering in over the city he eyed it speculatively and wondered if this was the one that was going to crash.

He was trying to get the sight of Constance's death out of his mind when the wind began to blow; it blew with pressure from the south and the Venetian blind began rattling and he got out of bed and adjusted it. Too restless to sleep he put on his slippers and walked on tiptoe into the living room and again he went out the French doors into the garden. The warm, moist air smelled of tropical waters, the garden quivered nervously and the stars seemed a little clearer than they had been before. After a while he went back inside and was groping toward his room when a flicker of whiteness appeared before him.

"I really tried to sleep," Chantal said.

"I know. I couldn't, either."

The white shadow was still there.

"Gabriel dear, I'm not thinking of forever. You know that, don't you?"

He was speechless.

"You and Dad and so many of you felt you had to think of forever, and it's been so hard and tragic for you all."

"I know."

She was white and silent.

"When did you first want this with me?" he asked her.

"Years ago, I suppose, though I didn't really know it then."

Afterwards he honestly did not believe he could have helped himself. She was so blindingly young to him and he also had loved her for years, and probably in this way without daring to admit it. A silvery light filtered through the half-open Venetian blind and the warm air continued to flood the city. Then in his mind he saw the waves of a Laurentian lake running through the dark like ranks of white cavalry horses while the spruces and pines bent and the whole empty north gave tongue. Then again he was a boy on a ground sheet in an almond grove near Aix wakened by the mistral and for a half-awake, half-asleep second he was mistaking hummocks of earth for the slumbering forms of the Roman legionaries who had camped there the night before Gaius Marius so handled the matter with the Teuton horde that not even a messenger survived to take the news home to the yellow-haired women who had stayed behind in the German forests. "What is love?" said jesting Pilate and would not stay for an answer. With these words garbled in his mind, Gabriel Fleury lay with the new-found, new-lost girl in his arms and was afraid to think what he had done. "I have never yet found a hiding place for my heart," he thought. "I will never dare to." But she was peaceful there; he could feel from her breathing that she was happy there, at ease there, and that for her this had been good. She had been so shy until the passion had seized her but then she had lost herself and now she was just beginning to come back to herself again. She stirred against him and sighed and this time he sought to lose himself in her and he did lose himself more than he ever had with any woman in his life but the traitor thoughts went on, "She's very experienced at this," and he hated himself for the idea and, "Why not?" he asked himself,

"Indeed why not?" and again he thought, "I have just said no to death," and this was answered by, "How pompous can you be?" and finally he prayed to a God in whom he did not believe to give him some kind of sureness that he had done her no harm and he was still trying to pray when he fell asleep.

FIVE

ALAIN AINSLIE left the concentration of offices sardonically known in the capital as The Department Store ever since the Prime Minister had permitted Moses Bulstrode to become—there was only one word for it and that word was used at least a hundred times a day in the capital—the "bottleneck" through which the plans and decisions of a variety of departments had to pour. The Old Gentleman had been an admirer of C. D. Howe, had considered him the greatest coordinator of departmental work in the country's history, and it was with Howe's example in mind that he had placed Bulstrode where he now was. But Bulstrode—as was also repeated a hundred times daily in the capital—was no C. D. Howe. After spending nearly two hours with him, Ainslie felt as though his normal conditioned-reflexes had broken down.

A quarter to five on the hottest Saturday afternoon in seven years and the city looked empty. But not quite. A young man in an Ascot topper, a morning coat with a gardenia in the buttonhole and gray gloves in his left hand was bowing to Ainslie from the center of one of the parliamentary lawns.

"Good afternoon, Mr. Minister. I've just come from a wedding. Where did you come from? The bride, Mr. Minister, had been the great and good friend of all eight ushers, including me, and my heart is broken, Mr. Minister."

This country is getting very queer, Ainslie thought as

65

he walked past. Very queer, and everything I learned in my life seems to disqualify me from being effective in it. His old civil-service friends blamed all of his troubles on Moses Bulstrode, but this was an exaggeration. He would have been in a bad enough position without Bulstrode. Since the Prime Minister had also appointed Bulstrode as House Leader, capital gossip was blaming most of the country's troubles on him as well, and Bulstrode himself talked at times as though he were the Prime Minister in fact.

The man invited attention, though for most of his life he had obtained very little of it. To begin with, his appearance was extraordinary. He had a face and head that reminded many men of Roman emperors; he also had huge hands that could twist horseshoes and a torso that made children think of bears. This mighty body was supported by a pair of unusually short legs so that however imperial he looked when seated behind a desk, the moment he rose and walked he appeared top-heavy and low-slung. He had a twanging voice and eyes and eyebrows that had a tendency to flicker and jump up and down and a habit of staring at people. But he also possessed, as Ainslie and others had recently found out, a strange but enormously effective animal power.

Ainslie was suddenly accosted by a bald-headed, square-jawed man who had emerged from a doorway in the East Block. His name was McCartney and he accosted Ainslie in a voice very close to a snarl.

"That was a nice effort of yours this morning. What do you think you're doing—giving your French-Canadian friends the idea the rest of us are scared to death of them?"

You hard-nosed bastard, Ainslie thought, and looked at the man without answering.

"I just asked you a question."

"Sorry, I didn't understand that you had."

The older man flushed. "All right, Ainslie—you keep on talking like that and see how long you last here. Some of

66

us who've been here for years appreciate a little thing called loyalty. Those punks burned old Moses in effigy and you treated them like heroes."

Ainslie lifted a shoulder and walked away. This was a sour parliament and a sour government. Conditions in the country would have produced sourness in any case, but the Prime Minister's refusal to lead, combined with the general belief that he was on the verge of retirement, had split the government into half a dozen factions, all of them scheming with an eye to the succession. Bulstrode had the fanatical support of most of the veteran back benchers who saw hopes for themselves if he ever did succeed in becoming the leader, while the more sophisticated ministers detested him. Bulstrode increased the frustrations of everyone by reducing all issues to personalities because he was unable to think in abstractions. He seemed incapable of relaxing tension, and Ainslie, remembering the contradiction between his forehead and his mouth, thought that if he had to sustain inside of himself the conflicts this man had to live with, he would be torn in pieces inside of a week.

It was said of Bulstrode that he loved power but did not know what to do with it when he had it. Ainslie simply did not know. He did not even pretend to understand the man, and he had an idea that Bulstrode was much more intelligent than most people believed he was. He was certainly adept at changing the subject if it ever seemed likely to take him into areas where he did not wish to do anything. After Ainslie had spent half an hour explaining what it would signify in Quebec if the government made the federal civil service bilingual, Bulstrode had suddenly leaned across the desk at him and said, "You know, Alan, the first time I met you I knew we had something very deep in common. You know what I'm referring to, of course?"

Off his guard, Ainslie had said he had no idea.

"We both saw our parents killed before our eyes when we were little children."

Ainslie had gasped and turned pale, and his first reaction was to believe the man was clairvoyant. Then he remembered that Bulstrode was one of the few men in the government with access to the secret files of the R.C.M.P. There was no malice in Bulstrode's interruption, quite the contrary.

"A thing like that," he had continued, "changes a man's view of everything. But of course in the case of my parents it was an accident. There's no question it was an accident."

A recent article in a national newspaper supplement had told the whole country about this accident. As an infant Bulstrode had been carried like a papoose on his mother's back over the Chilkoot Pass into the Klondike with his father bent double beside them under a hundredweight and a half of provisions and gear. Long after the Gold Rush petered out, his father had lingered in the Yukon searching for the motherlode. One day an avalanche carried the family cabin down a mountainside and buried it in snow. It was four days later before a pair of wandering prospectors saw some protruding wreckage, dug themselves inside and found both of Bulstrode's parents dead and the little boy half-conscious with his legs broken. They dragged him on a sledge through mountain passes to Dawson City and there a rough-handed doctor set the legs as best he could. But though they were strong enough, they had never grown normally.

The second chapter in Bulstrode's saga was almost as strange as the first. He had only one relative in the world, a preacher-uncle who lived in an Ontario bushtown. Months after the accident, this uncle appeared in Dawson. He was a somber man with a heavy beard—the newspaper supplement had published an old-fashioned picture of him. He took young Moses home and raised him as his own son in a house where the only literature was the Bible, religious tracts and *The Dictionary of National Biography*, and Bulstrode claimed that he had read them so often he practically knew them by heart. Tom McCartney, the man who had snarled at Ainslie, who worshipped Bulstrode, was fond of saying, "If you want to know what makes old Moses tick, it's those books he read when he was a kid. The kind of people he took for heroes were the kings and judges of Israel and men like Wellington and Gladstone. That's why when he looks around here, all he sees is pretty small potatoes."

In the bushtown Bulstrode had done more than read his uncle's modest little library; he had also taken strong-man's courses by correspondence and at nineteen years old he joined a circus and competed with Sandow and Louis Cyr. He had never married and his name had never been mentioned in connection with any woman. He did not drink but on Saturday nights he made a ritual of smoking a single large cigar. Though he lived almost like a monk, his mouth was heavy and sensual. Was this why, when he was angry, he was apt to vibrate like an overheated boiler?

At any rate, here he was now and Ainslie had to deal with him, and after two hours with him he believed he would never learn how. He decided not to return to his office and walked toward the hotel where he was staying until he could move back into the rooms he had rented when he had first come up to the capital. The Ottawa valley was so humid in this heat wave that his brain felt as though wrapped in wool that had been dipped in hot water. He strolled into the little park behind the hotel, found an empty bench and sat gazing out across the toy-sized locks of the Rideau Canal. From this position it made him think of a combination of Westminster, Edinburgh Castle and a château of the Loire. But not even here could he get Bulstrode out of his mind.

"What gives the French Canadians this idea they've had it so tough?" Bulstrode had suddenly demanded. "It was twenty times tougher in the Yukon than it ever was in Quebec."

When Ainslie had tried to get the subject back to the point of interruption, Bulstrode had continued as though he had not spoken.

"It was the cold up there. You know, the only place in the world lower temperatures have been recorded are around the Yenisei River in Siberia. I've seen spirit thermometers frozen solid. I've seen snow turned into concrete ribs by the wind. We had wolves too. One winter they were starving and they used to howl around our cabin at night—and the nights lasted most of the twenty-four hours. Poor father! To cheer us up he used to play us tunes on his mouth organ. He knew all kinds of tunes—hymn tunes, jigs, march music. Mother used to love them and so did I. But wolves or no wolves, Father always went out prospecting. Many a time Mother and I wondered if he'd ever come back alive. Can you imagine what it was like for a little boy to try to sleep knowing the wolves were out there waiting to eat his father?"

When he finally got back to the subject, Ainslie made his biggest effort of the day.

"I tell you, Mr. Minister, no people in history has ever tried to break with a strict Catholicism without turning to nationalism or some other kind of ism as a surrogate religion. As I see it, that is the essence of the situation in Quebec today. The problem there isn't economic, it's psychological. That's why these little things I try to remind you of are so important. What's happening in Quebec—whatever it turns out to be to a large extent is going to depend on the rest of us—is something deeper than we've ever seen before in Canada. It's a genuine revolution in a way of life, and I don't have to remind you that all revolutions have neurotic roots."

While he was saying this, Bulstrode picked up a paper from his desk and began reading it. He was still reading it half a minute after Ainslie finished. Then he took off his glasses and rubbed his eyes.

"That word 'neurotic,'" he muttered. Then he chuckled heavily. "You know, a lot of people these days make me laugh. That word 'neurotic.'" Bulstrode's wide face spread apart into an enormous pumpkin grin. "Know what I saw in the paper only the other day? Seems like some fellow in Winnipeg robbed a bank and got caught. Seventh offense. Well, his lawyer didn't have any case at all, so what did he come up with? 'My client,' he told the court, 'needs psychiatric treatment, not jail. You ask why he robs banks? If you don't want him to do it again, I beg the court to send him to a psychiatrist.' "

Bulstrode stopped, pondered and looked depressed. "If it wasn't so serious, all this stuff, you could laugh at it, but it's all over the place." He jerked his head up and a mischievous expression appeared in his eyes. "Now here's a story for you. A while back, in the library I happened to pick up one of those magazines the college professors turn out—you know the kind of stuff. Nobody reads them but other professors and maybe not even they read them. Dull—you know—full of words—professors. Well, just by the sheerest chance my eye fell on something a professor out in Vancouver had written about politics and this man had a brand new idea. It was accepted, according to him, that public men should have regular check-ups by their physicians. So why not make it compulsory for them to have regular check-ups by psychiatrists as well? I kept on reading and suddenly I spotted something. This professor had me in mind when he wrote that. According to him, *I* needed a psychiatrist. Of course he didn't mention me by name, but who did he think I was—a fool?" Bulstrode rubbed his hands together. "Right then and there I decided to have a little fun. I called Brown first thing next morning and I said, 'Brown, now is the time for all good men to lighten the heat and burden of the day.' To cut the story short, I told Brown to get that man here as soon as he could. At his own expense, of course." Again Bulstrode rubbed his hands. "Alan, you've just got no idea how conceited these intellectuals are. They say all kinds of things about men like us behind our backs, but if we meet them and ask them for their advice, they go right back to their colleges and tell the other professors we're wonderful. I told Brown we wanted this professor for consultation and did he come? He came on the jet flight two days later."

Ainslie sighed; Bulstrode leaned back with his hands clasped behind his head and rambled on.

"Well, when this professor was in here, I knew he didn't think I'd read his article. Men like him scare at the drop of a hat and if he'd guessed what I knew he'd never have dared face me. There he sat, nodding and agreeing with everything I said, and pretty soon I got tired of him and decided to let him have it. I told him I'd read that piece of his in the magazine and that it seemed to me a very original idea and that he had a very real contribution to make to good government in this country. Now the first problem I wanted to turn over to him—'Don't be too surprised,' I said—strangely enough is in the Department of Agriculture. If he could do something there, I said, he'd find out this was a government that knew how to be generous. He was purring and then I let him have it. 'Professor,' I said to that man, 'here's your problem. Find out, will you, how neurotic the cows of this country get because farmers milk them instead of their own calves?' "

Bulstrode let out a roaring, molar-showing laugh and the discussion was back to where it had started.

"It would help," Bulstrode growled, "it would help a lot if these intellectuals and journalists got around to the idea that I'm not as stupid as they think I am. Only this morning I read an editorial suggesting that the party ought to raise a fund to pension me off. It was time for me to resign, according to this editorial. *Me* resign!" A short, barking laugh.

By this time Ainslie had been reduced to helplessness by sheer confusion, but Bulstrode seemed to be enjoying himself. The next thing he did was to reach into one of his drawers and take out a newspaper clipping with some sentences underlined in red ink, which he handed to Ainslie. "Here's another editorial about me," he said.

"I'm coming to the conclusion that I'm keeping half the editorial writers in this country in business. *They* ought to be the ones to get up a fund for me, and the cartoonists could chip in too. Anyway, read this one. Just read it."

Ainslie read: "The principles of this man of principle are at constant war with the instincts of this man of instinct. Need anyone be surprised if the instincts win the battles whenever the chips are down?"

When Ainslie handed the clipping back, Bulstrode shook his head and muttered something unintelligible, and when the interview finally petered out, Ainslie felt like a suspect in the back room of a police station after the police have studiously pounded the muscles supporting the weight of his head. He also felt that a hand had reached inside of him and disconnected the balance wheel of his character. Strangest of all was the knowledge that Bulstrode felt no hostility to him whatever.

Now Ainslie was sitting in the humid heat trying to assess his position, but he could not do it. What confused his soul was something far more obscure than this obvious split within the country; this much at least he understood. A change in the human climate seemed to be occurring everywhere. Only a few years ago he had believed he understood this country as well as any man, but three nights ago, clawing at sleep that danced away whenever he gripped it, he had found himself overcome by a sensation familiar and ominous. Once before, when very young, he had felt like this, though on that occasion there had been no mystery about what was causing it.

In his college years Dr. Ainslie had arranged for him to take summer jobs on freight ships, his idea being that in this way Alan would see some of the world and have time to study when he was off watch. In the last of these summers at sea he was aboard an old vessel of Belfast registry ploughing across the Atlantic from the Mediterranean to Jamaica and everything went normally until they neared the Caribbean and found themselves in a huge swell that

73

glistened like oil under a haze turned pinky-gold by an invisible sun.

They battened down for a hurricane; they rigged hand-lines inside and outside, but no storm came. For two days and nights they wallowed on through twenty-foot waves that hardly ever broke. The water seemed to have the texture of oil as it sluiced languidly over the foredeck when the ship plunged. In the breathless air the ship creaked and groaned and occasionally there was a loud interior crash as some object carried away. Still nothing happened. After they passed through the outer fringes of the islands and entered the Caribbean the sea fell considerably, the vessel no longer shipped water, but Ainslie heard the captain mutter to the mate that he had never been more nervous in all his years at sea. The ship wallowed on and the crew ate their meals in unnatural silence. Another night fell and at last the wind began to blow. It came from a direction contrary to the motion of the sea and it blew with such force that it was possible to stand on deck and lean against it. It had the effect of flattening out the sea and when Ainslie came up to stand a bridge watch he found both the captain and the first officer already there. "This is shredding out from something very big," he heard the captain mutter. "I wish to God I knew where it was."

By this time the wind had pressed the ship into a noticeable list, but still nothing happened, and the sea was calmer than it had been in days, yet within the wind there was now a high, dog-whistle keening. It was eerie in the darkness with the warm, moist wind pressing the ship over, making the shrouds wail, blowing and blowing but still no storm. By midnight it began to rain and the windows of the wheelhouse streamed so that it was difficult to see properly. The mate took a look at the glass every ten minutes and did not like what he saw. At half-past midnight it read 28.72 and by one in the morning it was down to 28.25. Suddenly Ainslie heard the captain shout, "Watch that, Mister!" and he felt an agitation under his feet as though the ship were being shaken by a submarine upheaval. He pressed his face against the glass but saw nothing at first but the reflections of the dim lights inside the wheelhouse. Then something loomed at him, something absolutely enormous came at him out of the dark shaped like Kilimanjaro with snow solid on a long, humped crest. A huge, soft-muscled something alive scooped the ship up, held her an instant, trembling, then threw her over on her starboard side with a roar of water and a crash of breaking gear. Ainslie was knocked off his feet and bruised his cheekbone, but instantly was kicked erect as the huge sea passed under the keel with the rumbling of a volcano. The ship dropped with a crash into the opposite trough and came up shaking herself. After that Ainslie remembered nothing but hanging on while the quartermaster with aching arms kept her head to the seas and the skipper searched the darkness for shifts in the wind's direction. He could see next to nothing because the ship's searchlight had been knocked out by the first sea which had nearly capsized the vessel. Dawn came finally and revealed a sea like the Rocky Mountains in *delirium tremens* with spume blowing through the twisted valleys like snow.

This had been years ago and it was perhaps fanciful to compare his sensations here in Ottawa to his sensations before that storm broke. But however often he repeated to himself that his imagination was running away with itself, he could not persuade himself that it wasn't. The time he was living in was too fantastic for anyone to look it square in the eye. Hurricane weather but no hurricanes. Nuclear confrontations with serious-minded men seriously wondering whether there would be even a blade of grass left on the planet inside a few years, but so far no bombs. Full employment but no security. Knowledge in unknowable quantities but never so many people telling each other they could not understand. All the ideas that had guided and inspired Ainslie's life—socialism, education, the faith that science and prosperity would improve man's

75

life, even the new psychology which everyone so glibly talked—the best he could say now of any of these hopes was that they had foundered in the ancient ocean of human nature. Meanwhile people like himself kept doing the familiar jobs. They talked, they debated, they planned, they went electioneering, they docketed, classified and appointed commissions of inquiry. So far as he himself was concerned, he knew he was never seriously listened to by any of his colleagues when he repeated his storm warnings and implored them to do something before the storm broke.

Then crash—the riot in Montreal. And yesterday when the news of it came, he and Laurent Saint-Just, his first assistant, had looked at one another just as Ainslie remembered the captain and the mate looking at each other in the wheelhouse of the Belfast freighter years ago. But all either of them could think of saying was, "Well, it seems to have arrived at last."

He wished Gabriel Fleury were living here. Gabriel as solitary as himself, in Montreal, with his skiing and golf, his books and gramophone music, his old furniture from France and his perpetual sense of *déjà vu*. Since Gabriel had come to Canada, Ainslie had thought of him as a member of his own family, almost as a younger brother. Yet in his heart he had known that Gabriel's spirit was much older than his own. At least until a year ago.

"When he brought me the news about Constance I felt like a chunk of metal under a lathe that screamed when it carved strips off me."

For days his soul had been nothing but pain and he had dreamed savagely of women's bodies, but of bodies without faces, and he could not understand why this was. Then had come a numbness and he had thought that if he had a woman or two it might help, but he had been afraid to try for fear he would find himself impotent. A queer clairvoyance had come to him, a little like the clairvoyance of alcohol, but he could not trust it because, like alcohol, it stimulated one part of his brain while paralyzing another. Sometimes he had the sensation that parts of his character he had believed securely screwed into place for the rest of his life had broken loose and were tumbling about inside of him. Sometimes he looked at familiar landscapes and seemed to be seeing underneath the mask of their trees and grass to the bones of the earth itself. Lately had come a different sensation. He felt that instead of flying in an engine-driven aircraft, he was sitting in a glider adjusting to this or that air current, flipping up and down and sideways, unable to steer any true course of his own, just keeping the glider afloat while knowing there could be only one end to any flight like this.

Constance—he understood this now as he had never dared understand it before—had been the governor of his life's engine, though this was a ridiculous metaphor to apply to what he had felt about that woman. They had met in his early days in Montreal, met by accident in a group of people where she had known nearly everyone and he had known only two or three, and the flash between them had been instantaneous. He had always been an impulsive man, but never with women because he had been too unsure of his future to risk being caught and tied down. Nor had he had much to do with women though he had wanted them badly enough. Yet that very night he and Constance had gone to bed and made love and it had seemed the most natural thing he had ever done—without fear, without guilt, without doubt. It was after several love-makings in the white peace of sexual exhaustion that she had told him a story which normally would have shocked and horrified him, for in those days he did not consciously recognize—he did not dare—many of the contradictions which together make a human personality.

She was a daughter of one of the oldest established families in Quebec City, which meant one of the oldest established families in North America. Deeply traditional,

Catholic, conservative, such an entwinement of blood relationships that after he knew them better he suspected they would make even the family of Gabriel Fleury seem simple by comparison, for nearly three centuries they had sent their sons into the Church and the professions and their daughters to be educated in convents whence a regular quota each generation emerged with a vocation to become brides of Christ. To know such a family was to know an ancient flesh. Ainslie had thought them wonderful just as he had also thought them frustrating. He had found it impossible to talk to any of them except the old judge, Constance's father, for any length of time about things that deeply interested himself. They were profoundly, yet flexibly, moral. Though divorce could not and did not occur among them, mistresses and lovers occasionally could and did. It was a way of life, her family. It was a different, older, deeper, yet more inarticulate way of life than any he had ever known before.

But these were things he learned later over the years. What he learned on his first night with Constance was the thing which had made her so different from all the others, different from them as long as she lived, though none of the others seemed aware of it. Nobody alive knew of it except she and himself.

At the age of fourteen, on a summer vacation from her convent school, she had become the girl-mistress, almost the child-mistress, of a distant cousin old enough to be her father; indeed, this man was the relation her father had liked more than any of the others. He had roamed the world for years trying to be an artist and had come home defeated. He had seen this lovely girl (and Ainslie could understand what he felt when he saw her) and had made himself her Pygmalion in the only way he could.

"Old families," she said, "huge Catholic old families—the strange things that sometimes happen in them are not really as strange as they seem."

This older man had initiated her into love as into a subtle, complex, exquisite, demanding art, had done so with poetry, with respect, but also with a hard, firm expertness.

"He told me I'd never regret it. He told me that when I got married my husband would thank him forever if my husband was a proper man. Are you shocked?"

Ainslie had not been so shocked as incredulous at himself because he was *not* shocked.

"Did you regret it yourself?" he asked her. "Do you regret it now?"

"At first it was like finding myself awake in a dream. I had been taught to respect older men, to believe they were right, and ever since I was a child I had heard my father speak of André with admiration—and my father was not given to speaking of many people with admiration."

"Did this go on for long?"

"For three years, though of course only on and off. He was the one who finally ended it."

"Why did he end it?"

"Because he loved me for myself. At first, when it ended, I was terrified. I couldn't sleep properly and Maman and Papa became worried because I was losing weight, and I was very slim anyway. André left the country and wrote me a long letter from Italy and I still remember every word in it. 'If you ever let them see inside your soul,' he wrote me, 'to see what's really inside your soul, they'll crucify you to save themselves from seeing what's inside of their own.' I met him only once again and by that time I was twenty-four. He died in Italy only a year ago. Meanwhile I had been living with the feeling that surely anyone could look into my face and see what had happened. In my last year at the convent I suspected that the Mother Superior knew, but she never even hinted at it. She was very fond of me. But I was sure that anyone could look into my face and see how different I was from all the other sex-frightened girls of my own age. Oh yes, after André left I wanted it, but I didn't dare. Sometimes I'd see older men looking at me in a curious way and I knew that they had seen it in me. More than once they made suggestions to me, but I froze them. I was terrified that if I ever started again I'd become promiscuous. You see, I still felt pure. I think I still am pure. I decided I'd never marry, never have an affair with any man I could not tell this to and know he would understand and accept it."

"What made you think I would?"

"I didn't think. I saw you and talked to you and after five minutes I knew." And then she had said, "Alan darling, I already know you better than you know yourself. We're both like artichokes—layers of self-protection woven into still more layers of self-protection hidden inside. You only *seem* impetuous, Alan. You aren't—not when it really matters to your life."

The dawn had entered the room by this time and he saw on her face the peaceful smile of somebody who had been lost for years and had come home. It was what he felt also. He asked her if she had loved this older man and her smile was elliptical.

"At that age—love?"

A silence, and she asked if he ever wanted to see her again.

"I want to marry you," he said.

She put a finger on his lips. "Give me a little while, dear. You see, I come from a huge family and they're all Catholics and you aren't."

"Are you still a Catholic?"

Another elliptical smile. "In a certain way that certain Catholics understand how to be."

"Do you go to confession?"

"No."

Shortly afterwards he discovered that what bound him to her was something far deeper than the physical thing which with her was an intoxication he had never believed could exist even within his imagination. The poetry and expertness of her love-making had behind it something mysterious that released him from an interior terror he had not known he had harbored.

"When you saw André again," he asked her, "what did you feel?"

Again her smile. "Only a sense of gratitude because I knew that it was over, like my childhood."

It was then that he had sensed why she had given him such peace. It was because nothing he might ever do or wish to do as a man would horrify her. Anything he did as a man she would understand and accept providing it was honest. She would never have to forgive him for being a man.

There had been fear in her also, but fear of what? He did not know, unless it was the living, suppressed fear she had experienced as a teen-aged girl. Though she assured him that her father never suspected what had happened, Ainslie often wondered whether she was right. The old judge was an extremely shrewd man, tolerant of other men's sins in the Latin way though relentless to crime when he was on the bench. He did not have to learn the difference between sin and crime; he was born knowing it, as not many Protestants are. But with women he was a double-standard man, no doubt of that. What would he have done if he had known this about his favorite daughter? Ainslie had once asked Constance this and her face had paled slightly. "It would have been terrible—terrible for the both of us."

Ainslie got up from the bench in the park and strolled to the railing above the canal and again he looked across at the pile of Parliament on its little hill. Now he admitted that he would never have run for that Parliament if Constance had been alive and beside him. He had accepted the Prime Minister's offer to run in that by-election when he was still in a state of shock. The Old Gentleman—even the newspapers were calling him that now—would never have deceived Constance with his Old World courtliness and his famous reputation for integrity and philosophic wisdom. She would have cut straight through the façade to the vanity underneath and have recognized the truth about him, that he was one of the many men who would have been perfect leaders if only they had never become leaders.

It was now after six o'clock and he strolled out of the park to the hotel and in the lobby he encountered Moses Bulstrode once more. Bulstrode gave him a fatherly smile and reached into his pocket and took out tickets for something.

"I'd forgotten to give you these, Alan. The circus is coming to town next week. It's my old circus. They always give me all the tickets I want—these days they do."

Ainslie loathed circuses but he took the tickets and thanked Bulstrode.

"You know," said Bulstrode, "there's nothing like a circus to take a man's mind off his troubles." But he did not stop there; he went on. "Besides that, Alan, besides that, the circus is the greatest teacher of life any man could ever have. It's got just about everything, including the animals."

Low-slung, bulldog-faced, heavy-jowled, horseshoe-bald, so enormous in the chest and shoulders that his suit bulged with him, Bulstrode stood there and suddenly an ancient sadness appeared in his strange eyes.

"The circus coming to town after all these years has set me remembering. It's been such a long road, such a very long road. I was with the circus in Rochester when the news came to me that my uncle had passed on. The rail connections were terrible then—they're still pretty bad—maybe one of these days I'll be able to do something about those rail connections—but they were really bad then and by the time I got home they were on the way to the graveyard with him. It was in the dead of January, forty below with the wind blowing. They'd had to dig his grave with dynamite. We all stood around in the cold—there were many mourners, the whole town was there, I think—and I can still see that coffin going down into the ground. It wasn't any of your fancy caskets you may be sure, just a plain pine box—the coffin industry is one of the worst rackets in the country and one of these days— when I heard those frozen clods of earth hitting the top of the coffin when they shovelled them in, it was like hearing a drum beaten in the earth. It was then that I knew what it was that I had to do. Since then there has been no deviation because there was no choice in the matter. It was all determined for me and no matter what happened I knew what it was that I had to do. That last speech I made in London—the one on the Commonwealth I made when you were on tour in the west—one of those British financial editors called me 'the sound and the fury' on account of that speech. He was a Common Market man, of course. I only laughed when I read it. What does he know of England who only England knows?" Bulstrode stopped and fixed Ainslie with his eyes. "On Monday in the House some of them are going to be waiting with you with their knives honed." With the index finger of his right hand Bulstrode made a stropping movement on the outspread palm of the other. "I'm going to do some thinking over the weekend about how I'm going to handle them. But don't you worry—I'll handle them all right."

Ainslie, shaken again by this second encounter with Bulstrode, wondered how much longer he was going to be detained by him. Other people in the lobby recognized them and he was conscious of discreet glances as they stood there in conversation, but Bulstrode seemed oblivious of this.

"The way I see it," he said with his forehead wrinkling, "about the French Canadians, they've got the wrong idea about how tough it's been for them. They don't know anything about the rest of the country. They think the rest of the country's like that rotten crowd of rich English in Montreal. That's not fair to the rest of the country. I can understand them, though. If all they see of their fellow-Canadians are those rich English in Montreal how can anyone blame them for feeling the way

83

they do? They see that English Establishment living off the fat of the land and—you ought to do something to correct that impression, Alan. As a matter of fact, if your department made the French understand that the rest of Canada is *not* like the Montreal English Establishment, I'd say your department was just about the most valuable department in this government."

Then Bulstrode scratched his ear, looked puzzled, said that he had to meet a provincial premier in his suite in the hotel, and went off toward the elevators.

Ainslie stayed a short while in the lobby wondering why tonight he was so much more depressed than usual. Suddenly the cause of it came to him. Of course—it was because Bulstrode had found out about his father and mother. He had hoped that nobody alive knew about that now.

He went out the front door and stood looking over the square with the monument to the dead of the First War and remembered that it had been dedicated practically at the moment the Second War began. This prim little capital that could be so terrible. The air was as hot and humid as it had been earlier and the sun, still quite high in the west, veiled by thin clouds, looked like the banked-up embers of a huge fire. This dull little place that had withered so many hearts. This little capital that had grown out of a lumber town with the enormous land spreading away from it from coast to coast and all the way up to the North Pole. Bulstrode's words shouted at him earlier in the day: "I'm going to hold this together if I have to do it with my bare hands!" And Ainslie muttered, "Maybe he's right. Maybe he's the only one who can."

He strolled along and leaned on the railing of the bridge and stared down at the little canal locks. It seemed very far from the sea here. There was more paper work to do that night. There was always more. There was a feud lower down in his department and he was supposed to settle it. His secretary was an old capital hand, and she was angry because her salary was not as high as the salary of one of her friends who was the secretary of another minister. On Monday a newspaper editor from the west was coming to see him—or perhaps he would telegraph at the last minute to say that he wasn't—and when he arrived he would be certain to ask meaningless questions about Quebec and perhaps might even be out to trap him to say something that would make a headline. It seemed months since he had talked to those students. Had he been wrong to talk with them? They had been so dedicated, so determined, so young and so desperately self-confident. "A tragedy is a comedy with a sad ending," he muttered aloud. "A comedy is a tragedy with a funny ending." If true, as Bulstrode might have put it, what difference would it make to any country in the long run? He returned to the hotel.

SIX

WHEN AINSLIE went to the desk to pick up his key the clerk handed him a heavy parcel which he took up to his room. In it were ten complimentary copies of a book he had completed seven months ago. It was the only book he had ever written and it was pleasant to hold it in his hands. He had begun writing it two years before Constance's death, using his rare moments of free time, and not even she had been aware that he was writing it because he had a superstitious feeling that if he ever told anyone he was writing his first book he would never be able to finish it. The title he had chosen was *Death of a Victorian* and the Victorian who had died was himself. This Victorian had been dying slowly for many years but he had expired for good the night when his chute came down into the flames of the German city.

He read five pages and was quite pleased with the movement of his sentences. Then he took a cold shower, poured himself a drink, read a few more pages and finally he laid the book down and descended to one of the restaurants in the basement of the hotel. It was almost empty and he saw nobody there he knew. After supper he strolled again in the little park behind the hotel. The massed outline of the Parliament Buildings was now purple-black against a sky that had gone the color of burnt-orange.

Ottawa was one of the loneliest towns he knew for a solitary man after dinner. It was a place where there was nothing to do but wander the streets and look into shop windows that were not very interesting or sit beside the canal, so he went back to his room again. *Voyage à ma chambre,* he thought. Now it occurred to him that the most significant thing in all this confused day was something he had seen without even noting it consciously. All the four students he had interviewed had worn Ban-the-Bomb buttons. Were they recognition signals, like the fish the early Christians used to scratch in the sand of crossroads and market places when people were beginning to despair of the earlier empire?

Across the river and opposite his window a neon swan was advertising toilet paper from the roof of the factory that manufactured the product. A deep, reverberant boom throbbed in the air and he knew it came from a SAC plane outward bound for Thule or the Russian radar-screens. In this thick atmosphere with its varying levels of density the engine-throb came down from fifty thousand feet echoing around in the atmosphere and finally reaching his ears. On clear days you never heard the SAC planes.

Oh, the megadeath man and the megaton bomb
Flew out into space to view it.
Said the megadeath man to the megaton bomb,
"Now is the time to screw it."

The plane boomed down, the sound going away very fast, the neon swan grew steadily brighter on top of the toilet-paper factory and he wished he were in his cottage at the lake. Those weekends at the lake just after the war when the children were growing up had been the happiest and most fulfilled, by far the richest, of his entire life.

The telephone jangled and he crossed the room and picked it up.

"This is Joe Lacombe, Alan. How do you feel?"

"You'd better ask my psychiatrist. Where are you, Joe?"

"Down here in the lobby—say, can I come up and see you or have you got company?"

"You're damned right you can come up and see me. I didn't know there was a human being alive in this town."

"Have you got anything to drink up there? Two hours with the old Kodiak bear sure calls for something to drink."

"How did you know I was with Bulstrode?"

"I've been tailing you around half the day. After what you did this morning I was sure he'd be after you. How did it go?"

"Over the phone, no comment."

"If this wire was tapped I'd know about it. Anyway, save it till I come up."

Ainslie left the telephone, smiling. He had not seen Joe Lacombe since early in January, nearly six months ago, when Daniel was in Ottawa and he and Daniel, walking to lunch, had run into Lacombe on Wellington Street. Alan had asked Joe to join them for lunch at the Rideau Club because he had wanted Daniel to meet another man from his old air crew. Joe was with the R.C.M.P. now, and it was hard for Alan to realize how rapidly this tough little kid from the lower St. Lawrence had grown into the man he was.

Ainslie had the whiskey bottle out when Lacombe came in carrying a briefcase and looking dapper in a brown tropical suit and a brown straw hat like Sam Snead's. They shook hands affectionately and Alan held up the bottle.

"Do you still like this stuff, Joe?"

"I still love that stuff. Question is, how well does that stuff still love me? Oh well, Marcelline's seven months pregnant, it's Saturday night and what the hell."

Ainslie poured two doubles, and said with a gaiety which once had come naturally to him, but now sounded rather desperate.

"I've just discovered something up here. I'll give you three guesses."

"Bulstrode exists," said Lacombe.

"*Salut*, Joe."

"*Salut, Alain.*"

"Let's drink to preserve love from reason."

"Let's drink because this looks like good liquor."

Lacombe had acquired a pair of very shrewd eyes; they were also trained eyes. His black hair was foxed and there were squint-lines in his face and a double set of parentheses at the corners of his mouth. He had a very long nose and a habit of tapping it with his index finger when he talked and wanted to make a point.

"How's old Gabriel these days, Alan?"

"I haven't seen him for months, but I expect he's the same."

"That Frenchman worries too much. He makes a science of it. No matter what it is about something, you talk to old Gabriel for five minutes and it's so complicated you don't know where you are."

Ainslie took a copy of his new book off the pile, inscribed it and handed it to Lacombe.

"You don't have to read this, Joe, but it has some nice pictures." He flicked through the pages until he found the picture he wanted. "Well, how do you look to yourself now?"

"Jesus!" Lacombe said, and the squint-lines sharpened as he stared. "Is that little squirt really me?"

"It's you, all right."

"Christ, that was a long time ago."

"It doesn't seem a long time ago to me, I'm afraid."

"I guess it doesn't to me, either." Lacombe stared at the picture of the crew grouped about the old Lancaster. "Even the old Lanc looks kind of primitive, doesn't she? Have you seen Jean lately?"

"Not for years."

"I saw him a month ago. *He'll* never recognize himself when he sees this. He's got a big garage in Chicoutimi—had it for years—and the last time I saw him his belly was spilling out over his belt. His favorite meal is spaghetti and beer." Lacombe closed the book and patted it. "Let's face it, Alan—those were the days."

"They damned well shouldn't have been."

"They were for me. Not for old Gabriel, of course. He really hated it. That last flight, Gabriel and me were the only ones had a hunch. I was scared pissless that night. I never had enough brains to be scared before, but that night I just knew we were going to buy it for sure. And if it wasn't for you I'd be down in hell right now with all that stuff the priests used to scare me with."

"Balls!" said Ainslie.

"If the wind in Lincolnshire didn't blow from all four corners at the same time, I'd have to say that England in those days was the best country for a man. Over there I really made it. Me, that used to think I'd be lucky to get a fitter's job in the aluminum shop, I really made it over there and I mean with more than the *équipage*. I had so many English girls I've been a pretty good boy ever since. It was revenge for the Conquest. But there was one, Alan, there was one I had lined up for the night after our last trip, and God damn, I can't even remember her name any more. She was Polish, and the Poles all have tough names to remember. But do I remember *her!* The long and the short and the tall in a single piece. Sometimes when I think maybe I can't make it with Marcelline I think hard about that Polish blonde and *Boum!*" He lifted his glass. *"Salut, Alain!"*

"Québec—oui! Ottawa—non!"

"A bas les politiciens! You know, this new one of Marcelline and me is going to make our fifth."

"Good work."

"Yes," said Lacombe reflectively, "it's been pretty good work. But after this one we're going to quit unless somebody makes a mistake, which is always possible, so they tell me, and so I thought I'd discovered the hard way more than once. Marcelline's mother had eleven and mine had thirteen. That's an awful lot of kids anyway, but these days who can even think about that many when he looks at the grocery bills? So far we've hit it about right—two boys and two girls, three of them normal except for Claude who's really intelligent. I don't know where he comes from. Every now and then he reminds me of old Gabriel." He pointed to the bedside table. "Is that the little girl you showed me the picture of when we were overseas?"

"That's Chantal. She's twenty-five now."

"Tabernacle, and look what she's grown into! That's a very lovely daughter you've got, Alan. Is she married yet?"

"No."

"And your boy—how has he been doing?"

"So far as I know he's been doing pretty well. He was always a good student."

"Have you seen him lately?"

Ainslie shook his head. "I know I should have, but he's busy in Montreal and you know what it's like up here."

"That boy—Daniel, isn't he?—he has the shoulders of a middleweight boxer. Or maybe a hockey forward like Johnny Gagnon. You remember Johnny—the Black Cat of Chicoutimi? He was my hero before I met you."

"Balls to you again."

"It's true, but not any more. You stopped being my hero when you went into politics. I don't feel safe having a hero when he lets himself get into this mess up here. Does Daniel play any hockey?"

"He's never liked any kind of organized games."

"He'd have made a dandy right winger. I noticed his wrists. Remember how Johnny Gagnon could cut through a defense and when they closed in on him how he could stand on his points and let them slide past? I used to dream of being able to do that. What ankles! He's the only one I ever saw could do that. If Daniel wasn't an athlete, where did he get those shoulders?"

"Canoeing, perhaps. Or maybe he was born with them. In the good days I bought a place on one of the lakes north of Montreal and he was taught to paddle by a man who could handle a canoe like a *voyageur*. When he was only fifteen he and another kid paddled up the Gatineau and got their canoe over the height of land and then they went all the way down the Lièvre to the Ottawa. I've always been proud of Daniel for that; for the Lièvre can be a very tough river in places, a very tough river."

"He's certainly not built like you. You're a funny guy, Alan. All the time overseas you never let on to anyone you'd run in the Olympics."

"Why should I have, when I never did?"

A slightly puzzled look appeared on Lacombe's face and Ainslie grinned.

"Now that really encourages me, Joe. I've always wondered how much misinformation you Gestapo boys accumulate in those files of yours. But what the hell have you been digging into *my* dossier for?"

Lacombe colored a little. "Think nothing of it. Merely routine. Anyway—you mean you didn't run in the Olympics? It says in the book you did."

"All I did was win the 800 meters in the trials. My father wouldn't let me go to Europe for the games. He had it fixed in his mind that I ought to go to sea in the summers and see the world and study. It was just as well I didn't go, for that was the year D. G. A. Lowe won the 800 for the second time in row. The best I ever made was six-tenths of a second behind what he made that year, and that was a second and a half better than the best I made any other time."

They heard the clock strike heavily in the Peace Tower and sipped their drinks, and slowly their mood changed as Ainslie's brief euphoria left him. Lacombe sensed the change in him and his expression turned grave and a little sad.

"Why did you get yourself into this, Alan?"

Ainslie shrugged. "I just did it."

"Why do you care so much? Not many do."

"You mean for the country?" Another shrug. "I've

often asked myself that question, as a matter of fact. I do that's all."

"You're only one man, you know."

"I don't believe that."

"You really think you can start a bandwagon rolling?"

"It may start by itself, you know. But if I can wake up even a quarter of a million people to what they're in danger of losing, I reckon it doesn't matter what happens to myself. There's a change in the air. I can feel it coming. Can't you?"

"Quebec, you mean?"

"Only partly. All over the rest of the country there's a change coming."

"When did it start with you? I mean, what made you suddenly throw everything over and get working on this? A lot of us have watched you and wondered why."

Ainslie smiled. "I can tell you the exact time and place when it started with me. I was on a late night plane flying up from the U.N. with a report to the new chief whom I'd never met before. It was on that plane that I heard those bastards talking."

"What bastards? Bastards are my profession and a lot of them fly in aircraft."

"The kind there always are. But a very special kind, Joe. They could have been tax farmers in the Roman Empire. The American south swarmed with them after the Civil War. They poured into South Africa when the gold and diamonds turned up, and those poor, bloody Afrikaaner farmers didn't even guess what it was going to mean to them. These are the kind of bastards who can smell easy money the way a shark smells blood a mile away in the sea. This particular set of them had bottles and they were talking as though this was a charter flight and they owned the whole plane for the evening. I heard one of them say —just about the time we'd left the lights of the American cities behind us—I heard one of them say, 'These boobs up here will do anything you ask them to. All you have to do is wave a contract in their kissers and they'll sign it without even reading the fine print.' Then I heard one of his pals whisper, 'Quiet, boy—Big Brother may be listening.' Then the first one laughed louder than ever and said louder than before, 'Big Brother's given *my* outfit his personal guarantee.' Then another said, 'This is better than South America ever knew how to be, and these are nice people up here. Real nice.' Then another of them said, 'That you can say again. Real nice people.' Then they all laughed together and then, Joe, I got mad."

Lacombe was watching him carefully. "You better not make a habit of getting mad, Alan. You better not let yourself get too excited about that sort of stuff. There's plenty of that right here these days. We don't have to import it."

"I felt that night like a ship's captain seeing a cliff coming straight at him out of the fog."

Lacombe nodded thoughtfully. "So that's what made you quit External? I always wondered why."

"What's the use of a country having a foreign service if the country's disintegrating and selling itself out so that soon it can't afford luxuries like that? I had to quit, Joe. This wasn't the old chief I was dealing with. This was the new one. When I tried to talk to him about those men on the plane, and all it added up to, can you guess what he said?"

"That this was no concern of the Department of External Affairs."

"His exact words. But what made me feel sick at my stomach was to discover that it wasn't the concern of any other department of the government at that time. I knew quite a number of ministers, or thought I did. Some of them are with the corporations now, as might have been expected. During one week of lobbying among them I lost more friends and failed to influence more people than I ever did in my life."

"They couldn't have done anything about it," Lacombe said.

"How can you say they couldn't have done anything about it when you know damned well they never intended to try?"

Lacombe frowned and stared into his nearly empty glass. "Well, Alan, at least you knew you were asking for it. When you made that speaking tour of the country a few years ago you laid your head on the block every time you opened your mouth. I'd only been in this town two years then—you remember in my early days in the service I was up in the north—but two years was plenty of time for me to find out what kind of place this is. I used to read in the papers about what you were saying about the big sell-out and I used to say to Marcelline, 'That's my old pilot. There he is—going in for another run.' But even if you screwed yourself, I've got to admit you screwed quite a number of them too. That magazine of yours— sure they killed it. But people still remember what you printed in it, and some of those boys found out they couldn't get it both ways after all."

"Do you really think that magazine did any good?"

"It did this much good—they can't pretend any more that what's happening isn't happening." Lacombe grinned. "And now you've got *la belle province* on your neck. That was quite a riot in Montreal yesterday. Very well organized. I saw it. I was in the crowd."

"A fine job you did of stopping it too."

"I wasn't there to stop it. I was just there to look around. Do you realize what a well-organized riot it was, Alan?"

"Anything you say about it will be strictly off the record."

"Let's have another drink first."

Ainslie poured, they settled back, Ainslie lit a cigarette and Lacombe began smoking a cigar that looked huge in his small, quick face.

"You're lucky, Joe," Ainslie said. "Being younger than me, I mean. There'll never be the gap between you and your kids there is between Daniel and me."

A flicker crossed Lacombe's face but his voice was casual. "Do you really feel that way with Daniel?"

"Well, perhaps it's because he was born when I was at the war. I don't know. Every man hopes for a son, I suppose, and when I got home there my son was, a little tiny boy, but even then he had the makings of those shoulders." Ainslie looked away. "It was just one of those things. What happened to me happened in thousands of cases like mine at the end of the war. I don't suppose there was anything in it and I'm ashamed it's stuck in my mind. I was away nearly four years, you know."

Lacombe studied his glass, but his eyes had become a policeman's eyes again.

"The big, brave father came home to his family and I don't suppose I looked too well before this damned skin graft got itself used to the rest of my face. As a matter of fact, I looked awful. Anyway, the moment my son saw me, he pointed at me and screamed to his mother, 'Who's *that* man?' He'd learned to talk very early. He's clever, Joe. He's got much more imagination than I have. Of course you know he's got more background on his mother's side too, not that any of that sort of thing ever worried me. You and I are a little alike—there was only one direction we could go from the places we came from, and that was up. But it was different with Daniel. There were so many more choices open to him. He seemed aware of that even when he was a little boy. He's always lived a lot inside of himself. Then there were all those years I was in New York with the U.N. That's no city for a growing boy, so I arranged for him to go to the same classical college his grandfather had gone to. They give a fine education but it's also a religious education and for a time Daniel was very religious and that was another thing." Ainslie looked thoughtful. "You see, I was brought up without any religion at all. My—my father didn't believe in it even though he himself had had such a dose of it when he was young that it never seemed to me to make any difference whether he believed in it or not. He called it superstition and he used to say that superstition was the cause of all the trouble in the world." Ainslie smiled. "If it was only that simple, how simple everything would be! The odd thing about myself is that by nature I'm a religious man. When Daniel wanted to be a—"

"A man has got to have a religion," said Lacombe.

"Anyway, Daniel's lost his now."

"A lot of them say they've lost theirs now. Me, I'm waiting to see how long they've lost it."

"Naturally, with the classical college and his mother's family and all his friends, Daniel's *du côté français*. I'm glad he is. He has good reason to be. He said a very interesting thing to me once. You see, French is really his first language even though he speaks English perfectly. He likes French better. It suits his temperament better. Anyway, he told me once that no French person will ever give up his language the way so many other Europeans do when they come to North America. There was a lot of sense in what he said. He said French is the only language you can talk to a baby without making it ridiculous by talking baby talk. You can make it croon and still be speaking good French. And at the same time it's the most intelligent and discriminating language there is."

Lacombe grunted. "That's not what old Gabriel said about *my* French." Then he chuckled, "You really like us, eh, Alan?"

"Like you? What's the matter with you people? Why shouldn't I?" Again Ainslie refilled their glasses. "I suppose I drink too much these days. I never used to."

"This has been a tough year."

Ainslie said, a little sheepishly, "This is something I haven't even told Gabriel. Lately I've been finding it pretty hard to sleep. When I turn out the light I go into a panic pretty often. It can be pretty bad. Even overseas, no matter what was coming up the next day, I was always able to sleep. But now this panic comes the minute I turn the light out."

"Why don't you leave the light on?"

"If there was somebody else in the room it would be all right with the light off."

A silence fell between them and Ainslie got up and crossed to the open window and stared out.

"That damned neon swan over there across the river," he said. "Right in front of the Houses of Parliament, that swan advertising toilet paper. Could you name me another country in the world that would allow a toilet-paper advertisement to stare right into the windows of its Houses of Parliament?"

"A buck is a buck."

"And if that's how you value it you'll find out pretty soon it's not worth ten cents."

He stood looking out and the air felt dead-heavy, hot and stale.

"Did you have any idea of what Bulstrode was going to be like when you came up here?" he heard Lacombe say.

"I don't know what he's like even now."

"Don't try, is my suggestion."

"He's not so bad, really. I don't begin to understand him, but there's one thing you've got to say for him—he's done something to wake things up. In the old days I was so used to the atmosphere in this city I thought it would last forever. But you can't run a country indefinitely as though it was a civil service. Bulstrode pounded on that point for years and nobody listened to him."

Lacombe's sole response to this was a grunt. Outside, the neon swan had the whole night to itself. Ainslie felt a growing weight of apprehension, but he tried to shove it aside with a grin. "I've just made a very original discovery," he said, turning around. "I've just found out that I'm too naïve for the profession of politics."

But the weight of apprehension crystallized into one of those flashes that came to him sometimes and made his life so much tenser than most men's, and he asked quietly, "Joe, is there something about my children? Is that why you're here?"

Lacombe started but looked him in the eye. "Alan, you always were a funny guy, sometimes."

Lacombe saw resignation appear in his friend's face and with it an air of tired and defeated nobility.

"*La belle province* is becoming a very queer place these days, now that Jean Baptiste has gone to town."

"Go on, Joe. Whatever it is, tell me."

Lacombe's forehead wrinkled and he picked up his briefcase and took from it a large, glossy photograph which he carried over to the table where the light stood. The photograph curled a little at the edges and he pressed it flat on the table with his hands. Ainslie joined him and looked down on a blown-up picture of a small section of the crowd which had rioted in Montreal the day before.

"We made several dozen like this," Lacombe explained. "The boys gave us all the encouragement in the world. They thought we were press photographers giving them publicity, and by the end we had the whole mob cased from back to front and from left to right." He glanced up at Ainslie with his forehead wrinkling. "Now please listen carefully, Alan—this may not mean a thing. Not a thing. But I wouldn't be your friend if I didn't let you see it, understand? You'd better examine the faces in this picture. Just look them over and tell me if you recognize anyone you know."

Ainslie frowned, bent down and after a few moments he stiffened and started back. The color drained out of his face and the wounded side of it looked like lead. He sat down and began breathing as though he had asthma.

"As I was telling you," Lacombe said, "this maybe doesn't mean a thing. Maybe he was just there looking on. That's what most of that crowd was doing anyway—including quite a number of Montreal's finest."

After a silence, Ainslie said, as if to himself, as if he were all alone in the room, "So this is how he's chosen to execute me!"

Lacombe's hand froze in mid-motion as it was transferring the picture back to his briefcase. He saw Ainslie's face contort as though a knowledge that was not a knowledge had just exploded inside of his brain, and for an instant his policeman's training deserted him and he had the feeling that he had done something indecent to a human being. He crossed the room and put his hand on his friend's shoulder. *"Doucement, Alain—doucement!"*

Ainslie's face was in his hands and Lacombe thought he was crying until the face emerged from the hands with dry eyes.

"I'm not sure I'm going to be able to stand this," he said very quietly. "In the past, when I said I wasn't sure I was going to be able to stand a thing, I didn't really mean it. This time I do."

"I'm sorry, Alan. God, I'm sorry. But for Christ's sake remember what I just told you—this may not mean a single thing."

"You know it does or you wouldn't be here."

"I don't know it does. I don't know that at all."

Ainslie just looked at him. Then in a numb voice that unnerved Lacombe, he spoke as though a darkness had come up from somewhere inside of him and enveloped his soul, as though the whiskey which a few moments ago had relaxed him had unlocked a door inside of himself and let out the beasts, and the beasts were hidden in the darkness that had come out of the door with them. He talked to himself softly as though he were all alone.

"I did everything I knew how to do, Joe, I swear I did. I thought we used to be so happy, our family. At the same time I always had the feeling that something awful was going to happen and spoil it. You see, I come from nowhere. That's one thing Bulstrode and I have in common, I suppose." He looked at Lacombe inquiringly. "For some reason or other, Bulstrode's been digging into my file. Were you the one he asked to give it to him?"

Lacombe said sharply, "Alan!"

"What is it?"

"You've got to snap out of this. I know you're tired and it's been hell, but this city can be a damned cruel place to anyone in the spot you're in. Right now you can't afford anything except to protect yourself. Bulstrode's not shown any quarter to the people on the other side of the House, you know. Give them a chance and they're not going to show any to people on your side."

Ainslie picked up the bottle but, after poising it above his empty tumbler, he laid it down without having poured out any liquor. Then Lacombe saw concentration appear in his single eye, saw the swollen, diffuse look fade out as his features firmed, and then he heard him speak in the tone of one government official talking to another.

"How free are you to talk?"

"To you, as free as you like."

"Your chief said that, too?"

"A lot of people up here like you, Alan. A lot of them are pulling for you. I can talk as free as you like."

"Then you're the first of your people who ever have. The rest looked wise and played it so close to their chests I didn't know whether they knew anything or had been ordered by somebody not to answer any questions I asked them."

"The first rule of any force there ever was—if you're not sure about something, you can at least look wise and play it close."

"So they weren't holding out on me? Nobody had given them orders?"

"Nobody. There hasn't been anything backstage. They weren't holding out."

"So now I take it you know something at last?"

"We haven't infiltrated anything yet, if that's on your mind. It's not big enough yet. Or maybe it's not come out and started working yet. We just know something's there."

"Who doesn't know something's there?" Ainslie grunted. "Bulstrode chewed me out this morning because I couldn't tell him who's behind this. Can you tell me?"

Lacombe shrugged impatiently. "Look Alan—this is queer. To begin with, you can forget the Commies. Any old card-holders who are still around have been zombies for years. Some of the kids who are going that way—they may call themselves communists but it's not the same thing at all that it used to be. Some immigrants from Algeria? You hear a lot of talk about them, but I don't put much in it."

Ainslie eyed him carefully. "I've got to ask you this—what about the Church?"

Lacombe grinned. "Everybody knows they've been nationalistic for years, but this is different. Or maybe you can put it this way—something can get started and turn out completely different from what the men who started it wanted. A bishop here maybe, a few priests there. I can tell you this much for sure. I've got an uncle who's a priest and he tells me the Church is scared of this. I never thought I'd live to see the day when the Church in Quebec would be scared of anything, but this time they are. The ones with brains are."

"I wasn't thinking of it that simply."

"I don't get you."

"I just said I wasn't thinking of it that simply."

"Well, I've told you what I know."

"And a great help it's been. Now tell me what you don't know."

Lacombe grinned, relaxed and his face became informal again. "Listen, Alan, before you came up to this God damn town you'd never have asked me questions like this. You'd have known the answers yourself before someone like me would even think of asking them. You'd have been sure of them too. You know it's never made any sense to talk about Quebec as though it was like any other place on earth."

Ainslie looked at him rather grimly. "You know, Joe, I swear this is true. If one of you people got lost on the ice cap over the North Pole, and after wandering around for a month ran into another man, the first thing you'd wonder was whether he was a French Canadian or not."

Lacombe picked up his half-empty glass and lifted it. *"Salut, Alain!"* He took a sip and laid it down. "Okay, how would you like this? How would you like it if you just sat there and said nothing and let me think aloud for a while?"

"I'd like nothing better."

"Okay, let's forget that riot for a while. Let's forget Daniel for a while. *Ecoute, Alain!* First of all, remember I'm a cop and that the first thing a cop looks for is the most obvious thing anyone can think of, and that's money. *Eh bien,* here's a queer thing. In this separatist movement so far we haven't found even a *soupçon* of real money, and that's the truth. A few *piasses* here and there, but nothing that's *money*—understand? *Ecoute, Alain"*—Lacombe tapped his long nose with his index finger—"you know better than any *Anglais* I ever met how it was with us before the change."

Better than any *Anglais*—Ainslie smiled but said nothing.

"You know how stupid the Protestants were when they said the priests used to tell us what to think. Most of the time they never even had to do that. I go to Mass every Sunday and I'm going to Mass tomorrow morning, but that doesn't stop me from saying they fixed it so there was only one way we knew *how* to think—and about damn near everything. All this stuff they used to keep preaching against *les Anglais*—what did it really amount to? It was their way of looking after us and keeping us together, that's all. Any time any bright boy tried to do something about it beyond the talking stage, they pulled the rug out from under his feet so fast he never saw it happen. You knew all about that, didn't you?"

"Naturally. But this time doesn't look to me much like any of those other times."

"That's right. It's not. No matter what happens, it's not going to be automatic this time."

"But the Church goes on."

"Sure it goes on, but it's not going on the way it used to, and, speaking as a good Catholic, I'm glad it isn't. In the old days it was in the air we breathed and the priests thought nothing would ever change the air we breathed. But the smoke of the cities changed it. Television changed it. The new money changed it." Lacombe shrugged. "For the first time a lot of us are prosperous enough to say no for a change. For two centuries we were too poor even to dare to think of saying no. That little word 'no.' Some of us would like to shout it at the tops of our voices these days."

"Some of you have been doing it for quite a while."

"That little word 'no'—a boy says to himself, 'Me, I'm not going to have to live like my father did. I'm not going to jump every time a priest speaks.' He says this, this boy, and he listens for the roof to fall and, God damn, it doesn't, and he's almost scared because it doesn't. Then he says it to his friend, and he finds out his friend has been thinking the same thing." Lacombe paused. "I guess that was the first step in what they're calling The Movement."

"Go on, Joe."

"This time take a girl. She says to herself, 'I'm not going to be like *sa mère,* till I die all torn up inside from having a dozen kids. I'm not going to be like *grand'mère* I once saw tying a piece of salt pork fat by a string around the neck of her latest baby so he could suck it and keep quiet in the cradle that was still warm from the baby before him. With two or three kids, any husband I take, him and me can live like *les Anglais* and *les Américains* we see on the television and in the west end of Montreal. So I'm not going to turn this nice, pretty body of mine into a baby factory to keep the priests happy. I want nice clothes and to go to shows and take holidays just like English and American girls. And I want to enjoy it in bed with my husband or with any man I like without them making me feel it's dirty.' " Lacombe paused and tapped his nose with his finger. "That's the second step in The Movement."

"Go on."

"After that"—a quick shrug—"this boy and this girl find out that everyone they know is saying the same thing. They meet each other maybe, a well-brought-up boy and girl, and they make love without getting married, perhaps. At first maybe the talk is only in the *espresso* spots and taverns in Montreal and in the university, but it spreads out fast into the small towns and even into the villages. *Ça change! Ça change!* And the feeling's wonderful. *Tabernacle,* haven't we suffered enough? Supported enough for more than two hundred years? Prayed enough? Gone to Mass often enough? Given the Church enough? Taken the lousiest jobs and eaten pea soup long enough because there were too many mouths to feed on much else except once a week and sometimes not even that often? Why should it always be us to carry the load for everyone? Be tired all the time like *sa mère,* smile like *sa mère* because there wasn't anything else she could afford to do? Work for the English boss all the time like P'pa, speaking English always to him in our own home? Or suppose we want to work in our own *milieu*—what then? In some dirty way with our own dirtiest politicians because they were the ones the English always liked because if they took money they knew they had them, took money under the counter and then did the opposite to what they promised the people who voted for them? Why can't we be free and clean and proud of ourselves? *Why can't we succeed as French Canadians* and not as imitations of the English and Americans? Why should they be the ones to judge whether we're any good or not? Why can't we judge that ourselves?"

Lacombe stopped abruptly. Ainslie offered him a cigarette and Joe took it. He squinted when smoke got into his eyes and smiled—a little sadly, a little grimly, a little proudly.

"Now Alan, you remember this. You know it, of course, but remember it just the same. You just heard what I've been saying and, coming from me, maybe it's surprised you. You know I've never had a damned thing myself against the English, but just the same I meant every word of what I just told you. *Ecoute, Alain*—this is where the difference is this time. In the old days, anyone who talked and felt the way I did left his people and went over to the English and disappeared among them." He stopped, and pointed his cigarette at Ainslie's face. "This time that's not going to happen. This time we're staying *chez nous*. We want a *patrie*, and for the most of us Canada will do fine if the rest of you will ever get around to letting it become a *patrie* for all of us and not just for *les Anglais*. What have we got now? Is it a *patrie* when we can't speak our own language and be understood in it even by the boss? In business, what kind of promotions do we get when—"

"All right, Joe," Ainslie interrupted. "You don't have to tell *me* anything more about that part of it."

Lacombe tapped the side of his nose again and said quietly, *"Nobody started this movement.* Nobody had to. It just happened."

"And a lot of things you don't like are going to happen with it?"

"It looks like that."

Ainslie sat in silence and finally Lacombe broke it. "I made quite a speech, I guess. Quite a speech for a dumb Peasoup like me!"

"Don't call yourself that," Ainslie snapped at him. "I can be insulted too." Then, after a short silence, "Well, Joe—*que faire?*"

"Que faire? Live with it. Try to wake *les Anglais* up. Stop Bulstrode from doing something stupid and in the end things will turn out. Don't forget—*la belle province* is a woman."

Ainslie let the familiar remark slide by him. What was in his mind was nothing Lacombe was likely to understand or find helpful. All over the world these little neglected peoples were thinking of their own pasts as jails and were kicking at the doors without stopping to think they could very easily kick down the door of the old jail only to kick themselves into a newer one ten times harder to get out of. And why limit it to the little peoples? The big powers were doing pretty much the same at home and abroad, so far as he could tell.

"I've talked history to Daniel by the hour," he said, "and Daniel isn't stupid. I don't know why it is, but all these things keep happening again and again. Mice and men. Men and mice. Can't anyone ever learn from anything?"

Lacombe grinned. "If they did, us cops would be out of work for sure. But when do they ever? Every time a boy or a girl loses the virginity, it's the first time since Adam and Eve. Every time a smart boy robs his first *caisse*, it's the first time since somebody stole somebody else's sheep in the Old Testament." Lacombe's expression sharpened and his voice became decisive. "Listen to this carefully, Alan. There's nothing I hate worse than rumors, they make me waste so much time tracking them down. But last week in Montreal I picked one up with the real smell of oil. Sure, this movement started with talk. Everything starts with talk. The kettle may have been set simmering by the St. Jean Baptiste Society and the priests who've been pounding it in for years against the English and what they do to our rights. But when people talk for half a century, and even longer than that, and nothing ever happens but talk, the time comes sooner or later when people begin to scream, and then some of them say, 'How about a little action for a change?' " He paused. "Promise me you won't breathe a word of what I'm going to say to anyone? Not to Bulstrode and not to anyone else in your department?"

"You know I can't make that promise indefinitely."

"I wasn't thinking of indefinitely." Lacombe shrugged. "You're right—yes, of course you're right. If you kept anything away from Bulstrode and he found out afterwards you'd done it—But there's something forming, Alan. I ought to tell you that much anyway."

"What is it?"

Lacombe's forehead wrinkled. "After all the build-up I've been making I know it sounds pretty poor to say I can't tell anything yet for sure. All I know is, it's really there. It exists. We're guessing it's going to stay underground till it's gathered more strength. It's very queer. This talk of cells forming all over the province—I think it's real enough, but at the same time it may be only a whispering campaign. Are they coordinated? I don't know. Somehow I don't think they are. But behind it there may be a coordination and there probably is, and, if so, then it's really something formidable. Behind it there's some kind of control but I can't see exactly what it is or how it's working. Guess—oh sure! But know? That riot yesterday —I told you it was well organized. All this painting of *Québec libre* on the walls and on rocks along the roadsides —that's not happening by accident."

"And Daniel?"

Lacombe's sudden grin was searching. "It's just occurred to me that you may not even know what he's been doing lately."

"Evidently I don't, so tell me."

"You mean you don't know he's *en route* to becoming a television personality?"

Lacombe laughed. "Well, you've been out West for a couple of weeks and you wouldn't see any French network shows out there. But I thought somebody would have told you about it since you've come back. I thought he might have told you himself."

Ainslie shook his head and looked puzzled.

"Of course, all I said is that he's on his way to becoming

a TV personality. You know how it is with the networks —they burn up scripts and personalities like an incinerator. They're always looking around for something to fill the program time with. Last winter some guy in Radio-Canada got the idea of interviewing young men and asking them how they thought the world ought to be run. Soon they were asking the kids what they thought about this or that politician and what he was up to. Daniel appeared on one or two of those shows and they liked him so well they kept asking him back."

"I saw him on one of them. He was with one of those boys I interviewed today. It all sounded pretty innocuous. Anyway, I never look at television much."

"Well, a little while ago—two weeks ago, I think it was —they set him up permanently. He's the moderator of some kind of youth program—*La Jeunesse Parle,* they call it. He asks the questions and the people he interviews answer them." Lacombe gave him a sharp look. "What makes the difference is that Daniel *sets up* the questions."

"You mean, he loads them?"

"It's not a very new idea, is it?"

"No," said Ainslie grimly, "it's not a very new idea."

"*Les Anglais* don't seem to have heard of it yet, but I'm guessing they soon will. It's that nasty instinct of mine. So far he's played it fairly safe, but in Quebec it's taking on because they've got the same kind of instinct I have. My wife is very fond of the television and last week she turned it on after dinner and I saw your boy looking at me sitting beside Ti-Jean Levac. Well, I don't have to tell you anything about Ti-Jean's record in the old government or how dumb he can be sometimes. Ti-Jean would do anything for publicity and he walked right into it with his head down." Lacombe made a face. "You see, Alan, these kids—a lot more of us than the kids, too—they've been really shocked by what those investigations turned up about the graft and payola in *la belle province* only a few years ago. A lot of them suspect their fathers were taking it and they're right—a lot of their fathers were. They even think some priests were in on it. Well, you know how they'd all been taught to respect their elders and any kind of authority. When I was sent to work, my father said to me, 'Joe, the boss is English, but you respect him just the same so long as he doesn't turn out a bad man.' Well, it can be a pretty bad shock when a young fellow finds out that men he's been taught to respect are crooks or grifters or liars. Anyway, let me tell you the job your boy did on Ti-Jean Levac was a beautiful thing to watch. He damned near ruined what little was left of Ti-Jean's career."

Lacombe paused and his forehead wrinkled again. "I don't know whether I ought to tell you this or not. Yes, I guess I better had. The minute that show was over, I said to Marcelline, 'If that wasn't Alan Ainslie's boy, I'd swear for sure he was an active separatist. And a smart one, too.' "

"What gave you that idea?"

"My nose. No, it was a little more than that. It was how he shaded the questions. It was how he picked some of them and how he looked when he asked them and the expressions on his face when Ti-Jean answered them."

"And this show's on the government network? It's not on a private station?"

"Sure it's on a public network. I told you it was. There's plenty of separatist talk around Radio-Canada these days. You know that as well as I do. Bound to be, considering that using the French language is how they earn their living. But Daniel's good at what he's doing. Don't ask me how long this show of his is going to last, but if it lasts another five or six weeks, and he keeps raising the ante from one show to the next—and I've got a hunch that's exactly what he intends to do—then he's going to be a famous man in Quebec and perhaps outside of Quebec as well." Lacombe paused. "If he never told you

110

about it, it's damned funny none of your colleagues did."

Ainslie's face was set in a heavy frown. "Damned funny—or is it? I guess you know I'm not exactly popular with them. But of course, I've only been back a couple of days."

Lacombe picked up his drink. "Well, there it is, anyway."

Ainslie was still thinking. "Laurent Saint-Just would have told me—but no, while I was out west he was in the Maritimes. He could have missed it easily enough. It's a relief to remember that." His mouth became a straight line and for an instant the skin-graft on the left side of his face looked stiff and ugly. "This thing you told me about a while ago that has the smell of oil— does it call itself *le ralliement à mort*, by any chance?"

Lacombe's face had the expression of a poker player's when a man he thought had two pairs lays down fours against his own full house.

"Now how in hell did you find that one out?"

"I didn't find anything out," Ainslie said impatiently. "I just heard the name and I admit I didn't pay much attention to it. I hear a dozen new rumors every day and sometimes I wonder if they won't drive me crazy. Rumors —rumors—rumors and hardly any solid facts. If I got together all the people who've been giving me inside information about what's going on in Quebec, they'd fill the ballroom of the Château Laurier. What more do *you* know?"

Lacombe got to his feet and moved about the room. "Nothing. Nothing solid. Only I'm told, and I think it's right, that they're pretty close to making a move. For that matter, they already have made one. That riot. I'm sure they were mixed up in it, but that doesn't signify that any but a handful of the rioters were in the *ralliement*. It's the state of mind, Alan. It's the feeling that something you never imagined could happen. Just happen out of nowhere. And something a lot more than talk and flag-burning."

"*Le ralliement à mort!*" Ainslie grunted. "Is there a name like that in a French-language comic strip? They must be kids."

"Kids may be the ones who'll start taking the risks. In anything like this, they usually are."

"And Daniel—do you think he's a member of this?"

Lacombe hesitated. "I don't know who's a member of it, but Daniel? Somehow I don't think so. Not yet anyway. It might depend upon how intelligent they are. If they're intelligent"—Lacombe shrugged—"I don't think they'd take him even if he wanted to join."

Ainslie got to his feet. "You told me months ago I ought to get out of this place more often. You told me I ought to go home more. Of course I should have. It's— well, anyway I didn't. But I'm taking your advice right now. If Daniel's really mixed up in this it must be because he's been left alone too much—I mean, after his mother died. She was always closer to him than I ever was. Maybe than he ever let me be. It's hard to say. It must be ghastly to be an intelligent, sensitive kid these days and I must have failed him as a father—you know, talking about the depression and the war. Oh, everything. So I'm driving to Montreal to see him and I'm leaving now. Do you think I can make it before one o'clock?"

He telephoned to the desk and asked them to have his car brought around from the garage. Then he put some toilet things into a flight bag and picked up a briefcase stuffed with papers he intended to study over the week-end. While he was doing all these things Lacombe was quietly observing his movements.

"How about letting me drive you, Alan?" he said.

"I know I've been drinking a little, but it's passed off now. I'll be all right." He held up his right hand with a finger raised and sighted on it. "Okay?"

"I'd still like to drive you."

"Thanks, but I'll manage it."

"It's not the liquor—that's nothing. It's just that you're tired."

"Not that tired."

They went to the door, but abruptly Ainslie came back into the room and sat down at the table where lay the stacks of his new book. He picked up two copies and wrote two separate inscriptions on their title pages. The first one read: "To dearest Chantal from her father." The second, over which he hesitated, was longer: "To my dear and only son, Daniel—if you can bear to read this, perhaps you will discover a little of how the world seemed to your father when he was younger and more confident than he is now." He picked up the book and made a face. "Even Shakespeare sounded like a stuffed shirt when he wrote a dedication."

They went out again, Ainslie closed the door behind him and as they waited for the elevator his face softened.

"Please forget some of the damn fool things I said tonight, Joe. Even with a very little liquor these days I find myself saying things that aren't true. Or maybe things I'm afraid *are* true. Daniel's a very sweet boy, really. I don't believe he hates me. I'm sure he doesn't, as a matter of fact. If I was his age I'd probably be feeling and doing the same things he's feeling and doing now. It's when people know one another very well that they get panic-stricken about each other and begin imagining that they don't know each other at all. They think all kinds of things of one another that aren't true. Daniel was very religious once and I think he still is. He was a boy who was genuinely religious by nature."

They went down in the elevator and stepped out into the lobby, which was empty except for a single man. Moses Bulstrode was advancing toward them as he emerged from one of the side corridors and they watched him come on, low-slung, hands hanging far down his thighs, domed head surrounded by white hair, eyes curiously fixed and staring. He passed them as though

113

they were a pair of potted palms and proceeded to the revolving door in the front, passed through it and disappeared.

Lacombe let out a soft whistle. "He went by as though he didn't know who you were!"

"He's like that sometimes."

"Where is he off to at this hour of night?"

"He's going home. The only home he has, you know. He's lived in the same two rooms in Ottawa ever since he was first elected, and that was nearly thirty-five years ago. He's lived an incredible life, Joe, when you stop to think about it."

"I'd sooner think about something else, please. He didn't have to live that kind of a life, did he?"

"As he sees it, serving the country is all there is for him. He's never had a family since his parents were killed when he was a child. You knew that, didn't you?"

His car had just been brought to the front door when they stepped outside and felt the humid, sticky heat of a very hot and airless night. Ainslie tipped the man who had brought it, crawled inside and settled himself behind the wheel.

"Thanks, Joe. Thanks for just about everything I can think of."

"You're okay, Alan. Just keep remembering that—you're okay. You're still my old pilot. Your only trouble is that you try too hard."

"Do I, Joe? I suppose it's all I ever learned. I can't even begin to tell you how much I've envied your ease in life. So many of you people have it, you know. Do give my best to Marcelline and ask her to forgive me for keeping you here on Saturday night."

Lacombe stood watching the tail-light of the car until it disappeared around a corner. He smiled to himself a little sadly. Alan Ainslie was the only man he had ever met who made remarks to him like that last one and he thought, Sometimes I think he's on the wrong side of the fence in this country. He might have found it easier if he'd been born among us. And then he thought, But the poor old bastard's not on either side. He's got the fence right in his crotch.

SEVEN

FLICKERING HEADLIGHTS jumped at him, solid headlights glared at him and his car throbbed eastward at seventy miles an hour. At this rate he could be in Montreal soon after midnight. He drove entirely by reflex, for his mind had gone far away.

This middle-aged man was also a tiny boy on a faraway beach with his mother. The white shirt and green pants of the boy, the pants secured by cloth braces with white buttons, were bright between the water and the promontory whose shadow lay like that of a giant resting on his elbows with the back of his neck to the late-afternoon sun. Facing the sun was a second-quarter moon white in the cobalt mass of the sky, and the whole cove was awash with sound as the cliff caught and magnified the noise of the water and the screams of sea-birds while the air rushed in cold from the ocean and a black schooner, white sails cracking tight, plunged through the waves in the direction of Newfoundland. The boy and his mother were talking about the father who had been away so long the boy could not remember what he looked like. They were on the beach talking of his homecoming as they did every day and how wonderful his homecoming was going to be. He had not known that his mother was lying because she loved him.

A horn blared and he heard the scream of tires as a doubling car dodged, swung, passed and was gone. Peace was within him. This promontory, this perfect recollection of the sunny sea for a moment filled his soul with cool fresh air. How often over the years he had seen this vision return and smelled the ocean in his mind. The scene had come back to him on the first night he had loved Constance, and the whole promontory had taken off and swung up into the sky, turned itself upside down and fallen and become Constance herself, and the high clouds of childhood had rested still. Later he had seen the rivers and plains and mountains of the empty, enormous land, but the little island had never ceased to be an island within his mind.

Now the night through which he drove was harsh and ghostly, harsh where the neon signs smoldered over barbecues and filling stations and headlights stabbed and tires rushed and screamed, but far over to his left where the Ottawa River widened out, the mist was filled with starlight and ghostly *voyageurs* were gliding through it to the west in their canoes. His new book came into his mind and the cool air left it.

Could Daniel ever, ever understand how it had been for men of his age? How events had happened to so many of them and how some, like himself, had been driven to do irrevocable things not out of any fate created by their characters—at least so far as he understood his own character—but because such things had come with the rations of the epoch into which they had been born; that these things had come from the outside like Western imperialists invading helpless peoples who did not know them, want them or understand them and had changed their lives and twisted them. Now the glow of Montreal in the night sky was reminding him of something. What was it? Yes, of course. This was how the dawn had looked rising out of Denmark the morning they flew home over the North Sea from the first perfect operation, the raid on Hamburg that had set the pavements afire and, so they were told later, killed eighty thousand people. What a friend we had in Hitler, all our rage and sins to bear!

Dr. Ainslie had not lived to see his adopted son in the sky-blue uniform. The doctor, that strange intruder into his childhood whom Chantal and Daniel believed was his real father, had died several years before the Hitler war began. The son-hungry man did not live long enough to know whether the educational experiment he had performed on the adopted orphan had succeeded or failed. The doctor's wife, the foster-mother, had outlived her husband by only a few years so that he had been totally alone, no kin anywhere, when he and Constance had married.

"But I *have* been happy!" Ainslie cried aloud. "Many, many, many times, and while she was alive my life was often glorious."

Yet he still felt a failure, still felt a young man with his way to make. He wished he had accomplished something that existed in its own right, had written a poem or built a house that would last for generations. All of his work was written on water. He had held positions. He had made contributions to general plans, but the contributions were all blurred and mixed with those of other men. Only a handful of men knew about the one valuable thing he had done and it was by pure chance that he had been able to do it. In the nature of things this was something that would never go into the history books, but if he had believed in an anthropomorphic God it would have made him happy to hope that this action, at least, was recorded in the Book of Heaven.

It had begun late one afternoon in the huge lounge of the U.N. Building in New York in the coldest season of the Cold War. The famous Russian had entered alone and sat down near to Ainslie and somebody had brought him a glass of Russian tea. Ainslie could still see the slice of lemon in the glass and the tiny wince of the Russian's tight lips when the first sip of the tea had been too hot. He had sat there looking obliquely at the Russian and suddenly a memory had come to him: he was in a train with his foster-father and the doctor, after staring hard at another passenger across the aisle, turned and said to Alan under his breath, "That poor devil over there has cancer and doesn't know it yet."

Looking at the Russian, Alan Ainslie knew that this man also had cancer, and something in the grim resignation of the parchment face told him the Russian knew it too. On one of his impulses he rose, crossed the floor and asked the Russian if he might join him.

"Vous voulez quelque chose?" the Russian said with an expression which really said, "Go to hell and leave me alone."

"I had the pleasure of meeting you three months ago," Ainslie answered in French. "My name is Ainslie."

The Russian gave a formal smile indicating that he considered him a fool of no consequence, but a current must have established itself between the two of them, for, surprisingly, the Russian asked, "Is it difficult to grow roses in Canada?"

"In the part where I live it is very difficult to keep them. Last year I lost half a dozen bushes from winter-kill."

"Only half a dozen bushes, Mr. Ainslie? A modest garden—but then, you are a modest man."

"With much to be modest about," Ainslie said with a smile.

The Russian relaxed a little and almost chuckled. "That old Churchill—how you people love to quote him when he is rude." Then he looked hard at Ainslie through pince-nez which magnified a pair of the coldest gray eyes Ainslie had ever seen, and said in a tone of sardonic relief, "I see that you are not stupid, Monsieur. It has been our error to think that you people generally are. You have observed something, *n'est-ce pas?*"

Ainslie said nothing to this, his instinct telling him to wait, and the moment seemed strangely luminous. Lights were coming on in New York, but though they shone through the high windows of the lounge, he did not really see them. He seemed seated in a still luminosity with this old, cold, gray man whose name was so hated and feared. Neither of them spoke for nearly five minutes. The Russian ordered another cup of tea and took his time over it. Then he got to his feet, made a short, old-fashioned bow—it occurred to Ainslie how very old-fashioned the man's appearance was, as though he had never left the nineteenth century—and said, "Would it be an imposition if at some time I were to telephone you at your apartment?"

"Would you care to make a note of my number, Your Excellency?"

The gray old face wrinkled like a lizard's for an instant. "That will not be necessary. Remember, however, that it is extremely unlikely that I will ever speak with you again."

"Should Your Excellency desire to, I shall be at your service at any time."

The Russian bowed again and walked stiffly out of the lounge alone, but Ainslie noticed that two big men in stiff dark suits appeared from nowwhere and walked out after him. He remained where he was, nursing the kind of feeling that he used to have before a good race—that something was going to come of this.

In the days of the Old Chief his department had exercised an influence far greater than the strength of its nation warranted. This was because none of them had any illusions about the nation's importance in any decisive matter. Service in the foreign office of a weak power was different in kind from service in a great one, and in the days of their competence none of them were tempted by flattery to forget it. Ainslie was always embarrassed when the home newspapers of the time called Canada "a middle power." There were no middle powers any more, only small ones and a few gigantic ones. No decisions involving life and death could ever come the way of the Department of External Affairs. The consciences of the men who served in it were not strained as were those of the men whose decisions and advice were translated into actions in which the stakes were hundreds of millions of lives and perhaps the world itself. The best the men in External could do was to keep themselves informed and play the role of honest broker if any of the powers wished to use them as such. The Old Chief knew that their influence would disappear if they ever boasted or became self-righteous. Now in the change of climate in Ottawa, the department's influence had become almost nugatory.

Ainslie's instinct about the Russian turned out to be accurate: at eleven o'clock on a Friday night the call came and Ainslie asked Constance to go out to a newsreel theater so that the Russian would find him alone when he arrived. His Excellency appeared at half-past eleven accompanied by the two big men in their stiff dark suits, who did not even trouble to apologize when they cased the apartment before leaving their master alone with his host.

For half an hour the conversation was more ambiguous than any that Ainslie had ever participated in. Finally the lizard's eyes concentrated and their owner said, "It has become too difficult. We all must try to do something. It has become impossibly difficult, but so has the situation."

Ainslie asked himself, "Dare I say it?" and he did say it, before giving himself time to think.

"In other words, Your Excellency, Marx was understandably ignorant of certain future developments within the science of physics?"

The Russian answered with a frigid smile.

"Do you regard the situation as insoluble, Your Excellency?"

The Russian shrugged. "What important thing in this life is ever soluble?"

Before leaving, he took Ainslie's hand in finely-shaped fingers and said, "Small countries, if they are discreet, can occasionally afford to be intelligent."

"Occasionally perhaps—in small things."

"This time it may not be a small thing."

The next day, without telling even Constance a word about the nature of the interview, Ainslie flew to Ottawa and reported the conversation to his superior. The Old Chief occasionally showed signs of clairvoyance, though he profoundly distrusted it both in himself and in others. He ordered Ainslie to keep his interview secret even from his colleagues but to be ready to take any opening the Russian might offer. Weeks passed and though he and the Russian exchanged an occasional bow in the corridors of U.N., nothing happened between them.

Then the Russian acted. At ten o'clock one weekday night he telephoned Ainslie and informed him he was sending a memo which he was to read, and afterwards, if he saw fit, do with it whatever he liked. Ainslie smiled to himself, for he had noted that the Russian had spoken in the tone of a man who had known he was at home that night before he had called him. The memo was delivered by a messenger with a face you could hardly remember even while looking at it; it was delivered without a single word and without a request for a reply or a receipt. When the messenger left, Ainslie read and re-read the memo, whistled softly to himself and noted that it was typed and unsigned. The next day he flew to Ottawa with the paper buttoned up inside a special pocket of his jacket.

After this the matter was taken out of his hands, but things began to happen. Ainslie believed that his role in the affair was unknown to anyone except his chief, but in the curious intricacy of such matters, the Americans found out and one of their men—a very important one—angrily accused him of having gone behind the back of his ally. For a few weeks Ainslie wondered whether he would have to be sacrificed by his department, but if any demand was made for his head, he was never told of it. Then came a night when he was present at a function at which the American Secretary of State was the guest of honor and, after the speeches and the dinner, the Secretary had drawn him into a corner and shaken hands. "You were right," he said, "the man really did have cancer and knew it. We also noted the significance of your observation that he had been raised as a Christian. It may not have been a decisive factor, but who can ever know? At any rate, you have made a most remarkable and valuable contribution."

Out of this curious, hidden chain of accidents and plans had emerged, fashioned by many brains more important than his own, the first of the various conferences which had led to such co-existence as there now was. "It would have happened anyway," Ainslie had said to Constance. With a wife's pride in a loved husband, she had smiled confidently and said, "Would it have?"

The strange things like this, the obscure rain of details that make up a life and career—how small they all seemed now to him! Now it was the moments of personal joy that mattered and as he drove into Montreal he remembered the best of them.

It was the week of his embarkation leave in 1941, a fine July week when Constance, Chantal and he had driven together down to the Gaspé. Gulls, gannets and puffins were diving for fish and Chantal was watching them in delight. The cool brilliance of the afternoon entered them all. In his little family that day he felt a radiance and he knew it was also inside of himself. Now, years later, he could watch that moment as though he had become a spectator of the happiness of strangers, the shining in the parents' eyes when they looked at their child and then at one another and were silent because silence said more than any words could utter. That summer the daisies were like snow in the high Gaspesian meadows. The smells of the sun-warmed land, of the ice-chilled sea, the diving birds, the feeling of the sun on their skins that afternoon when they were parents and still young.

It was on the night after that afternoon that he begot Daniel and Constance conceived him and they were both sure it had happened. "It will be a son," she whispered, "and I'll keep him for you till you come home."

During the nights of danger over Germany an unreasonable confidence had made him braver than he had ever expected to be, for he had always been a man afraid of many things. He had an inner conviction that he would survive in order to see his son.

The city was coming around him now. He turned on the light in the roof of his car and glanced at his watch and saw it was past midnight, well past it. He was tired, but peace had returned to him. How right Joe Lacombe had been that he should have spent more weekends in Montreal with his children, and righter still when he said that he worried and fretted too much. The country existed, didn't it? The rain of contributions made to it by millions of people for so long a time were infinitely more important than the gossamer ideas the clever ones invented to understand the meanings of countries. As Gabriel Fleury was so fond of saying, men can talk themselves into anything, deceive themselves with the words they use to control others, believe in their own propaganda almost indefinitely, but in time reality can talk them out of the word-meshes they spin. So play for time. Soon he would be with Daniel and this time he would try to understand his son and obliterate whatever it was that had risen between them.

He drove slowly now that he was in the city and nearing home. Then suddenly the panic was on him again and he was afraid to go home. He had been away so long and what had happened to the children in the interval? He drove wanderingly about the streets: pools of light at the corners, young people standing in them finishing their Saturday night. He drove up the mountain and the city

125

seemed to have grown even larger than it had been six months ago, a quivering carpet of light for miles, more than two million people now, and in Ottawa the politicians believed they could govern those unknowns invisible under that ocean of electric light.

He was still afraid to go home. Then the wind that had been heard by Gabriel Fleury began to blow moist and tropical and he realized he was sticky from sweat. The heat of this day seemed to have stupefied his brain and he could not stay on the mountain any more. He got into his car and drove back down the switchbacks and for a wild moment he thought of driving into the heart of the city and entering some night club where there were women without faces and noise without music . . . .

Run, run, run till you die,
fox at your heels and crow in the sky.

EIGHT

DANIEL AINSLIE spent most of that hot afternoon in a broadcasting studio making a videotape for his next broadcast. The engineers were now setting up the tape for a replay and Daniel was sitting in the semi-darkness with the man he had just interviewed. Aimé Latendresse was glacially calm, gray-calm, and he was one of those men whose age is so difficult to determine that he could pass for any age between thirty and forty-five. His lanky frame seemed like a case containing an inner pain that had frozen long ago inside of him and had become his sole companion, and the closest he had ever come to mentioning it to Daniel was to say, once, "I used to wonder why they had called me 'The Loved One' and why their own name was 'Tenderness.' It was years before I found out that both names had been chosen for me by the Sisters."

When Latendresse was thirteen a neighboring priest took him out of the orphanage and raised him in his own *presbytère* in a village on the shore of the lower St. Lawrence. He read all the priest's books, he studied woodcarving and became skilful at carving images of saints for the church; he served as an altar boy and when older he entered a seminary. Later he studied with the Dominicans and won a scholarship for a year's study in France. When the year was up he did not come home, but roamed through Europe and the Mediterranean countries supporting himself as an electrician and studying in any public libraries he could find. It was only a year ago that he had reappeared in Quebec, but he made no effort to visit the priest who had befriended him, though the old man was still alive. From occasional things he said, the young men who came under his influence believed that he had left the Church for good, but they knew very little about him. He lived in solitude and supported himself by working at an electrical-appliance shop.

The engineer signed that he was ready, the camera began to roll and Daniel and Latendresse sat in semi-darkness and watched themselves on the monitor screen. Daniel asked the questions and Latendresse answered them in a voice so cold and emotionless that it might have come out of an ice box.

Q. M. Latendresse—what's your opinion of yesterday's riot?

A. It was the most important single event in the life of our people in years.

Q. Why do you say that?

A. Because it was one of those spontaneous acts that mark a change in history—like the taking of the Bastille. It signifies that our people have had enough. Believe me, there will be more riots after this one. This is not the last we shall see. There will be more and more until independence has been achieved, for where else can independence be achieved except in the streets? That riot was produced by the strongest instinct in the world—the instinct of self-preservation.

Q. Against what are the people rising?

A. Against their own past.

Q. Can you be more exact?

A. I can and I will. Against—for the time being—the evil alliance between the worst elements among ourselves, the most slavish, despicable and venal elements among ourselves, and the Anglo-Saxon System.

Q. But in Quebec aren't all our politicians nationalists?

A. [*A thin-lipped smile.*]

Q. But aren't they? Don't all of them get elected on nationalist platforms?

A. We live in the grip of aliens who are a tiny minority here and yet rule us. This they do indirectly, by buying our politicians. That is why we are now prisoners in our own home. That is why we will lose even such a poor home as we have left unless we act.

Q. By "home" do you mean the country at large? Or do you mean Quebec, our particular *patrie*?

A. Naturally I mean Quebec, our particular *patrie*, but I also mean more. I mean the French language, the French culture. Since the Conquest amputated us from our motherland, our language and culture have been all we had left to call our own. Now the Anglo-Saxons are on the point of taking even these things away from us by the time-honored Anglo-Saxon technique of assimilation. I ask you—any of my people, any of my language, who is listening—am I not right? Essentially our home is the French language, and here, in our own land, in old Quebec itself, the Anglo-Saxon System makes it more and more impossible for us to use it except in the privacy of our own homes. The purest proof of what they have done to our spirit is that we have been made so meek that we tolerate this. We must speak the conqueror's language if we are to earn our bread. A little more of this and our language will disappear in North America—*our* language, the first European language ever spoken in North America above the Rio Grande. A little more and we ourselves will be swallowed up and become as though we had never been, as though our ancestors had suffered for absolutely nothing, and then our mission in the world will disappear.

Q. How can you put it so drastically, M. Latendresse? So simply?

A. Because it is exactly that drastic and exactly that

simple. Try for a job above the workman's level and see what happens. You will have to speak English. And what does this mean beyond the degradation of it? It means something more than that. It means that your *ability* will be judged in a foreign language, and this means that you will automatically be judged inferior. They call this officially a bilingual country. They put a few words of French on the dollar bills. But at the moment there is not a single French-Canadian high official in the nation's entire railway system. Is this because our people lack ability? It is not. It is because they are French Canadians. Now for the first time thousands of young people are attending our colleges. What awaits them when they try to market their knowledge and skills in the Anglo-Saxon System? Inferiority awaits them. They will be judged inferior, and in fact they will *be* inferior forever unless we become masters in our own house and Quebec becomes an independent state.

Q. A different kind of question, M. Latendresse—are you hostile to the English?

A. That is like asking me if I am hostile to human nature. People always tread over the rights of those who allow their rights to be trodden over. The English only do what others do.

Q. But there are so many of them and we are so few! In this whole English-speaking continent we are only about two and a half per cent.

A. What movement that ever changed the face of the world was ever begun in a majority? Yes, they are successful now. So were the Romans once. I even admit that theirs is the most successful culture in the history of the world. No other has ever been so successful in making other cultures feel helpless without actually dominating them by troops and secret police. They rule by a method of corruption so subtle it escapes the victims' notice. The strength of the Anglo-

Saxon System lies in its incredible simplicity.

Q. I'm not sure I understand what you mean by that. Could you explain?

A. Easily. People want to do things the easy way, don't they? The Anglo-Saxon System understands this, and it turns the entire human race into a producing and consuming machine. Enough for the inferior not to make them desperate. Enough for the inferior for them to say they have it much better than their ancestors did. But more—much, much more—for the rich masters. The Anglo-Saxon table is so richly and luxuriously furnished that the crumbs from it are much bigger than any crumbs from the tables of cruder tyrants in the past. But crumbs they are, just the same. Look at this province! Our forbears settled it, they endured the harshness of the winters for three centuries, they went out from here and explored most of the continent long ago. Then the Anglo-Saxons took it away from them. And this land, which our sweat developed, is now one of the richest there is. But do our people own it? You know, don't you, that at the moment the Anglo-Saxon control covers more than eighty-five per cent of our entire economy? [*A pause, followed by a slight change of voice.*] In the past century patriots in France used to say, "Speak of it never; think of it always." But I say to you, the time has come here to think of it always, to speak of it always, to think and speak about nothing else at all until we have overcome. We are capable if we know we are capable. Just that—if we *know* we are capable.

Q. With your permission I will change the subject slightly. Do you believe—as many of our people do—that we can gain our rights within Confederation if we press for them?

A. If nearly a century of Confederation has left us in our present condition, how can you even ask such a question? This can go on forever as it has gone on in Latin

America. What do free elections signify if they never touch the economic root? There is only one way to heal the wound in our race and that is by becoming independent. [*A slow, grim, grudging smile appeared for an instant on Latendresse's pinched face.*] The Anglo-Saxons honestly believe they benefit everyone they exploit. That is the secret of their power. They are good at production and business and they know it. They insist that what is good for themselves must be good for everyone else—even when it destroys their meaning.

Q. But isn't there more to it than that? Haven't the Anglo-Saxons in this country changed greatly in recent years? Don't many of them blame their own ancestors for the injustices they did us, and work to restore our rights? Aren't there many who sincerely try to do this now?

A. The ones who pretend to like us—I'll go farther and admit that some of them really do like us and want to help—are now our most dangerous enemies. They do not understand the nature of their own System. They do not understand that the controllers of the System are happy to use men of good-will to weaken our purpose. There will always be some Anglo-Saxons eager to cooperate with what they call our moderates. It is this combination of weak-minded good-will that I particularly dread. If we allow such men to soften us, we will lose our last chance, because the next few years will tell the tale. If we make accommodations once more, we will soon see how they really regard us. We will become what they say among themselves we are now and always have been—talkers, whiners, complainers. [*Again Latendresse paused and stared at his unseen audience.*] This you must never forget—they take it for granted, the Anglo-Saxons do, that everyone wants to copy them. In Asia the Americans are bombing and burning alive helpless people—and for what? They tell us exactly for what—to compel those people to sit docile while the Americans pour in money and equipment to destroy the ancient Asian cultures and turn them into the culture of Coca-Cola and the supermarket. The English here are always asking what we want. I can answer them. Dignity is what we want. The right to be ourselves is what we want. Even the right to be allowed to make our own mistakes is what we want.

Q. Do you think we are alone in wanting that?

A. Alone? When the Anglo-Saxons together make up less than nine per cent of the world's population?

Q. Two more questions, M. Latendresse. First—if we separate—won't they accuse us of destroying their country?

A. If they do, I have a simple answer for them. Messieurs, your sudden interest in us comes too late. You have let a century pass without ever having tried to understand us, without ever showing us the least affection. You have not been cruel—no. You have merely been indifferent. You have merely taken us for granted and taken it for granted that we would never change. You have not even paid us the ordinary courtesy of trying to learn the language of those your own constitution boasts are your compatriots. We owe you nothing more, Messieurs. There is nothing you can say now, nothing you can do now, nothing you can think now that can possibly interest us.

Q. My final question—can we become independent without bloodshed?

A. I sincerely hope so.

Q. But do you believe it?

A. I believe that we should face whatever may be necessary to gain our independence—no matter what it may be, that we must accept it.

Q. But do you believe our independence can be achieved without bloodshed?

A. [*A long pause, then the glacially expressionless eyes stared out from the screen.*] In the entire history of

133

the human race, has that ever happened? Now—have I made myself clear, or not?

There was a crash of music, the producer's voice repeated the names of Daniel and Latendresse, identified the program, then the images faded off the screen and Daniel and Latendresse looked at one another in the darkened studio.

"You were wonderful," Daniel said.

Latendresse permitted himself a slight shrug. "Was I? What I just said must be repeated a million times by others before it can be called wonderful. It will not be wonderful until the time has arrived when we no longer have to persuade but can give orders and people will spring up from all sides to obey them." He changed the subject. "I suppose you know some of the boys interviewed your father in Ottawa this morning?"

Daniel, also on his feet, was aware of how stifling the studio had become; klieg lights earlier and the heat that had entered from outside.

"I haven't seen my father for months," he said.

Latendresse moved toward the door. "Arrange a debate between your father and me."

The tightness of steel bands seemed to press Daniel's chest. "Can't we leave him out of this?"

"How is that possible, considering who he is?"

"He'd never agree to debate with you, Aimé. He'd say there couldn't be anything to discuss between himself and a separatist. He'd give his life for Confederation."

Latendresse smiled ever so slightly. "I am aware of that. That is why I am sure he would agree to debate with me."

They left the studio together and parted company at the first corner without shaking hands. Daniel watched Latendresse moving away and thought how thin he was, how meager his physique, how narrow his shoulders, how heroic he was to have endured with so few advantages. He thought of Gandhi and tears came to his eyes. Then, as he watched, he saw Latendresse stop, turn around and come back to him. Daniel moved forward to meet him again.

His eyes more opaque than usual, yet strangely glowing, Latendresse said, "I gain much comfort from something Lenin said once. Revolutionaries are dead men on furlough. It gives me great happiness to think that. But there's not much time. Now they have the power to blow up the whole world. They've never been so strong as they are now, but if a man is too strong—" Latendresse did not finish the sentence. He turned and walked away and Daniel stood and watched him go. If you did not notice his eyes, he thought, you would never notice this man in a crowd, not even in a room. Daniel did not know where he lived, though he had his telephone number, but as he watched him move away among the throng on the sidewalk it was as though the passers-by made a path for him without knowing they did so.

NINE

Twilight had not quite disappeared when Daniel Ainslie parked his second-hand sports car (he had bought it on installment at a bargain price only a week ago) in an over-lived-in district where shadows cast by street lamps filtered through elms onto curving outside-staircases (one or two apartments above, one or two below) and there were one-room shops surviving from a simpler age which sold beer, tobacco, candy, soft drinks, newspapers, comic books, girlie magazines, canned goods and packaged groceries. Families were sitting on the steps of the staircases and on rocking chairs on the platforms of the second stories, some of them with beer or soft drinks, some of them fanning themselves with folded newspapers, most of them talking quietly so that the twilit street seemed to be murmuring. In a puddle of light in front of one of the little stores was a cluster of boys and girls drinking pop and fondling one another. The boys wore jeans and T-shirts and the hair of most of them was long and shaggy. The girls were in hip-and-thigh stretchies of thin material and bright colors so that their lines were as clearly drawn as though they were naked. A girl giggled as Daniel walked past and the expressions on the faces of the boys made him think of calves. "Sexacola and Saturday night," he muttered to himself as he passed, and added the local slogan of the year, " 'Y a d'la joie!' "

Daniel was intoxicated with the feeling of power and wonder at himself that comes to a very young man who has succeeded suddenly and beyond expectation and believes he is becoming famous. He told himself that it was quite possible that his program would change history. As he walked along he felt omnipotently detached. Everything was falling into its slot in the scheme of things. He also saw women.

On this fantastically hot night the city was a bargain basement of raw sex on display, with thousands of females of all ages in those skin-tight garments that had come into fashion, and he understood the significance of it. Latendresse had explained that in the *fin de siècle,* in the trance of desperate pleasure before the cataclysm wipes away an old order, there is always a sexual explosion, a Mardi gras before another of history's Lenten seasons ushers in the day of retribution and atonement. So it had been in France before the Revolution, in St. Petersburg before the Revolution, in Havana before Castro came down from the hills and took the city. Even some of Daniel's friends in the movement were part of it. One of them had begun with girls when he was thirteen, his explanation being that he had discovered that his parents were unfaithful to each other so why shouldn't he do as he pleased? He boasted that he had had fifty-one girls— he had kept a count of them—before he was eighteen and now he wanted something more exciting. Drinking beer in the tavern where the young political folk-singer strummed his guitar, this boy made bitter jokes against the priests, imagining how jealous they were of the young these days when they could no longer get compensation for their own celibacy by making those who enjoyed their sex feel ashamed of themselves. But not many of the others were like this one. Some were almost sacredly dedicated. More girls were ahead of Daniel, buttocks and thighs, plump one wobbling and a lean one popping up and down. He felt a claw in his groin and thought, It would be like peeling oranges to get at that one.

Over the roofs and not far away he saw the tops of the

new skyscrapers built by the corporations out of glass, chrome and ferro-concrete, one of them completely illuminated and gleaming with the cold purity of an immense ice palace. Yes, he thought, yes! If you chose that thin one you could do it. Anyone could obtain a plan of it and you could do it. If you placed the explosive at exactly the proper balance points you could bring that thin one down. You could bring it down screaming and grinding and trembling—no, something better! If you did it with absolute perfection you could hang it at a twenty-degree angle as the students in Budapest made Stalin's statue hang, the great tryrant seeming to kiss the ground in front of the students, and if you did that here, with this thin one, the businessmen would shower out the windows like the larvae of caterpillars out of their tent when you put the torch to them.

His body was strong, his shoulders sloped and his jaw thrust forward out of a short, robust neck. His hair was cut close and brushed forward like a Roman's. He wore a light, close-fitting suit made in Paris and in its lapel was a Ban-the-Bomb button; his shoes were light, pointed and had been made in Italy. He reached his destination and mounted an outside-staircase, and on the platform in front of the upper apartment he emerged into a maze of light and shadow caused by a street light half-hidden in the branches of an elm. He saw a cloud of insects in the light and there were more insects trying to get through the screen of the door, attracted by the light within. He loved this old street where French people lived. He pressed the bell button and soon a woman appeared in the light and greeted him in French. She had a contralto voice which suited with her rich black hair, and her French was exquisite to listen to.

"Daniel—but how charming to see you! Did you expect Clarisse to be here? I'm afraid she isn't."

He followed her through a small vestibule into a living room hung with reproductions of Braque and Chagall and two original oils by good painters without a reputation. There was an Arabic rug with a thick pile on the floor, and bronze Arabic bowls standing on tables reflected the light. One wall of the room was lined with books from floor to ceiling, many of them bound in calf.

"Clarisse was expecting me, wasn't she?"

The woman bent down to pick up the book she had been reading and had left spread open on the floor beside her chair, and as she did so a light summer blouse parted from her old-fashioned dirndl skirt and he saw honey-colored flesh at the small of her back. She rose and smiled with a kind of grave welcome, though her eyes were shrewd and observant. She had prominent front teeth and her underlip was also prominent, but her face was slim with very soft, creamy skin. Her eyes were large in it. Daniel admired her as someone exotic yet profoundly, anciently French in her culture and grace, for the language as she used it was like music, its shadings at times a kind of *pointillisme*, and she spoke it with a formality that sounded strange over here yet with her was completely natural.

He repeated his question about Clarisse. Was her mother expecting her back soon?

"You've been doing such exciting things lately it is small wonder if you got your dates confused," she said.

"But she knew I was coming. I'm sure of it."

"Then it is very bad of Clarisse. But you know how vague she can be."

A flash of anger went through him; frustration, and tonight of all nights he thought he had earned the right not to be frustrated by anyone. He had wanted to take her down to the studio and play back the tape he had made with Latendresse and after that . . .

"She disappeared after breakfast with some of her friends," her mother went on. "I'm not sure just who they were, but there were two cars and they went north to some lake. There was to be swimming and water-skiing, she said. I thought it would do her good. She said not to

140

expect her befo e midnight but when she left and I was standing on the balcony she called up to say she'd be out all night and not to expect her till sometime tomorrow."

He sat down, his nerves tightening, and said nothing.

"I'm afraid there's nothing in the house but beer," she said. "Good wine is impossibly expensive over here and not even the beer tastes as it should."

"They don't mature it any more," he said without interest. "They save money that way."

"But since it's all we have, let's pretend it's nice."

"You have one. I don't like drinking."

"On a night like this it would do you good, Daniel." She smiled and stretched and as she did so her bosom arched. "Everyone I've met today has complained of the heat but I've felt alive for the first time in months. I thought that awful winter would never end. No wonder you're as gloomy as Russians, you Canadians."

She went out to the kitchen and Daniel, restless, got up and crossed to the window and looked out. He could smell a faint odor of car-exhaust. Some elderly couples were rocking on balconies across the street and he looked at them and thought how the System had used them up and wasted their lives and left them there on their balconies to draw their old-age pensions and pray to the saints. They were expendable; it was a pity, but they were. The teen-agers were still at the corner drinking their colas and fondling one another, those meager boys with their girls, and one of the boys let out a whoop like a mating call. They were expendable too. You could never do anything with people like them.

He heard her return and gestured toward the window. "Look out there, Marielle. Those kids down there, look at them."

She was carrying a tray with glasses, a small pitcher of ice, a tall bottle with a red label and two splits of Schweppes.

"Look what I found—a whole unopened bottle of Cinzano! Clarisse must have brought it in. Try some, Daniel. On a hot night it goes deliciously with tonic."

"Those kids out there," he said.

She poured some Cinzano over the ice she had placed in the glasses and poured tonic in afterwards and it fizzed up red and looked cold and frothy. She held out a glass and he accepted it automatically.

"Those kids down there," he repeated.

The woman went to the window, looked down and smiled. "How lovely! The good time of life. I love to see them like that together, thinking the old lovely thoughts."

He was astonished. Of all the people he knew, she was the last he would have expected to say a thing like that.

"The good time of life?" He stared at her. "The lovely thoughts? Them?"

"But of course! For ones like those, what other time is there? Do you mean you grudge it to them, Daniel?"

His eyes began to smolder but he kept his voice quiet. "That's the beginning of the new serfdom, what you're looking at there. The serfdom *à l'américaine*. Don't you see the poverty they came from and what's in front of them? Inside a few years they'll all have babies. They'll be hooked to the System the rest of their lives. There's an organized, scientific conspiracy against them and they're too stupid to know it. Sex is the new opium of the people. The only ambition any of those are going to have after a few years"—he gestured fiercely—"is to be able to make the last payment on the washing machine and the car they never owned in the first place. Buy now—pay later! Have you never looked at the notices of the bailiff's sales in the papers? These days there are pages and pages of them."

She smiled. "Does the world end with a bailiff's sale?" She sipped her Cinzano. "Daniel, what makes you so tense tonight?"

"I don't think I'm tense."

"You always are, but tonight the tendons are sticking out on your wrists. Are you angry with Clarisse, or is it because of yesterday?"

142

His teeth flashed in one of his rare smiles. "Did Clarisse tell you about yesterday?"

"Oh yes. She was very pleased and excited."

His ardent face strained forward out of his short, taut neck. "Yesterday was only the beginning. You should have seen their faces. Their faces at the windows. This was the first time men like them ever noticed our existence. Those buildings they're so proud of are practically made of glass. Yesterday I bet they wished they'd been made of steel. A row of American-made bastilles in the middle of the city, that's what they are. You should have seen their faces. We scared them, Marielle."

The frown-line that had appeared between her eyes was making him feel uncertain. He admired her so much, her mind and her old-world dignity of speech and carriage.

"Daniel," she said quietly, "do you think it intelligent to frighten men like them?"

"We frightened them all right. You should have seen their faces."

"I can very well imagine their faces. I can also imagine what they said among themselves afterwards."

He grinned. "So can I."

"Can you? I wonder if you can. They have much to lose, men like them, and they don't often lose it."

"They lost it in your country."

"Did they?" That smile of hers. "Well, the country certainly became independent, if that's what you mean. Now it has its little vote in the United Nations and those so very necessary things, and a few politicians we remember not having two francs to rub against each other are now living in hotel suites with their mistresses. But when it was all over, one noticed that the ones who'd been rich before were still rich."

"What are you trying to say to me?"

"Forgive me, Daniel. I'm being *méchante*."

He looked at the floor in frustration, then up again, and she was calm in her chair. She had come out from

Morocco a few years ago with her only child, whom Daniel had met at the university, and the two women were so unlike one another it was hard to believe they were related, much less mother and daughter. Marielle Jeannotte was the daugther of a professor who had been killed in the war; she herself had studied art, but now she was a dress designer in a new, small and extremely expensive *boutique* which had been opened some years ago by one of her friends from Europe. She was astonishingly young-looking to be the mother of a college student.

"Clarisse agrees with me," he said.

"She's been here only two years and how can she possibly understand such a strange country in that time?"

"She understands perfectly how we feel."

"I'm afraid I know my poor Clarisse better than you, *mon cher*."

"It's got to come!" he cried at her. "It must come! There's no other way. There's a wound in our race."

She shook her head and he broke into a litany, ending with, "Just to be ourselves at last! For once not to feel this awful weight! Is that asking too much?"

"Where does this weight come from, Daniel!"

"It comes—it comes from everywhere. We're born with it."

She looked away. "Suddenly you make me feel very old and futile and disappointed."

He was taken aback. "You old? Marielle, you're as young as—" he almost said "as young as Clarisse." Then he was stopped by the thought that Clarisse often looked older than her mother, on account of her expression and the sallowness of her skin.

"Daniel," she said quietly, her voice sad and serious, "when you talk this way you remind me of a boy I knew. He was very like you too. He even looked a little like you. He was an idealist like you. He had shoulders and a head like yours, though his hair was darker. He had a lovely mind, but he's dead now. So is the cause he died for."

"But that was in Europe. It's not like that here at all. We could make it work here. It's been proved we can make it work here."

Her hands made a quick arabesque in the air. "By whom has this been proved?"

"Experts have been working on it. Working quietly in cells."

"Oh my dear, life is so short and precious and youth is almost all there is. So experts are working on this in cells! Experts always are working on something in cells." She looked away and said thoughtfully, "When I decided to come over here I knew there would be many things I would find disagreeable, but one thing I was sure I would never see again, and that was people ruining their lives for political ideas." She looked at him sternly, yet with great uneasiness, anxiety and fondness. "Clarisse is a turbulent girl, Daniel. She's always been neurotic and self-willed and I find nothing so terrifying as self-willed ignorance. I wish you would stop being romantic about Europe and the Old World. People there understand things it will take you North Americans another century to learn. You are all puritans over here and you don't even guess what it does to you. Now I want to tell you something, Daniel, and I want to tell you it honestly." She paused and the look in her eyes troubled him. "Young men never plunge into movements like this without some kind of personal reason. Usually they don't understand what it is until it's too late and sometimes they never understand it. If you were poor—if you'd come from an unhappy home or a deprived one—then I could understand you easily." A shrug. "But you come from an educated home. Your father is a distinguished man—I've seen his picture in the papers. And people have told me he's a very kind man. So what is it with you, Daniel?"

His face was troubled and he looked away. "Well, all right," he said. "It's him. I mean, it's my father."

"How so—your father?"

"What they've done to him. He's thrown away his

whole life for this rotten country and what reward has he got? Now he doesn't seem to know what he's doing any more. He reminds me of some well-meaning American in Viet Nam. I see what they've done to him and I—"

He got to his feet and roamed the room, talking in an intense voice and repeating himself, until she interrupted him.

"Do you really believe you are fond of Clarisse?"

He stared. "What's that got to do with what I've been saying?"

"My dear boy, can't you even guess what Clarisse's trouble is? That poor child of mine can't even like herself. How can anyone expect her to like anyone else, least of all a man?" Another flux of gestures. "It could be said that this is my fault. Possibly it is. But if it is my fault, does that alter the fact?" She paused and added quietly, "I'm sure you are not normally hostile, Daniel. Unfortunately, she has been hostile ever since she was a baby."

He stared at the pointed toes of his shoes and wondered why he was so unhappy, why he felt as though ropes were binding him. Why so many of them felt it, all the ones who were able to think. Then he saw her smiling at him with affection and this strange, uncomfortable understanding.

"You see, Marielle, my father—well, I don't know how to put it. Maman's family is one of those wonderful old French-Canadian families related to all kinds of others, but the truth is that they never really knew where my father came from. He came from another province none of them had even visited. And he was all alone when he came here—no family of his own at all. Of course he was awfully well educated. His father was a doctor and seems to have been a remarkable man in his way. When I was studying, Dad was always pleased. Nothing ever made him happier than when I got good reports. He used to talk to me about the necessity of this country *earning* its way into civilization and I never understood what he

146

meant. *Earning* its way into civilization—can you understand what he meant by that?"

She smiled quietly. "I can very easily understand what he meant."

"But what is this wonderful civilization he keeps talking about? This confederated Canada—he loves the very idea of it, but I tell you it's just plain crazy. The English have sold nearly all of it out to the Americans long ago. That department of his in the government only proves what I'm saying. The English don't want him and the time's soon coming when the French will have to turn on him as well. It's horrible. Bulstrode has turned that department of his into a national joke. It's terrible what they do to a man like him and he just lets them do it."

She said nothing to this. Instead, she crossed to a table in the far corner of the room, opened a drawer and returned to her chair with some needlework. She put on the glasses she used for reading and her fingers got busy.

"You said you saw his pictures in the paper," he burst out. "But nobody knows what he really looks like from them. You see, one side of his face got burned in the war and he lost one of his eyes as well. The eye doesn't show —I mean it doesn't bother you—but the left side of his face has this skin-graft that looks queer and glazed. It's not as—well, it isn't ugly any more as it was when he first came home from the war, but it's—well, anyway, Marielle, when they take his pictures he always turns the bad side of his face away from the camera."

"Why should he not, if it got burned in the war?"

"He never got over the war. All the men of his age are like that. That war—they never got over it and they never will. The war and the depression they're always talking about. They have no idea what it's like for us now or how we feel about anything. It's all right for him. He was a hero in the war. But the fathers of the boys I know, the French boys, hardly any of *them* wanted to be used by the English in a war to save England. And what did the

English do here? They insulted them and called them zombies. They conscripted them and made them ashamed. French-Canadian regiments were wonderful in the war, but the English called us cowards because we didn't want to be conscripted to fight for another country. Did French Canada have any stake in the war? When it was over, did anyone ask us what we wanted done afterwards? Can't you understand what it's like to be a French Canadian?"

"Perhaps I can—if you can explain it to me."

"It's hell. It's plain hell. We suffer and we don't know why. But now—yes, now we know why and we're going to change things unless we're sold out once more." He strained forward. "I've met a marvelous man lately. He's older than any of the rest of us—much older. He's been everywhere—French, Italy, Algeria, South America—he's even been in China. He told me only today that in a situation like ours, a friend like my father is more dangerous than the worst and most open enemy."

She glanced up. "How original this new friend of yours appears to be! I suppose he's this Aimé Latendresse that Clarisse is always talking about? Tell me something else, Daniel—was your father very strict with you?"

"What's that got to do with what I've been saying?"

"It might have much to do with it."

"Well, no—not exactly. But he always had plans for me. And he can't understand. If I—if I have to do what I know I must do—look, it's not him, it's this horrible System. And he talks too much. He used to be a professor for a while and I think he'd have been happier if he'd stayed one, but before the war, in this depression they're always talking about, they kept him as a lecturer at a miserable salary without promotion because they thought he was a socialist and he'd gone out on the end of the limb for the unemployed. He nearly enlisted in the Spanish Civil War, and if that doesn't prove—look at what's happened in Spain since then! Franco's the only

148

one who's kept them *all* out. After that, when Dad had gone into External Affairs, he left it to fight against Hitler though he was over-age and was supposed to be indispensable. He nearly got killed doing it. And what did *that* war do except turn over the whole world to the Americans and Russians and leave us more helpless than we ever were? Inside twenty-five years nobody will be able to tell the Russians and Americans apart unless he uses a microscope. The Americans are betraying all their allies and the Russians are betraying all theirs and—"

"Latendresse again?"

"It's true, isn't it?"

"Daniel, is this Latendresse a spoiled priest by any chance?"

"What's that got to do with it? In the old days, the empires went after slaves and raw materials, but now what the Americans are after is consumers. That's their famous Way of Life—turn the whole world into consumers of American products. If they keep on getting away with it, it will mean they've turned the whole world into a colossal American supermarket with cheap copies of Americans in there, buying. You haven't been over here long enough to see how they operate. Even Dad understands how they operate. They've taken over the English in this country completely, and now they're after us. Those products they sell here—do you know the way they do it? They hire French Canadians to go down to the States to translate their advertising slogans into French. That's their idea of culture—advertising."

He realized that his eyes were following the curves of her body as they flowed down into the narrowing curves of her waist and out again into her hips. Her body made him think of a soft river pouring into the lake of her hips.

"You see, Marielle, even though Dad never went to church, in a funny way he's really a saintly kind of man. He's willing to put up with anything they do to him so

149

long as he thinks it's for the sake of the country—of his idea of it, which isn't theirs. For instance, suppose I went to him and said, 'Look, Dad, you've done the best anyone could possibly do and it's all been useless,' do you know what he would say? He'd say—and he'd really believe it—that if we can keep the peace for another ten years the crisis will simply disappear." Suddenly his voice rose. "That swine Bulstrode! He's making a fool out of my father! It's horrible for me to see a man like him used by somebody like Bulstrode. That effigy we burned yesterday was so life-like you'd think it was Bulstrode himself. He burned well, Marielle, he burned brilliantly."

She laid down her needlework and removed her glasses. He felt she was watching him, yet he realized that she was not looking into his eyes. A smile he could not fathom had formed at the corners of her full mouth. He felt that something was rending and cracking inside of him and then he heard the deep, bass voice of Montreal in the night.

"It sounds like the lion house in the zoo at feeding time," he muttered.

"What sounds like the lion house?"

"The city. Can't you hear it too?"

"I can even feel it. I've had this sensation in cities before and it frightens me. Tell me—why do you pretend to have so little respect for your father and men his age?"

"It's not my father. It's not him at all. It's the others he goes along with. How can anyone respect them? They don't even respect themselves."

"Do you really believe that?"

"They're a pretty awful lot, Marielle. They keep telling us they've given us everything, but what everyone sees is that they've given us everything except the chance of being ourselves. They're so generous they make me vomit. Generous! I call it bribery. Cars, bank accounts, trips to Europe—if we want to get married they'll furnish the

150

support. But what's the price-tag on all this? The price-tag says we're to turn ourselves into carbon copies of their own corrupted, dishonest, useless selves. They offer us a world no decent person can possibly respect. In the States they're conscripting high-school drop-outs to fight against helpless people. Why? Because if they haven't got a war going somewhere, their whole rotten System will collapse and they know it. They're liars and professional liars, into the bargain. Their advertising is lies, their propaganda is lies, their politics is lies and their lives are the worst lies of all."

She was still watching him with an expression he could not understand and he felt an overpowering desire to justify himself. But before he could think of anything to say, she interrupted him.

"You haven't even tasted your Cinzano."

"Well, if it would please you." He looked at his glass but did not move his hand toward it. "I'll be perfectly frank and admit I'm scared of drink. You see, little by little Dad's got into the habit of drinking too much. That's part of the System too. They can't do business any more except over lunch and with cocktail parties and that means —I find it very disgusting, the English and Americans of Dad's age. Their masks fall off and they remind me of overgrown babies with their bottles. Of course Dad never looks like that, but it sneaks up on him and he begins talking too loud and then—well, something's worrying him and he begins to boast. Of course it's not real boasting. It's as though he had to prove to people—maybe even to himself—that in spite of everything he's really done something important after all. He can never relax."

She looked up from her needlework. "Why are you so afraid of being a man, Daniel? It's not such a terrible fate, and you can't avoid it anyway."

Exasperated, tighter than ever with a new kind of fear, he cried out at her, "Why do you keep saying such things to me tonight?"

"Because you keep saying such things to me, dear," she said gently.

He buried his face in his hands, his shoulders hunched and rigid. Staring down through his spread fingers he saw the toes of his Italian shoes and he began talking again as though a dam had burst inside of him, burst wide open.

"Lately I've taken to walking the streets after dark. It's fantastic, the truth you can see in this city at night. You can go for miles without seeing a single *Anglais*. They know no more about this city than the English knew about India. When I learn more about television techniques I want a program about this city after dark. About *la nation* after dark. The camera spying. The camera working as if it had a mind of its own. The camera just telling me what to do with it. The people speaking in broken sentences. That's where the truth is, in broken sentences. Their expressions when you catch them with the truth on their faces. The people are smoldering. There's not enough room for them any more. They live in the city like a huge African kraal with the forests all around them. The lights on the snow in the streets, the dirty snow in the streets, when the men come drunk out of the taverns. The businessmen slinking into the night clubs to see the girls take off their clothes and wiggle and despise them. The girls prowling around the streets for the only thing left that means anything to anyone any more. They never see what controls them now. What controls them is like the spirits in the jungle. I know a student from Africa and he says that when people leave the village and go out into the jungle to defecate, it's taboo to utter another person's name. Somebody else may be there in the dark and hear you. The people here never made this city. They don't own anything in it. They're just here. I want background music of a new kind. No tunes, just noise. A new kind of noise. I can hear it in my mind but I don't know how to play it yet. The people are ready to explode. They want to smash things."

Her face remained tranquil while she listened to all this and when finally he stopped, his hands quivering, it was as though his eyes had come in out of the dark and at last he really saw her. He saw a woman who was like a girl wounded, and he saw that this calmness of hers was only a dressing over the wound, and now he was certain that underneath her blouse and skirt she was entirely naked and that her body was as youthful as his own. Except that once for nine months Clarisse had lived and grown inside of it. How could a stranger like Clarisse have—

She tucked her needlework back into her basket and got to her feet.

"It's too warm even for me to do this kind of work tonight."

As she moved across the floor he felt a sudden wave of exultation and clarity as he saw the beauty of her. She was his idea of a Mediterranean woman who had been trained to walk with jars of olive oil on her head. She returned to her chair without speaking.

"I get so worried about this I get sick," he said. "A few nights ago I thought of it and I actually vomited. I see what's bound to happen and I can't help it. You see, any time now Dad is going to be used as the key to unlock our prison door. Unless he gives up and gets out of the government, I mean. He's going to be attacked and ridiculed and burned in effigy like we burned Bulstrode yesterday."

She looked at him in alarm, and her face twisted with anger and contempt. "Daniel, this Latendresse you and Clarisse so admire is a wicked man."

"Latendresse?" His eyes opened in astonishment. "Latendresse never said anything to me about burning Dad in effigy."

"Then who did?"

His hands twisted and his face distorted. "Nobody did, but if things go on—and they're bound to because nothing can stop it now—somebody's certain to think of it because—listen, it's inevitable that somebody will think of

153

it. The English have got to be made to move, you see. If our movement turns on Dad, the English will say, 'Now at last we know where we stand with those French bastards.' I can hear them saying it. 'Alan Ainslie was the best friend they ever had. He's leaned over backwards for them for years and now look at what thanks he's got!' You see," he went on explaining, "at least half of the English want to join up with the Americans anyway and this would give them just the excuse they're looking for. I can hear them—'To hell with those damned Peasoups! Let them stew in their own juice and see if we care. Let's *us* be the ones to separate from *them*!' "

Unconsciously he had switched into English and his final words had come out with a harsh, mocking American accent.

He watched her reach to a side table and pick up a blue packet of cigarettes.

"Have one with me?" she said, extending a package of Gitanes.

He took a cigarette and bent forward with his lighter to ignite hers, and as he did so she steadied his hand with her own. He saw the soft fullness of her bosom, full and soft and curved, and then the bitter smoke of the cigarette made him cough and he returned to his chair.

"Daniel," she said quietly, as though she had never even heard the last things he had said, "I'm not going to ask you if you have ever made love to Clarisse because I know you haven't. Nor will you ever. She dislikes men. Don't think from this that I'm suggesting that she is a lesbian. She is simply cold and hostile to men."

With a spasmodic movement he put out his hand to his Cinzano, picked it up and swallowed half of it in swift gulps.

"So it would be a relief to me," she went on, "if you and Clarisse admitted that not only do you not even like one another, but that you frustrate each other as well. You do one another no good, you two."

He sat in silence and she let him keep it as long as he wished. It was minutes before he began talking again.

"If we give up now," he said, "the last spark of resistance will die out. We'll be absorbed. Our children will be conscripted to fight the Chinese for the Americans just as their fathers were conscripted to fight the Germans for the British—unless the generals incinerate the whole world first, as they probably will."

As he looked into her face he again saw that expression of sad, understanding affection.

"Poor dear!" she said. "I suppose it's natural that so many of you young people take so much pleasure out of the Bomb."

"Pleasure out of the Bomb! Marielle, what next are you going to say to me?"

"Nothing more than that it's natural that you should. It's one of the most natural things in the world that you should."

She sat very erect and calm, she sat stately, and he thought of another woman who had sat that way.

"I wish you'd known Maman, Marielle. Gabriel Fleury —he's from France and he was Dad's navigator in the war—he's been practically a member of our family and Chantal and I call him Uncle Gabriel—he used to say that Maman understood people better than anyone he'd ever known." Daniel was smiling now, almost relaxed. "She was wonderful with everyone. Dad and she adored each other. He was perfectly safe so long as she was alive. If she was alive she'd never have let him be taken in by those politicians. When we were living at the lake in the summers I remember how they used to go out walking in the lane among the birch trees. They always walked hand in hand."

"It must be very hard for your father now."

"He's pretty lonely. He's worse than that—he's just plain lost. He never comes home any more. I don't know why."

"No wonder," she said, "with a marriage like that, your father should think that this country could have a wonderful future. For that matter, it's done pretty well as things are. Considering everything, the record is formidable."

"That's what the English are always saying. What I say is, 'A fine ride—said the rider to the horse.'"

Her lips pursed slightly, but soon they smiled again, smiled with affection.

"Daniel dear, I'm going to say something I'm afraid you are not going to like. But you must remember where I come from and what I have seen. You people in this movement of yours—you have no idea how provincial you sound. You talk as though Quebec were the center of the universe. You talk as though nobody ever had feelings like yours before."

"That's unfair."

"I'm thinking of something else you keep harping on," she said, still smiling. "About not respecting older people. Well—do you respect me?"

"Of course I do."

"And do you think Clarisse does too?"

"She certainly never said she didn't. Of course she does."

"I wonder," she said with a strange smile, "if the time has not come for me to tell you certain things about Clarisse and me."

It was her tone that alarmed him more than her words.

"It is so different here. Perhaps it's the long winters. I don't know. I wish you could see the Mediterranean sometime, and especially North Africa."

"Yes," he said, "yes, I dream of going there."

"The odors themselves are full of history. There was the dryness of the desert behind us, but in front was the sea, and in the Arab quarter there was a curious acridity. Some of the landscape is the color of a lion."

He would not and could not depart from his obsession.

"What I dread," he went on as though she had never mentioned North Africa, "is that nothing will happen at all. That some of the English like Dad are going to extract enough concessions out of the rest of them—minor concessions—that our people will fall for them. I can see it beginning to happen already." His eyes gleamed. "So there's only one thing, and that's action. Somehow the English must be made to strike back at us."

She looked at him thoughtfully. "Have you any idea of what you're saying? All this sounds so exciting, so very intelligent, so dramatic when it's at the talking stage. But don't you understand where that kind of talk leads? The world is full of people with a grudge against it—not idealists like you, but a kind of person you know nothing about yet. This movement of yours will lead directly to bombs and shootings in the streets."

"Yes," he cried, "to bombs and shootings in the streets! That's what Aimé Latendresse says is inevitable. He doesn't want it, but he says we must accept it for certain. Otherwise we'll die in our sleep."

He felt as if his words had dropped with a plop into a bottomless well, and then he felt a strange force coming from her.

"I've made up my mind," she said. "You children here in this lucky country, what do you know of war—least of all of civil war? What do you know of bombs and shootings and what they do to people? Your father would know. He knows what bombs are, even the little ones of the last war that could only destroy a city block or break a battleship in two. I tell you, Daniel, the time has come for you to change your dreams or they will destroy you. But first—before I tell you what I intend to tell you—are you still a virgin?"

He flushed. "What's that got to do with it?"

"It has this perhaps to do with it, that you are afraid of loving a woman, and if a man fears that, then it is very natural for him to talk and dream about bombs and war."

He said to her sullenly, "I thought you were going to tell me something about yourself and Clarisse."

"About our life. A little about it—since you make such a great thing out of self-respect. But first of all you might tell me what you mean by self-respect. I'd really like to know what you mean by it."

"Not being ashamed."

"The only people who are never ashamed are the dead—didn't you ever think of that?" She gave him a curious smile. "Didn't it ever occur to you to wonder how it is that a woman as young as I happens to be the mother of a girl as old as Clarisse?"

It had often occurred to him, but he had been too shy to mention it.

"When Clarisse was born I was only three weeks beyond my sixteenth birthday," she went on. "My father had been a professor of mathematics at Aix. He was deeply interested in philosophy as well. I was a carefully-reared young girl. Does it not seem curious that one like myself should have become a mother at that age?"

He felt the blood rising to his cheeks but said nothing.

"Did Clarisse ever mention to you that her father was an American?"

"What?"

"A young American lieutenant from Ohio. He bought me for two dozen tins of Spam and half a dozen cartons of cigarettes, which I sold for more food."

"The—the—"

"Stop, Daniel. He was a reasonably nice boy but he was very immature. He was also frightened and was sure he was going to be killed, and as a matter of fact so he was—three months later in Tunisia. He was just an American boy in the army who was sent to Casablanca in the war. He tried rather pathetically to act tough, but he wasn't tough at all. He'd been brought up to think

158

that in a situation like ours the man is always to blame and the minute he found out I was pregnant he offered to marry me. But even at fifteen I knew enough not to marry a man for the sake of easing his conscience."

He was staring at her. "But you! You yourself! I can't believe this. It's untrue. You're making it up. This damned American, this dirty—"

"We were talking about bombs and shootings in the street and self-respect. So let me tell you a little about my father.

"In the war of 1914 he was just old enough to be called up to the army for the last few months, but that was enough to make him hate the very idea of war. He was a pacifist for years. But then Hitler came, and my father believed that not even war would be as bad as the Nazis. In the Second War he served in the navy and, as my mother came from Casablanca, he had her take me there with her when he went to his ship. Well, when France fell so suddenly, the navy was not surrendered and his ship was ordered into Casablanca. So my father was with us in Casablanca until the Americans invaded Morocco more than two years later. Have you ever heard of a battleship called *Jean Bart*?"

He shook his head.

"Have you ever read anything about the invasion of North Africa?"

"Everything about that war bores me to death. Dad can never get it out of his mind, but—"

"I'm going to tell you a little about it, just the same. After all, it's responsible for the existence of Clarisse and she's responsible for you being here tonight." She smiled obliquely and lit another Gitane. "It was my father's particular dread that his ship would be ordered by Vichy to fight the allies. He was very proud of the *Jean Bart*—he might hate war, but sailors become attached to their ships. Even I, as a little girl, knew a great deal about her. She had been built to be the equal of any battleship afloat and she was brand new. She was so new they didn't have time to install all of her big guns. She was supposed to have eight huge, fifteen-inch guns, but when she arrived in Casablanca from Lorient she only had four. They were all in a single turret on the foredeck and it was in that turret that my father served. She was a very unusual ship, very long in front. I can see her still.

"It was incredibly strange then, Daniel. I can still feel the strangeness of it. We lived in limbo. Day after day the same, the climate wonderful in the spring and fall and tropical in the summers, but always we had the feeling that something awful might arrive at any moment. Nazi agents were there quite openly and some Americans too. However, when the Americans entered the war, we knew that no matter what happened Hitler would never win it.

"My father and all the officers he liked longed for the day when they would be ordered to sail out to join the allies, but their ships were hostages for unoccupied France and the order never came. It was not easy for a Frenchman to be clear about things in those days— much harder, I assure you, than the Gaullists would have people believe now. It was not easy for any Frenchman to retain his self-respect then. There was always this atmosphere of a loyalty within a betrayal and of a betrayal within a loyalty—and you know, Daniel, a great deal more of ordinary life is like that than most people dare admit. It was incredibly strange, the atmosphere of those days when I was a growing girl. Just think—when my father joined his ship and Mother and I left Aix for Casablanca, I was only twelve. In the autumns at Casablanca, when the hurricanes blow on the American side of the ocean, there is a great turbulence in the sea because the storms throw the ocean against the side of Africa, and Africa throws it back upon itself. The air is moist and the palm trees rattle in the winds. It was at just such a time that

160

the inevitable happened and the war came to us at last. In those days in Europe, all the civilized people who hoped to escape the war knew in their hearts that finally it was certain to discover them. It was like that then.

"The city was full of rumors. It was always full of rumors. But this time the allies had kept their secret perfectly. One night just before the invasion my father came home to supper and said he had heard in the wardroom that a convoy had sailed from England against Dakar. If this was true, the convoy would have to sail right across in front of us and there was talk that our ships might be ordered out to prevent them. Dakar, of course, was under the jurisdiction of Vichy. But that was not what happened. One night—it was morning actually, but in the late autumn it was still dark—I heard planes and knew from the sound of their motors they were not ours. Then the telephone rang in our apartment and the next thing I heard was Papa shouting to my mother. I got out of bed in time to see him run out of the house with his naval cap on his head and his tunic still unbuttoned. I ran out into the street in my nightdress and saw him bent double over the handlebars of his bicycle pedalling down to the harbor. I went inside and threw some clothes on and followed him, and when I reached the wire fence about the naval property I found many other people were there before me, most of them women. They were the wives and families of sailors and there were also sailors who had shore leave like my father pushing through, and the naval police at the gates were keeping the crowd back. An officer appeared and shouted through a megaphone to all of us to disperse, to go home and go into shelters if we had any. I saw some sailors running up the ladders on the side of the *Jean Bart* and boats going back and forth between the smaller ships and the shore. This officer kept shouting, 'Go home, you fools, go home! Get away from here! The bombs and shells will be coming any minute!' There was a great confusion of voices and people were shouting, 'Who is attacking us?' and the officer and some people in the crowd shouted back, 'The Americans have dropped leaflets! The time limit is nearly up!' I don't yet know whether they dropped leaflets or just attacked by surprise. It was like that then. The officer was beside himself, jumping up and down and stamping his feet at our stupidity, and I can still hear him screaming through his megaphone, 'Get away from here or you'll all be killed!'

"A little after this there was a roar in the sky and something that felt like an earthquake and the whole harbor seemed to shudder and then it jumped up to the sky with a roar in enormous white fountains. I heard somebody shout, 'American battleships are firing from out at sea!' The shock of those first shots had knocked me and a lot of others off our feet. Then all the smaller guns on my father's ship began firing together at airplanes. There was a pile of empty petrol drums and I crawled behind them for shelter and I watched the four big guns in the turret where my father was on duty pointing up to the sky and moving slowly back and forth as though they were searching for something, and I thought, How unfair this is for Papa! His ship has only four guns instead of eight and they have not been allowed to practice." She smiled ruefully. "That's what I remember thinking then, exactly. Then I saw the guns fix themselves and there was a jerk and four huge flashes of fire and a roar and a shock of air, and I thought, How terrible for my father, what he had dreaded most of all, to be ordered to fire his guns against his allies, but at the same time I crossed myself and I prayed that those shots he had fired would strike an American ship. If I have picked up all these horrid military terms it is only because as a little girl I heard them used all the time. Another salvo came down from the American ships and some of these shells struck the *Jean Bart* and others struck the water and the docks, and even before they exploded I felt the shock of them driving into the steel and the concrete. Everything was so full of noise and smoke and I couldn't tell shells from bombs, but my entrails and heart and the loose parts inside of me were being churned by the explosions. Then suddenly I saw my father's turret cracked open and heaved out of place on the deck with bright-orange fire and smoke pouring out of it and I think my soul went out of me in a scream of pain. The whole front deck of the ship was buckled upward from the explosions and she seemed to have been lifted halfway up on the shore." She stopped. "Later when the Americans inspected the ship they washed the remains of my father and his men out of the turret with hoses."

He avoided her eyes and looked at his shoes.

"There were also the smaller ships that day," she went on. "There was a cruiser called *Primauguet*. Her captain knew my father well and he was often in our apartment. He was ardent for the allies. But now he was ordered out to fight them and he steered his little ship against the whole American fleet and the American battleship *Massachusetts* blew the *Primauguet* out of the water and the captain died shooting his useless guns at the men he had always wanted to fight beside.

"I can't remember anything clearly after that. American soldiers arrived in their funny-looking helmets, walking in that long-legged way so many of them have. There were more leaflets. I remember hearing grenades bursting and rifles firing and there were some dead and wounded, but all I was really seeing was the fire and smoke coming out of that broken turret where my father was. He was a handsome man, Daniel. He was such a gentle man, and I was thinking there was not even any skin left on what had been his body on account of the fire. Then it was all over and the American commander announced that we had been liberated, and soon American soldiers were passing out candy bars and Coca-Cola to the children."

Daniel could not speak. He could not even look at her.

"Well, Daniel, we were talking of self-respect, were we not? I was a carefully-reared girl in a cultivated family but after all this happened, what remained of me? But I learned one thing in those days—I learned that people can accept almost anything. They can do unthinkable things just because they do them."

Daniel standing with his back to the room not looking at her and outside, the night. Couples were still rocking on the balconies across the street and he knew they were speaking together in French. What did they know about anything? The boys and girls had disappeared from the corner, but the pool of light remained there. The glow of the city, the voice of the city, the two million strangers in the city on this hot night. His watch told him it was only eleven o'clock but surely he had been here much longer than that. A wall seemed to be swaying away from him, then toward him, crumbling, hardening again, and his body felt molten when at last he turned and looked at her.

She was the enormous unknown. She was the huge world of the things men and women had done to each other and had seen each other do. What did the Jesuits know of women like her? She was the enormous unknown and all of her was inviting him in. He sensed it. He knew it.

"Daniel dear," she was saying, "this world we live in is supposed to contain more than two billion people. What they tell you in college about governing, about changing it—all that is false. There is so little time to enjoy it, yet what else is it here for? I'm very lonely here and you are lost. I'm worried and anxious about you. I love you, Daniel. I think I loved you the first time you came here. Oh, not to interfere with your life, but just to love you and let you know what love can be. I'm not being wicked. This has nothing to do with Clarisse. If it could affect her in any way at all, I would never consider it.

164

But I know her and I know you better than you know yourself." She got to her feet. "Come! Do what you've been longing to do for weeks. When the truth can be so good, why do we resist it?"

His mind seemed to split in two and he saw half of it disappear into the dark as those broken ships had sunk into the ocean off Africa. The life of her body was stirring against him and her tongue was lingeringly, flickeringly, moving in his mouth and he did not know who he was any more and soon after that he exploded. But he was young and the first time was only a prelude to a chain-reaction that finally exhausted her.

The warm, moist wind that rose after midnight was pouring into the room and caressing the skin of his back. The wind was sonorous and steady in the city. She sighed in her sleep and he wondered who she really was and if the things she had told him were true. This is what they know, he thought, and now I know it. For a time he was grateful to her. I have an idea now, he thought. Why didn't it come to me long ago? I must persuade my father to join us. We need him and now I don't think we can succeed without him.

The dawn came very early and she grew visible in it and he traced her lines with his eyes. No two snowflakes were ever precisely alike, neither were the forms of any two women. And the world was full of women. He felt a cool dawn-peace, the coolness of very early morning after the tautening heat of a tropic day, and, with the coolness, an uncoiling of the whirlpools of his soul, a deepening and a spreading out of their whorls into the surface of a lake clasped by hills in the gray-white innocence of the dawn before the trumpet of the rising sun marshals the soul back into war. He studied her wonderingly. She had taken him into the deep unknown and now that he had been there he would never be the same again. Was this all there was? Was the remainder gestures merely? He wished she would wake so he could ask her that. Those things she had seen and done and known, those unsayable things she had seen and done and permitted. "I think I know more now than my father ever knew," he thought. "Maman could never have known what this one does." She seemed helpless and frail curled up, with her black hair and closed eyes, her skin rosy from him, but he did not exist for her now. Soon he fell asleep himself.

TEN

ALAN AINSLIE was searching the rooms of his apartment and wondering why they were empty. Where had the children gone? Where was Chantal tonight? It was two o'clock in the morning and where was his daughter?

Every room was tidy, nothing had been left lying about. The beds in the children's rooms were neatly made, but where had the children gone? What was happening to them now and what was this throb in the emptiness of the empty rooms? Where were they and what were they doing and with whom?

Then it came to him—of course, they had gone north to the lake! Was he losing his grip that he should have forgotten something so obvious? But had they indeed gone to the lake? Daniel was on television and was a separatist and the frenzy was working in the boy, working against everything that gave his own life any reason for being.

His mind lapsed far, far back and he was in a cot under the cracked plaster of the upper room in the little cottage near the mine, the house on the outside painted iron-oxide red, one in a row of identical shacks where the miners lived. He was warm in bed and moonlight had come in through the dormer window and a mouse had come out of its hole and was crouching in the moonpath on the floor and he had lain still and looked at the mouse and dreamed of his father's homecoming.

So very far from there and then. To Dr. Ainslie's house, to the universities, to External and into Constance's bed and into Constance herself from there and then; into the dignity and old-worldliness of her ancient French-Canadian family from there and then; night after night over Germany with the flak floating up like pelleted stars exploding with blazes and crashes from there and then; drifting down through the flak into the flames of the German city, the people trying to murder him, the lizard-faced Russian in the U.N. lounge, the old Prime Minister begging him to come into the government, from there and then to Moses Bulstrode here and now, and he wondered what would become of him.

Through the open window he heard the drum and surge of the south wind. He saw the lights of the city washing in their cascade down to the ink-black band that was the St. Lawrence. When he left the living room he walked along a narrow corridor leading to the back of the apartment where his study was. It smelled musty as though nobody had entered it in months. The book bindings had the sharp, hot, dusty, musty glue-smell of book bindings in a closed room in summer. He passed his hand over the surface of his desk and it came away clean. Chantal kept everything spotless and dustless here. Where are you, Chantal? Please, please, don't do it! Wait a while longer, dear. But your mother began so much younger than you that you would be horrified if you knew. Or would you be? Yes, I think you would.

He opened the door that led from the library into the master-bedroom he had shared with Constance, and it was hot and close because the window had been shut against the dirt-laden air of the city. It was baking-hot in the bedroom and there was not enough oxygen in its dead air. He went to the window and heaved on it, but the wood had swelled in the heat and the window was stuck in its frame. In unreasoning anger he cursed and heaved as though everything that was thwarting him were concentrated in the window, and still it did not budge. He slapped it with the heel of his hand and bruised his hand with slam after slam until finally it cracked open and he heaved again and with a screaming creak the window went up in its grooves. He stood sweating, panting, feeling the hot dry air suck smellingly past him into the wind outside. Here in the back of the building he looked down on treetops and he saw their outlines boiling in the wind in the half-darkness.

The counterpane of the bed stared at him and he folded it back, folded it up, took it from the bed and laid it on a chair. The pillows were freshly laundered. He pulled off the solitary blanket and laid it on the floor. Then he undressed, dropped his clothes on another chair, went into the adjoining bathroom, brushed his teeth and sponged his shoulders and chest. The top of his head felt ready to fly off. His half-naked body was reflected in the full-length mirror. It was still taut with the long muscles of a middle-distance runner and his chest still expanded in a great arch when he filled it with air. Only his face with the glazed skin-graft and the dead left side did not seem to belong to him. He had never been able to get used to it. It was not his own, it was a borrowed face. Suddenly it occurred to him that this was the only face of his that Daniel had ever seen.

The idea came to him that he had no work that mattered any more, no love that mattered any more, no hope that mattered any more.

The idea came to him that the entire journey from there and then to here and now was over and that he had reached the end of its road.

The idea came to him that this country he was trying to serve was not a nation at all—that it was nothing but a huge wilderness with a few ant hills in it where the ants believed that the possession of their hills signified that they possessed the enormous land.

The idea came to him that nothing he could think, say or do could be of the least significance to anyone.

Then he was remembering the tweedy, grown-man and

ether smell of Dr. Ainslie the night the doctor had carried him away from what his father did when at last his father came home.

He returned naked into the bedroom, took a pair of fresh pajamas from a drawer and put them on. He lay on the bed and stretched, but the heat was too great under the sheet and he threw the sheet off. Then the heat was too intense in his pajamas and he took them off too and lay naked. Now he was glad the children were not here. He did not care, he did not care. But when he turned out the light, shadows made such violent movement in the room that he wondered if something were happening to him organically until he understood the shadows were real. They were being thrown into the room by some combination of reflections from outside, the light of the city sufficient to throw the shadows of boiling treetops onto his walls.

Now it must be three o'clock in the morning and the panic was still upon him. He turned the light on. No, it would be too brutal to waken Gabriel Fleury at an hour like this. But as he stared at the telephone he could not resist it and, because he remembered Gabriel's number, he dialed it. Then in a convulsion of guilty shame at his weakness, he put the receiver down and broke the connection.

Again he turned out the light and lay with open eyes and watched the shadow-dance until finally the tide lapped up to him and he smelled it, the clam and mussel smell of the island shore, the salt smell of long ago, the Grecian face of the slim woman with the dark hair and Celtic eyes whose tenderness had been flushed out of the world on the night when his father returned, his real father and not Dr. Ainslie, the father he had seen only once and that in the act of murder, and it was incredible to him that this had actually happened. Now Bulstrode, hunting through an R.C.M.P. file out of curiosity, had unearthed this fact that not even his own children knew.

But Bulstrode only knew the fact and the fact was nothing. He had not seen the woman, the gentle woman, flushed out of the world like water swirling down a drain when the plug has been pulled. Now there were no eyes and there was chaos again. He shivered in the panic, but after a time the tide of sleep crept up mercifully. Sweet and cool it lapped him, and before he sank into it he thought, How lovely it will be if death turns out to be white!

Intermezzo

THE SINGLE RING of the telephone in his study was not loud, but it was loud enough to waken Gabriel Fleury and make him grope for the extension beside his bed. He heard nothing but the singing of the dial tone and carefully replaced the instrument in its cradle.

Beside him Chantal had not stirred. She was lying on her stomach with her face on her forearms and her legs spread out like a baby's and in the faint light her lines were fragile. His lips lightly touched her shoulder and he eased himself down and closed his eyes and listened to the deep rhythm of her breathing.

Who had called him? This telephone linked him now to every region of the world. In this limbo between sleep and waking it seemed very important to know the identity of the unknown caller. Some frightened person wanting the police and realizing he had dialed the wrong number? Some drunken, lonely man? A woman whose husband had taken a heart attack in the night dialing the doctor's number and knowing it was wrong and hanging up? A ring in the night. He dozed off and what caused him to wake a second time he did not know at first. The sonorous blowing of the wind had fallen. Suddenly he knew what had wakened him—the echo of Chantal's voice saying, "This isn't forever."

There was light in the room now; outside the window the song of a robin was liquid and stirred a series of sweet images in his mind. Chantal's sleeping form was as fresh as a happy childhood, but would she be happy when she woke? Then Tarnley's voice saying, "Nothing has seemed real to me since then. That was when it all started."

What had started then was surely the rebirth of a kind of man who had perished two thousand years ago, a man who knew there was no escape from his own nature into religion or politics or science or even into his own skill. That was certainly when it began for himself, and he was not even six years old when he understood it as a child understands certain things as final and absolute facts. Yet in the years afterward he had tried to deny it. Only last summer had he ceased trying to deny it; last summer when he went home for a while to Dauphiné.

He had been told in letters to expect many changes and a few of these were obvious. The ancient walls of the city near the land his father had owned had been torn down to make room for the city's growth. Much of the farm and meadow country he remembered stretching from the city to the rampart of Vercors was built over with new factories and cement-gray apartment blocks. *"Nous avons maintenant le New Look,"* was how the hotel porter put it. *"Beaucoup de buildings—très modernes."* If Gabriel wished to see the real nature of the change he must inspect the new *supermarché* on the relatively new Avenue Maréchal Foch which ran over what had been farmland when Gabriel was born. Gabriel had arrived in the city by night from Paris and as he went up to his room he reflected that it was in obedience to Marshal Foch's love of *élan* that his father had nearly been killed in the first month of the war.

The next morning he rose shortly after dawn and walked through the old quarter of the city and it seemed quite unchanged. He had always resented the Parisian assumption that this city was dull; in the early-morning light it seemed to him clean and noble. The sun was still hidden behind Chamrousse, but its rays were flushing the snow that lingered on the high peaks of the Belledonne far away. The Isère bridges, caught by the sun at a low diagonal, were mirrored in the water of the stream. When he ate his rolls and drank his coffee in a restaurant in Place Grenette he remembered having been taken here when he was a child by one of his aunts and on that occasion a peasant from the mountains had been sitting on the pavement outside with a basket of vipers beside him. When they left the restaurant after lunch his aunt had given the peasant a franc; the man then took a viper out of his basket, held it up by the back of the neck and killed it. This was an old custom and the reason for it was the belief of the townsfolk that the mountain ledges would be safer for children if the killing of snakes was made a part of the local economy. On this more modern morning, opaque-eyed Algerians were moving along the sidewalks on their way to work and theirs were new faces in the old city. But most of the passers-by had the reserved expressions of Dauphinois and he saw several tall young men in the blue cloaks and sweeping bérets of the Chasseurs Alpins. Bicycles with pedals and bicycles fitted with motors streamed by, but at this hour in the morning there were no *voyous* loitering about. It was all so familiar that the anxiety rested in Gabriel and for a while he almost believed he could come home again.

At the beginning of this visit he had deliberately avoided notifying any of his relatives that he had arrived. It was the country itself he wished to recover, so that afternoon he took a bus out of the city and went up the valley along the Geneva road to the place where the mountains narrow down to the Isère, which had seemed such a mighty river before he had seen the Mekong and the St. Lawrence. The stream was putty-colored from Alpine limestone and its surface looked satin-smooth. It curved down the valley toward the city and the gap in the mountains on its journey toward the farms and vineyards east of the Rhône. There were films of mist on its surface and the sunlight flickering through them made golden patches that never stayed constant but shimmered like flocks of brilliant birds resting before they took off and flew away. Everything seemed permanent and dignified after the rawness of the New World. Again he felt he might come home.

But the man beside him in the bus took up the tale of the porter in the hotel. "The villages in the mountains grow emptier every year. Some of the men will stay but not the young girls." And he quoted the old saying, "The goat always climbs up and the woman always climbs down." He added, however, that in winter *les stations de ski* were as good or better than any in Europe. Last year many American skiers had preferred it here to Switzerland. There were also many American-owned factories with new labor from Italy, Spain and Algeria, though of course De Gaulle was ruining the nation's economy. And so on and so on.

When he left the bus he walked up a steep slope to a spot about six hundred meters from the river and stood there alone, breathing in the stillness of mountain air when there is no wind. A very abrupt peak lunged up behind him, and an even higher one—this was the one shaped like the dying Negro Warrior his mad aunt had told him about—bulged against the western sky several kilometers away on the far side of the valley. The scene looked older to him than any in the world, older even than Ankhor Vat, because it was the first his eyes had looked at, nor would this particular prospect ever change unless the scientists learned how to melt mountains. There were many fruit trees on the slopes and, though there was little good soil here, the whole valley smelled of summer, of the immense fertility of France herself. Farmers were getting in the first harvest, some working with tractors, others with scythes as in the old days. For the third time he felt he might come home again.

When he was studying architecture in Paris before the war he had met a Parisian literary critic who had said, "Your Dauphiné is as gray as the style of the only great writer it ever produced." Irritated by the condescension, Gabriel had answered, "In Dauphiné we never thought too much of Stendhal," and the Parisian had smiled in the way Parisians have and said, "In Dauphiné how could you?" France, the home of originality and stereotypes.

At last he forced himself to go to the house and ring the bell beside the front door. It was an electric bell now, not a pull as it had been in the old days, and when the door opened an old woman was there. She looked at him curiously, dropped him a suggestion of a curtsey and asked if he might be Monsieur Gabriel. He could not remember her but said that he was and then she smiled, her face russet-brown and wrinkled.

"I remember you when you were a little boy, Monsieur. You look so much like Colonel de Fleury I recognized you immediately. In your father's time I lived in the hamlet."

"Would the proprietor mind if I strolled over the property?"

"The proprietor is in Paris. That is where he usually is. His family also."

Her tone and expression told him that if this proprietor lived for a hundred years he would never be more than the man who paid her wages.

"Has the house changed hands more than once?"

"It has changed hands four times, Monsieur. This new owner is very rich and he and his family and his children's friends use it when they come here to ski. Naturally, they have installed central heating." She added, "It is very modern now inside."

She asked if he wished to enter; she was all alone with her husband—they were the caretakers and it would be perfectly all right. But he could not bring himself to enter and she nodded to say that she understood.

"I'll just take a look around the grounds," he said and left her.

These had been smartened up close to the house, but the fields were untouched. The proprietor probably let the local farmers cut the hay in return for wood for his fires. Gabriel reached the stone wall where he had come so often as a child and sat down on it, but he could not feel the place any more. For a while he felt as if a nerve in his life had been severed by some kind of psychical operation. Then the scent of wildflowers reached him and memory returned and he felt a tearing in his nerves as he remembered acutely the first time he had seen his father in the flesh.

He was five and a half before he saw his father to recognize and remember him, and the year was 1920. Several times during the war, his mother had told him, his father had returned from short leaves at the front, but the last visit had been early in 1917 and Gabriel had been too young to remember it. In the year and a half after memory became more or less reliable, he had learned to love his father as a Christian child learns to love God or Christ, from legends and a picture on the wall. His father's picture on the wall showed an officer in the uniform of the Chasseurs Alpins, the lean face stern and uncompromising, but not even the flamboyant sweep of the enormous blue béret disguised the baffled gentleness in his Velázquez eyes.

The shock of his father when Gabriel first saw him to remember him had never gone away; now, recalling it, he could finally admit that it was from this that he had been running away all of his life.

He had imagined his father as he had been told he was: a champion fencer, a mountaineer, a candidate for the Rugby team of All France, an officer leading his men into their first battle wearing white gloves. What he saw was a mangled, wheezing wreck, and he saw it with the merciless clarity of an appalled child. Though his father had first been wounded in Lorraine at the very beginning of the war, it was the offensive in 1917, launched by the general known to his men as *le buveur de sang*, that had reduced him to this. What his son saw was something that never should have been permitted to live. The right leg had been blown off just above the knee; a hunk of hot, jagged steel had gouged out some of his back and destroyed the right lung and part of the right shoulder; the face was greenish-gray and harsh with perpetual pain; the eyes were the worst of all.

When his father bent to kiss his son, his whole face broke into a pain-caused sweat, and for Gabriel the moment was terrible. It was then that he ceased believing in God or in mercy or even in truth. . . .

"What's troubling you, dear?"

Chantal had awakened and was watching his profile. He looked at her and her youth so stabbed him that he had to look away.

"Myself," he said. "Nothing more than that."

"What do you mean?"

"Because I couldn't get over it."

"Darling, what do you mean? I can't understand you."

The ancient statement when minds have leaped apart after the miracle of physical fusion.

"Can't you tell it even to me?"

In her expression he recognized the eternal mother in every girl.

"I'm a war and a peace older than you," he said.

"War!" she said. "War, war, war—can't you ever forget it?"

"I've spent a lifetime trying to forget it. So have millions who weren't even born then, who can't even remember it. So have you and Daniel, though you don't realize it."

"Did you ever tell Dad about it?"

"Partly, but I didn't really have to."

"Is that what's so deep between you two?"

"That's half of it."

"And the other half—what's the other half?"

"I doubt if either of us know."

"When you two were in prison camp did he tell you something about himself he never told us?"

"When two men are together in prison camp they tell each other all sorts of things."

"Tell me about yourself. What's causing that look on your face?"

After a long time he said, "It was terribly cold that winter my father was sent home from the hospital to die."

She lay still and did not speak. A few moments later he went jerkily on. "The year previous it had been the influenza, but that year when people died in the hamlet it was on account of the cold. They put up with things over there you don't put up with here. In this country the winters are so cold that people have to live in warm houses, but over there they save money and survive. Those stone houses in the winter are grippe and pneumonia traps. But most of the people who died that year in the hamlet were old. After, there were hardly any young men still alive."

That winter his mother seemed to age by twenty years. People said she had looked like Lily Langtry, but that winter with her mangled, dying husband come home after all those years, without enough nourishing food or wood for the fires because there were no men to cut it, his mother wore old sweaters and long, thick woolen stockings and looked little different from the peasant women in the hamlet who grew old in their thirties. There were turrets on either end of the house and when the wind came down from the mountains the turrets hummed and the old woman who helped her mother used to say to him, "Your father's towers are chanting tonight. 'C'est la bise, c'est la bise.'" Gabriel did not learn the truth about war in 1943 and 1944 in the Air Force; he learned it from people's faces in 1920.

Spring came finally and the land unfroze, the river foamed under the pressure of the run-off from the mountains, wildflowers came out on the slopes and in the city the pruned plane trees and chestnuts bloomed. Day after day soft airs streamed into the valley from the Rhône with the smell of the Mediterranean in them, and on one morning his father tried to take him over the property. It was horrible, for every move on the crutches made his father sweat with agony. After fifty yards he gave up and Gabriel ran back to the house and found the wheel chair and pushed it out to where his father stood propped on his crutches. Then a man was found in the hamlet to push the wheel chair down to the road-fork where three ways joined: one led northward to Geneva, another southeast toward the city and the Rhône; the third was the family road which ran up through the property and ended at the side of the mountain. His father wetted his finger and held it up to test the direction of the wind, then a violent spasm of coughing wracked him. When he could speak again he asked the workman who had pushed his chair to leave them for a while and then he told Gabriel that he was content with him. Tears came into the child's eyes and in a flash his father's face became an officer's face and his father's voice commanded him not to cry. Then he told Gabriel that it had been decided that he must leave them and go to his mother's family in Dublin.

Gabriel trembled with fear and asked why.

"There is no proper place for you here at the moment. Your mother's family has been very generous." He cleared his throat and added, "It has been arranged for tomorrow."

That night Gabriel was unable to sleep. The warm airs from the south continued to flood the valley and fill it with odors. When he went to the window of his room he saw the dark shadow of a large bird dip soundlessly down through the moonlight to the river. He left his room and wandered in bare feet over the stone floor of the upstairs corridor and at the end of it a shaft of light told him his parents were still awake. He felt so lonely he wanted to join them, but when he reached the door he heard a sound he had not believed possible. It was his father sobbing.

"It went out of me on the second day of the fighting." In spite of the broken sobs the voice was oddly factual. "It went out of me, I tell you, and it will never come back. There is nothing left for it to return to."

"Let me get you a pill to put you to sleep."

"I wanted to fall down but I couldn't. They'd sent us in waves and we'd been mown down in waves and we were all on top of each other. The bullet had gone through me but I couldn't fall. I was propped against the ones who had fallen before and pressed by the others they'd sent in behind. The Germans began firing into us to clear their sights for the others coming up behind, and when the shells broke in the pile the whole pile shuddered and . . ."

"It's over now."

"Never." A long silence, then a whisper, "Never, never, never."

Gabriel stole back along the corridor and closed himself into his room.

The next morning he was driven in a carriage down the valley with his mother beside him very pale and drawn. She put him on the Paris train, spoke to the conductor asking him to keep an eye on him, then kissed him and stood on the platform waving absent-mindedly as the train pulled out. He was met in the Gare de Lyon by one of his Dublin uncles, a big man with a ruddy face and a strong Irish accent whether he spoke French or English, a lawyer and prosperous, also an Irish nationalist who boasted that he had been "out in '16," and assured Gabriel that soon the English would be out of Ireland forever. But in the train on the way to Calais he said that on account of the troubles in Ireland, Gabriel would be sent to a school in England.

"But if the English are so wicked, why do I have to go to England?"

"In England they are not so bad, and their schools are better than ours, I fear to have to say."

In Dublin that summer there were assassinations and shootings in the streets.

Chantal wanted to know how Gabriel's father and mother had met one another.

"Her family sent her to our university to learn French. You know how it is—this feeling some of the Irish have for France. Father was much older than she was. Some of my aunts never got over his marrying a foreigner. They were jealous of her, of course, and among themselves they never referred to her by name. They always called her *'La Belle Irlandaise.'* She must have been marvelously beautiful when she was young. My aunts professed they could never understand how a man as disciplined as my father could have fallen in love at first sight. It never occurred to them that he was just the sort of man who was almost certain to." He added as though dismissing the subject, "He died the first winter I was at that English school. Three years later my mother remarried. She married an English officer who had arrested one of her brothers during the Troubles."

"And that's why you were sent back to France?"

"Yes."

"Why didn't you stay there?"

"It's very hard to put it into words. When I put it into words it sounds completely silly."

"Try to."

"Well, my father's family came to horrify me. They all loved each other—or was it that they loved the *idea of the family*? I don't really know and it doesn't matter, but I began to think of them as responsible for my father's death. I mean, because in that family a young man was expected to grow up to be a professional soldier. Of course, in the 1914 war, he'd have been killed no matter what he was. There was more than that too. When Father died, the family seemed—I can only put it this way—they seemed greedy for me. They wanted me to carry on and replace him when I grew older, and live exactly as he had lived."

"Is your mother still alive?"

"Alive and well. I spent a few days with her last year in London. She's had three children by her second marriage and now she has eight grandchildren. Meeting her after all those years wasn't easy. She had adored my father and he had adored her, but she barely mentioned him to me and I had the idea that months could pass without her even remembering him. She doesn't look like Lily Langtry any more. She's quite fat and easy-going and one afternoon she took me out to the tennis at Wimbledon."

Watching his profile, Chantal realized at last that he was just as old as he had said that he was. It was then she knew she was in love with him.

Daniel Ainslie opened his eyes and for an instant he did not know where he was. Then he saw the woman beside him and was hammered by a panic that swiftly turned into terror. He felt for a moment as though he had been condemned to death. The world lurched and he stole from the bed and went to the window. It was very bright. Had he been asleep only for a few hours? If so, time meant nothing because now he was seeing himself and this woman and what they had done in the cold light of the morning after with all lust spent. The face of the Jesuit at the seminary, the severest of them all, with the penetrating eyes, the lantern jaw, the total authority when he addressed the boys:

"Fornication is at once both a disease and a habit. It is a disease because it damages the body and ruins the soul. It is a habit because, like opium, once you have formed it you can never break it. Not until you are miserable old men will you ever be free of it, and then your fate will be ironic—you will crave it and be unable any more to pursue it.

"During your lifetime this abominable habit will make you ashamed before your wives and you will not dare reveal your shame to them. It will make you ashamed before God, Who will be looking at you every time you commit that sin.

"Just as every hair of your head is numbered, so is

186

every occasion of your fornications. And be sure of this—this sin above all others will find you out. You may wish to believe that it will escape detection, but your sin will be branded upon your face like the brand of Cain. Every man and woman of experience recognizes the face of the fornicator. You will deceive your wives again and again, not because this will give you any pleasure, but because it is the unfailing punishment of the fornicator that he is driven to do again and again that which his heart and soul destest doing. And always the eye of God will be watching, the hand of God entering each one of his sins on the eternal list. You will know this, but you will be helpless to stop it, you will continue onward in the path you have chosen until . . ."

How clean he had felt in the early mornings before the impure thoughts had come to him! Now he was lost. He stared at the sleeping woman and felt his very privates shrinking. Stealthily he put on his clothes and slunk out of the room, descended the outside-staircase and walked swiftly around the corner to find his car. He was almost surprised when it still was there. This at least was his; this he owed to nobody but himself. He patted the hood, got in and drove away through the empty streets to the top of Mount Royal, and there he got out and walked to the Lookout and stared down over the city and beyond.

Montreal lay silent and asleep on this Sunday morning of heat before the angelus rang. Looking out over that immense spread of buildings, over the river to the buttes of extinct volcanoes humping upward out of the plain, the fields deeply green in the distance, the air smokeless because it was Sunday morning, he felt the strong early sun strike against his face and heat it. The sun glared at him and hurt his eyes. He saw it shining through the glass of a new building and making the building seem on fire within.

Now he knew he had to liberate this nation even if it involved his own death. He heard his name mentioned with reverence by thankful people long after he was gone, as the Christians spoke the names of their martyrs. He heard the Jesuit speaking to little boys in the seminary: "Once he sat here just as you are sitting here now. Even then his face revealed his dedication. He had a very pure face. Only to serve God and liberate his people—even as a little boy this pure dedication was in his face." To liberate this people at no matter what cost, to cut the cords of the strait-jacket of this nation the people loved so desperately.

Exhaustion swamped him, the reverie faded and his legs felt dead as he walked to his car. He climbed in and instantly fell into a profound sleep from which he did not waken until he felt a hand on his shoulder and looked up at the jowled and heavy face of a policeman staring at him.

"So you're only drunk," the policeman said. "I thought you might be dead. All right, young fellow—" Daniel saw the policeman taking out his notebook and wetting the tip of his pencil with his tongue.

"I'm not drunk."

"Let me smell your breath."

Daniel puffed at him and the officer made a face.

"Your breath smells bad but it doesn't smell of booze. Are you a nut, or something?"

"Isn't a man allowed to sleep in his own car in this so-called free country?"

"Why not?" the policeman said.

The wide-haunched figure in blue walked away with no more interest and left Daniel with an idea that had never occurred to him before. Nearly all the cops in this city were enormous men. They were French and most of them had big, square hands strong enough to break a man's neck. He was fairly strong himself, but he could never be even half a match for a man like this policeman unless he learned karate. As for his friends, nearly all of them in the movement had meager bodies and lived on their nerves. They looked as if they came from a different race of people from these policemen of Montreal. The body of that cop walking away made Daniel angry just to look at it.

Then Daniel did something he had not done for several years: he drove down into the heart of the city and went to High Mass in the cathedral, remembering how wonderfully comforting it had been only a few years ago when he had gone to Mass and believed. When he entered the cathedral and saw them collecting money from those who had taken seats, he decided not to take one himself. It was as if sitting down among all these bourgeois would have chained him to something, so he stood near a font at the side of the nave. The Mass began and he watched the burning candles and the polished movements of the celebrant in his chasuble, but soon he wearied of it and at the beginning of the *Credo* he slipped out of the church. He went to a nearby restaurant in the square and ordered breakfast and was surprised to find himself ravenous. He ate a bowl of cornflakes, two fried eggs with bacon and a double order of toast and marmalade before he was satisfied. When he had drunk his third cup of coffee the morning opened up to him large and full. She had loved others; she had performed the act with strange and experienced men; she had chosen him, not he her, and her cries and movements had told him that ultimately he had satisfied her. He felt proud and strong, and seeing a telephone booth near the door, he went over to it and dialed her number.

Her voice came to him with the shock of a cold shower. "Where did you go? Leaving me like that without a word —where are you now?"

"Oh, Marielle—when can I see you again?"

There was a short pause. Then, with the factuality of a tired woman out of sorts in the morning, but at the same time relieved about something, she answered him,

"You certainly can't see me again today. It's close to noon and Clarisse may be home at any time."

"Tomorrow then?"

"I will be occupied all day tomorrow and tomorrow evening there will still be Clarisse."

"May I call you later? Will you let me know when I can call you?"

Her voice softened. "I love you, Daniel. I truly do. But don't you ever do a thing like that to me again."

He went out to his car and drove to his father's apartment, whistling as he went.

Alan Ainslie opened his eyes in the great heat of another day and saw by his watch that it was ten o'clock in the morning. For a few seconds he lay still, not sure where he was. When he recognized the bed he had shared with Constance he became wide awake and the anxieties returned like a swarm of mosquitoes. He took a luke-warm shower, ended it with a jet of cold water and realized that he was hungry. The apartment seemed less empty that it had been the night before and now he was certain where his children were and was going to find them. In a heat wave like this, where else would they be but at the lake?

He found eggs, milk and cream in the refrigerator and made himself breakfast, which he ate in the kitchen wearing nothing but a light cotton dressing gown. The thermometer outside the window, set in a place where the sun's rays never fell, registered eighty-two degrees and this meant that by mid-afternoon it would be close to a hundred in the city. He wondered what to wear and remembered a pair of Bermuda shorts that Constance had bought for him. He found them just where she had hung them, and wearing a short-sleeved sports shirt, and carrying the jacket of a tropical suit over his arm, his money and car license in the inside breast pocket, he was about to leave when he remembered that the bed was

190

unmade and the dishes were unwashed. He tidied up, made the bed, left one copy of his book in Chantal's room and the other in Daniel's, then he went out and drove north in his car.

The lake was shining in the sun when he reached it, but the cottage was empty and there was no sign of his children having been there. The veranda furniture had been set out as usual by the local people who looked after the cottage, closing it in the fall and reopening it in the spring. Every spring there was usually some minor thing wrong and this time it was the hook on the screen door or the screened-in veranda. It had fallen off so that anyone could enter the veranda. He went in and tried the door of the cottage proper and found it locked, so he took out his key, opened it and smelled the cool mustiness of a summer cottage that had been closed for a long time. He left the door open to air the cottage and sat on the veranda and stared at the lake.

This property represented one of the few continuances he knew. He had bought it at a low price in the 1930s when he was quite poor, and he and Constance working together had put in the gardens. Here the children had grown up in the summers, and as he looked around he felt again, as he had done in his first summer here, that he had come into a good land, a land somewhat different from any he had known, with the winters white and arctic and the summers dramatic with great heats and sudden storms and sunsets unbelievable over the pine-and-spruce-covered hills. There were bears, deer, raccoons and skunks in the forest and plenty of fish in the lake. Except in a few clearings, the land was much as it had been thousands of years ago.

The peonies had gone over in the garden, the delphinium were in bud, but nobody had planted any annuals this year and the gardens were half-choked with weeds. There was excellent soil underneath the weeds because it had been nourished steadily with compost for twenty-four years and had been fairly good to begin with, for once it had been a forest floor.

He took off his shirt and strolled around the property. He saw the lovely combination of pine and white birch lining the little entrance road and on the nearest point in the lake the stand of maples that flamed scarlet in the fall. He and Constance together here and the best memories of life. Driving out together from the city's heat, sitting together on evenings when the moon made a path on the lake. The children's voices laughing at six o'clock on summer mornings. Youth—his, hers—and the children's infancy. He hoped that Chantal and Daniel would always wish to come here, and the idea of them coming here after he was gone, and of their own children coming with them, was very pleasant to him.

After a while he inspected the woodshed and smelled the dry maple logs that Jean-Baptiste Provencher had stored there the autumn before. He never had to tell Jean-Baptiste anything he wanted done; the man knew whatever was necessary and did it. The garden tools, oiled by Jean-Baptiste last year, hung clean on their hooks, and he took a weeding fork and a basket and went back into the sun to clear some of the weeds from the garden. The mosquitoes and blackflies were not too bad at this hour of the day, but there were enough of them to force him to put on his shirt again and to rub repellent over his face and ears and the back of his neck. When he had weeded a quarter of the garden he walked down to the sandspit and washed the dirt off his hands, found a chip of wood and dug the dirt from under his nails, then he stripped naked and swam in the lake, floating on his back finally while he looked at the white cottage nestling among the trees. The evergreens were fragrant in the sun and the land was as still as the sky. It was such a fine land even though nearly all of it was useless for farmers. The birches, fed by underground springs, had grown enormously since he had bought the place. He wondered if fire-flies would appear that night in the woods.

He left the water and sat in the sun until his skin felt dry, warm and polished, then he put on his clothes and again sat on the porch looking out at the lake. Constance's spirit seemed present and he had the feeling that it was content and happy because he was here again. Something whispered to him that whoever and whatever she had become was at ease. This was a good land he had come to even though he thought of himself as its tenant and not as its owner. His life had been nothing, apparently, but a succession of accidents. Was that why he had felt compelled to find and create a coherence in the country he lived in? Thinking this, he realized that Constance and her family, though they had three centuries behind them of people who knew exactly who they were and where they had come from, were in fact more primitive than himself. For what else was he but another example of the modern man living as a human exile among abstractions?

Around half-past four he locked the cottage door and got into his car and drove back to the autoroute. It was only in the rush of the Sunday-afternoon traffic that his predicament returned to him with a crash and he cried aloud in the wind, "Where are my children? In God's name, where are they?"

Chantal had breakfast with Gabriel and afterwards they sat in chairs in the garden among the flowers, Gabriel quietening her fears about the possible appearance and disapproval of his landlady by saying that she always went to church on Sundays and that it was nearly noon anyway. Chantal told him she was in love with him and that this was the first time she had ever been in love with anyone. She sat on the warm grass with her head against his knee and they were both relaxed and spent. Though Gabriel was sure that this could never last, happiness was so rare with him that he made no effort to thrust it away. She was lovely to look at leaning against his knee, breathing in the flower-scented air, occasionally lifting her head to stare up at the blue sky through the branches of the pear tree in the garden.

About one o'clock she stirred and said she ought to go home and he realized that she was worried about Daniel and was wondering how to explain her absence from the apartment the night before.

"Just tell him the truth," he said.

"I wouldn't mind in the least telling him the truth, but do you really want him to know about us now?"

He smiled wistfully. "Would you mind keeping it a secret between ourselves for a little while?" Seeing a slight frown of anxiety on her face, he added, "I seem very old to him, dear. I'm Uncle Gabriel, the old family friend. If you tell him you spent the night here, he won't assume anything more than that you've spent the night here."

"He's very intuitive."

"Well—"

"I'd like to stay here forever."

"You wouldn't, of course. And for a while I think we ought to ration ourselves with each other."

"Why, darling?"

"Non sum qualis eram."

"Now just what does that mean?"

"It means that I also played golf yesterday."

Looking at him she thought she could see him as he had been when a little boy. Those French boys with their wise little faces as though they had a pre-knowledge of what life was going to do to them.

"Dear Gabriel!"

His eyes were full of gratitude to her, of love for her.

"Darling," she said, "do you know what I want more than anything in the world? I want to give you a son."

He breathed deeply, turned his eyes away, then bent and kissed the nape of her neck.

Aimé Latendresse, alone and inconspicuous as ever, had been wandering about visiting various churches where the people were at Mass. He noted with an expressionless countenance that the churches were almost two-thirds empty and that most of the worshippers were middle-aged or elderly. He entered his last church toward the end of High Mass and debated with himself whether or not to take the Sacrament. In his years with the old priest on the lower river, and later with the Dominicans, the Sacrament had always given him the feeling of being filled and satisfied. This last comfort was fading out of the lives of the young and soon it would fade out of the world. *Benedictus qui venit in nomine Domini*—they had taken it away at last. The youth of the world was over. The world's youth was made aged before it had grown up. There was no comfort left for the youth of the world. They had taken it away. The System had taken it away.

He left the church without offering himself for the Sacrament and walked back through the heat to his single room and sat down before a table to resume his study of a technical book on the manufacture of explosive devices.

Daniel was driving home to shave, bathe and change his clothes; after that he intended to drive north to the cottage, to swim in the lake, to sleep in the afternoon, to get out the old canoe and do some fishing and not return to town until around midnight. He felt a sense of physical well-being such as he had not known since the days when he was a canoeist. He drove with only one hand on the wheel, the left hand resting on the door-frame, and the wind whipped his hair. After a time he thrust the fingers of his left hand inside his open shirt—he was not wearing his jacket—and caressed the muscles of his right shoulder. He felt the powerful curve of them and grinned. He was so strong and she had known it. He thought of Aimé Latendresse and became serious, but again he grinned and said, "The revolution can wait till this heat wave is over."

When he found the apartment empty he was annoyed with Chantal for not being there. He felt she ought to have been there, otherwise there was no home, but his sense of well-being was still strong and he whistled while he took a cold shower and towelled himself and admired his trim, powerful body in the glass. His skin looked too white to him; he must get out into the sun and tan it. He wondered if he would soon make enough money to fly to North Africa or a Greek island where the sun could knock you senseless.

After he had dressed in a sports shirt, shorts and rubber-soled shoes and was about to leave, a quick apprehension came to him and arrested his movements. He had an idea that stranger had been in the apartment the night before, but there were no cigarette butts in any of the ash trays. Yet he was sure that somebody had been here very recently. He entered Chantal's room and saw that her bed not been slept in. "That's funny!" he muttered. Then he went to the rear of the apartment and entered the master bedroom. His feeling was right; somebody had been here because the window was open. He looked sharply at the big double bed and with a quick jerk he tore off the covers. The sheets were wrinkled and so were the pillow cases.

"You little bitch!" he muttered. "You God-damned little bitch! You took a man here last night—*here*, of all places! Plenty of room to roll around in, you bet!"

He was sour and angry when he set out in his car for the north, but soon his anger shifted into another sensation. If she could do it, why not himself? His father thought the world of her.

On the autoroute he drove the car so hard that its engine whined like a Viscount aircraft on a landing strip; old though she was, he pushed her beyond ninety miles an hour. She had new valves and rings and the engine was as strong as when the car came off the assembly line, though the body was beginning to rot around the edges. The miles reeled away under his tires; he had been careful to buy new tires for his first car. Where the autoroute by-passes Saint-Jérôme there was a sudden splutter and the engine died. Daniel swore and let the car run with its momentum for a hundred yards before he stopped on a apron beside the road. He got out and lifted the hood.

Daniel had always had a certain aptitude for mechanics which had surprised his father, who was no good with machinery, and though as yet he did not really understand automobiles, he understood enough to recognize that he was going to be stalled here for quite a while. The trouble was probably the coil or the condenser though it might be the timer, and if it was the timer he would have to have the car towed into Saint-Jérôme and left there for several days. He stood beside the car with the hood lifted while the traffic rushed past and it was three-quarters of an hour before an autoroute patrol car came around a curve, slowed down and stopped beside him and Daniel found himself confronting his second policeman of the day. The patrolman had neither a coil nor a condenser in his repair kit, but after a little tinkering he agreed with Daniel that it was probably one or the other. He offered to drive him to the nearest sortie leading into Saint-Jérôme. He could not take him all the way into the town because his job was to patrol the route.

Daniel had to walk half the way into Saint-Jérôme before a car stopped and took him the rest of the distance. He was dripping with sweat when he reached the nearest garage, and there the man told him he had no coils or condensers that would fit a foreign car.

"Why do you call this a foreign car?" Daniel said. "This is a French car."

The garage man did not get the point. "You ought to go with Chrysler or G.M. products," he said. "With these foreign cars, it's always the same story when it comes to parts."

"You mean there's no place in this town where I can get a part?"

"Yes, there's a place. I don't know whether it's open or not."

He gave Daniel the name and the address and when Daniel reached the garage it was closed. He walked several blocks before he found a phone book and thumbed the yellow pages, and finally he found a garage which could sell him a condenser but not a coil. It was ten minutes away, and after he had bought the condenser he telephoned for a taxi to drive him back to the autoroute. By this time his sports shirt was as wet as though he had been swimming in it.

After a quarter of an hour's work he fitted in the new condenser and the car started. It was now nearly five o'clock and he drove at top speed to make up for lost time, and after a few miles he heard a siren behind him and looked into the rearview mirror and a police car was chasing him with its beacon flashing. He stopped on the apron and waited for the policeman to get out and the policeman took his time. He turned out to be the same man who had driven him to the sortie earlier, and this time he demanded his license.

"I guess this is your lucky day," he informed Daniel as he noted down the essential data. He handed the license back. "Okay, you'll be hearing from us. Now get going and drive properly. You young fellows with cars like this, if I was the judge I wouldn't fine you. I'd put you in jail."

It was a quarter past six before Daniel reached the winding lane through the pines and birches and saw the late-afternoon sun shimmering on the lake. The hook was off the screened door of the veranda and he thought how careless Chantal had been to leave it like that until he saw that the hook had fallen off and not been replaced. It did not matter too much, for the cottage was farther north than the robbery belt nearer the city. So far as the local people were concerned, it could be left unlocked for years and nobody would take anything.

He turned on the tap and drank his first Laurentian water of the season. It came from an artesian well and its freshness gave his tongue a sensation of cool, pearly roundness. Pine needles were fragrant in the sun and it was cool in the shaded places. He stripped, changed into swimming trunks, took his fishing rod and went down to the little jetty in front of the cottage. The red canoe was upside down under a shelter and he dragged it to the water, took the paddle and pushed off and stroked for the center of the lake. He had it all to himself without a ripple. When he reached the deepest part he rolled out of the canoe and swam around, the cold, clean water delicious on his skin and with it the feeling that underneath him were nearly a hundred fathoms. When he was thoroughly cool he swam back to the canoe—he had never got far from it—came around to its stern and with a trained movement he flipped himself up and in and crouched forward with his hands on the gunwales steadying the craft until it came out of its rocking. Then he paddled to a point in the lake under a high promontory and began to fish. After half an hour he had caught a trout and a pair of bass, but by then the blackflies, mosquitoes and no-see-ums had come out from the land and were finding him. He gave up fishing and paddled back to the cottage. He beached the canoe on the little stretch of sand where he and Chantal had played as children and his mother had taken the sun in her bathing suit.

He gutted the fish at the water's edge, threw the offal into the woods for the crows and skunks to find, washed the flesh of the fish and took them into the kitchen of the cottage. He searched the shelves of the pantry for what he could find to make a meal. There was no butter, but he found an unopened bottle of olive oil, a package of dried bread crumbs, tins of vegetables and jars of herbs. He seasoned the fish with tarragon, dried out the crumbs in a pan, rolled the fish in them and cooked them slowly in the olive oil while *petit pois* heated on the burner beside them. It was a delicious sensation to be cooking his own supper in the coolness of the cottage with the heat outside, and when the fish began to sizzle he became very hungry. He served them up on a plate with the peas and ate his meal on the veranda while he looked at the lake. When the meal was over he felt deeply satisfied with the goodness of everything. He returned to the kitchen and poured boiling water over Nescafé and lay on the recliner on the veranda with his coffee while he watched the on-coming of evening, the insects outside the screen, the shadows of the hills reaching out over the lake and all the forest still. The landscape darkened as heavy clouds began to form.

He might have been a thousand miles from any human being. The birds scented the coming rain and were filling the air with warbling, liquid sounds. His father could identify every bird-call in the region, but the only ones familiar to Daniel were the robins, woodpeckers, phoebes and the hermit thrushes, the *rossignols* as they were called here, and while he sipped his coffee and smoked a cigarette a *rossignol* began singing in the birch thicket. It was a call he could almost see: it was like silver water cascading lightly through space, purer than joy and remote from the world. "On a night like this the twilight is so dense it ought to be called a gloaming"—more than once on evenings like this at the lake he had heard his father make that remark. It was a lovely word, "gloaming." Could the French language find a better one? *Le crépuscule*—better than "twilight," a shadow-shimmering word—but not for this present density of air, this absorption of daylight and of the world itself into dark velvet. The streets of the city seemed millions of miles away. *"La nation,"* he murmured. *"La nation!"*

The bird-songs dwindled off, the *rossignol* ending the chorus with a single half-phrase, and he remembered his mother telling him when he was a child that they slept with their heads tucked under their wings. Now the whole vast land was composing itself to sleep. Insects and frogs possessed the night. The insects hummed outside the screen; a June bug struck the screen with a boom. Frogs were ringing joyously as they mated among the reeds. The promontory where he had fished merged with the night without quite disappearing; it turned itself into a deeper darkness within the dark. The clouds had come between the lake and the stars.

He could not remember where he had left his cigarettes. There was a light installed on the porch and he rose and turned it on, blinking at its suddenness, and hunted for them. He had just remembered leaving them in the kitchen when he noticed something he had not noticed before: the filter-tipped butts of three cigarettes on an ash tray on a small table at the far end of the veranda. He picked one up, carried it to the light, examined it and saw it was a Du Maurier. He frowned, wondering how these butts had got here. His father smoked Du Mauriers. So did Chantal, of course. She had probably left them here the week before. He frowned again. One thing you could always say for Chantal, she was meticulously tidy; she was always after him for leaving his smoked-out cigarettes on ash trays. Oh well, the porch door had been open. Anyone could have got in. Some stranger had probably wandered down the birch-lined lane, found the porch door open and sat for a while smoking and watching the lake. Hundreds of thousands of people smoked Du Mauriers.

He returned from the kitchen with his cigarettes, shut off the porch light and sat down again. Lassitude filled him and he remembered the night before. He could not believe it now. It might have happened to another person entirely. Certainly it had not happened to the man he was now. Marielle seemed miles and years away, yet she had surely delivered him from himself. His nerves were quiet and cool and he was at one with the night.

He realized that if he tried to drive home to the city now he would fall asleep at the wheel. It was an effort even to climb out of the recliner before sleep took him. The sheets he put on his bed were slightly damp from the winter and the humidity, but they were clean and the dampness did not matter. His bed was built like a ship's bunk with drawers for his clothes underneath. It had been his father's idea to build him a bunk like this. His father must have lived a peculiar life before coming to Quebec. Funny that he spoke so little about it. Going to sea in the summers—he used to speak a lot about that. Funny his father coming here and marrying into *la nation*. Where does Dad really come from? Oh yes ... yes, I know. Daniel fell asleep.

The storm broke around three in the morning with a blinding flash of lightning simultaneous with a tearing crash of thunder as the first bolt split a pine. The rain followed it at once and after the rain came the north wind. The wind set every door in the cottage banging and rattling and blew the curtains out from the windows. Daniel rolled over and tried to get back to sleep, but this sounded more like a bombardment than a thunder storm and he got up and groped for the light-switch. No light came on. Either a transformer had been hit or they had shut off the power till the storm was over. But the flashes were so rapid that no artificial light was necessary.

He felt cold, wet air on his flesh and in the flashes he saw the curtains streaming away from the windows. Cold air gushed into the cottage in a torrent and he went out to the porch and saw the pattern of the storm.

It was almost three-dimensional, for the clouds extended up to the stratosphere. High up were huge, quivering illuminations among hidden clouds and the distant rumblings of a chain-reaction of electrical discharges. Lower down, the lightning was jumping through almost solid rain to the earth and the lake. He saw three simultaneous forks of lightning dart into the lake with a movement that made him think of the nerve in a tooth when the drill touches it. The blown rain lashed his skin and made him feel fresh and strong. It blew the soft feeling completely out of him, and sleep along with it. Now he wished Marielle were here with him; fiercely he wished it, so that he could make love to her in the storm and hear her cries in the thunder. Cold air gushed over the land, through the house, into his lungs, as the northern front ripped into the southern one and routed it. The forest neither wailed nor shrieked; it roared like Niagara.

Daniel stayed on the porch until the storm had rolled almost out of hearing into the south. The air was now so cold he needed a pair of woolen blankets on his bed. As he fell asleep he saw it was dawn and that the wind was still fresh but no longer violent. He remembered he had come up wearing nothing but shorts and a sports shirt, but that made no difference because there were woolen sweaters and an old pair of work-trousers in the drawers underneath his bunk.

When Alan Ainslie reached the island of Montreal from the north he decided not to re-enter the city. He was too tired, it was too hot and his emotions had burned out too much of his energy. Tomorrow might easily decide his fate in the government and he could not be sure what Bulstrode would do. It had come to him slowly that Bulstrode was the instinctive politician whose mind might appear to others to move in a haze, yet for that very reason was effective in his work as a politician. If the man has a genius, he thought, it is because he appears dominant and forthright when all the time he is as sincerely ambiguous as human nature itself.

He turned off toward the Ottawa highway and reached the capital about 7:30. The doorman of the hotel told him the temperature was ninety degrees and that it had reached ninety-nine during the mid-afternoon. He went up to his room and telephoned his apartment in Montreal and after three rings he heard Chantal's voice at last.

"Chantal dear, where on earth have you been?"

"Oh, Dad! So it was you who was here last night! Why didn't you tell me you were coming?"

"I came down on the spur of the moment. Where were you? I thought you might have been at the lake. I went up there today to see if you were."

There was an instant's hesitation before she said, "I'm so terribly sorry, Dad. How are you anyway?"

"I'm all right. How are you?"

Another hesitation and she said, "We just kept missing each other. Last night after you'd told me you were staying in Ottawa I went down to see Gabriel and it was so hot I asked him if I could sleep there and he let me have his spare room."

"Thank God you're all right! I'd been so worried about you. How is Gabriel?"

"He's fine. He'd—he'd been playing golf in the afternoon, as usual."

"In all that heat?" This time it was Ainslie who hesitated and sounded tentative. "Daniel wasn't at the lake, either. Is he home now?"

"He's out, I'm afraid. I haven't seen him all day."

"I want to speak to him very badly. . . . Chantal?"

"Yes, Dad?"

"Has Daniel been talking to you about things lately?"

"A little. He—well yes, the other night."

"So you know what he's been up to?"

"You mean the television show? Yes, I saw it last week. It's hard for me to get used to the idea of it. He's very good at it. It seems—well, it doesn't seem natural for anyone his age to talk with so much authority in public."

She stopped and Ainslie waited a moment before he asked quietly, "Is that all he told you?"

"Well, he didn't tell me much, but—Dad, do you know about it too?"

"I was told about it yesterday." He added, "In Ottawa."

"So they know there?"

"Certain people do. I must speak to him as soon as

possible, Chantal."

"Oh Dad, of course you must. I never knew the first thing about it till the night of the riot when he told me."

"Is he all right? I mean, does he seem normal?"

"Oh Dad, how can I possibly answer a question like that?"

"I can't answer it, either. Well, don't worry too much about it. After all, he's only a boy. This is an ugly and hypocritical world and if I were his age I'd probably feel the same way about it. But I do have to talk with him. Where is he sleeping these days if he isn't sleeping at home?"

"He usually comes home to sleep, but some of his friends have apartments and sometimes he stays with them."

"I'm not going to be critical of him or anything like that, but I must speak with him." Ainslie hesitated. "A lot of this must be my own fault. It's so long since I've seen him. It's not been easy for any of us. Will he talk with me, do you think?"

"You can make him talk with you."

"Not if he won't come to see me. I've not got much time of my own any more. The hours up here are awful. Chantal dear—do find him for me and tell him to ring me up. Either at my office or at the hotel. He can reverse the charges."

"I'd get in touch with him right away if I knew where he was."

"Even if he comes home at two o'clock in the morning, ask him to call me."

"Oh, I could kick the little fool."

"Don't think of him as a fool. He's only very young. He's young enough to see certain things very plain. The trouble is, of course, that he can't—"

"Dad, how are you yourself? How are you really yourself?"

"I feel very well now. I was up at the lake this afternoon and I had a swim and weeded some of the garden. It's pitiful to see the garden going to seed. Gabriel used to be fond of the place. Next Saturday why don't you get him to drive you up there and the both of you can do some weeding? It would be a change from his golf."

There was an abrupt silence from Chantal after he said this, but he did not notice it because he went on talking himself. It was five more minutes before he hung up.

Hours later Alan Ainslie heard the storm, but only for a moment. He was so tired he rolled over and slept through it. An hour later he woke shivering and pulled some blankets over him and slept again and did not stir until his alarm rang at 7:30. When he looked out the window the country seemed to have changed its nature —or, rather, to have cast off its masquerade and reverted to its real self. There were white caps on the brown water of the river and the sky was a hard cerulean with an invisible wind pouring through it. Not being certain of the kind of clothes to wear, he telephoned to the desk to ask what the temperature was and was told it had dropped to forty-four degrees. He decided on tweeds.

After breakfast when he walked through the cold, winy air he felt like a man who has just emerged from an anesthetic. He had spent an insane weekend careering down to Montreal in the heat in search of his children, chasing up to the lake and back again. Now his lungs were full of ozone and his mind was clear and fresh.

He reached his office just before the clock in the Peace Tower struck nine and was informed by his secretary that Mr. Bulstrode wanted a word with him immediately. Bulstrode always rose at five in the morning and usually he reached his desk by half-past six. Ainslie told his secretary to put the call through.

Book Two

ONE

"THEY'VE GIVEN notice they're going to be after you this afternoon," Bulstrode said to Ainslie over the phone. "You aren't surprised by that, are you?"

"Hardly."

"The press reaction to what you told those students hasn't been good. Coming after the riot, what else could you expect? It wasn't even as good as it might have been in Quebec, but I'll talk about that when I've thought it over." Bulstrode seemed to be in one of his fatherly moods. "Well, nobody can expect to find his way up here without experience, and lately this Parliament has been getting personal about everything. It's disgraceful. We're in a very bad patch right now. You say something, and everyone knows how you meant it, but some of them will twist it inside out in front of your eyes. It took me at least five years before—So long as a man's loyal to me, I'm loyal to him. There's so little loyalty left, so much of this P.R. image stuff that's come in from the States—so long as a man keeps himself like Caesar's wife, as clean as a hound's tooth—well, don't you worry too much about what that crowd can do to you. By the time I'm finished with anything coming from them, it's not going to be worth throwing it into the trash can even if it was any good to begin with. They've got spines like bananas. I'll call you later in the morning."

Ainslie hung up and contemplated the pile of bumpf

Miss Armstrong had sorted and placed on his desk and the sight of it made him think of the old anarchist slogan about incinerating the documents. But routine was built into him and he dictated letter after letter, adding to the pile this capital turned out mountain-high, and it was after twelve before he had completed his daily share of it. At 12:30 Bulstrode called him again.

"I'm having sandwiches for two sent up with milk and tomato juice and I want you over here right away."

Ainslie found Bulstrode prowling about his room low-slung with his weight-lifter's shoulders making him look triangular when finally he came to rest in front of the window and stood there with his hands clasped behind him. He stared across the river as though he were in private communication with the Gatineau Hills.

"This idea of yours about making the federal civil service bilingual," he said. "You and the French keep harping on that." Bulstrode turned around and his expression was puzzled. "You may be right, but I'll never believe the voter cares what happens in the civil service." Bulstrode returned to his desk and sat down heavily and scratched his ear. "The English provinces are in a bad mood about the French. The way they see it, Quebec's out to wreck Confederation and this idea of yours—it's a perfectly worthy idea normally—is going to look to them like appeasement. Their arteries are hardening."

"It's not appeasement to allow public servants in an officially bilingual country to use their own language when they're trying to serve it."

Bulstrode pondered and after a while he said, "There's something you haven't thought of."

Ainslie waited and said nothing.

"You see," Bulstrode said, "this hullabaloo about independence in Quebec could be catching. I've been in public life for a lot more than half of my life and my ear stays close to the ground and let me tell you something—it's not Quebec I'm scared of. It's the west. They've got the oil, they've got the potash and uranium, they've got so much water—and they've got a Pacific port. It would take most of the civil servants I know two years to learn enough French to order ham and eggs in a restaurant. They don't do much anyway. Are you suggesting we ought to promote a man just because he's bilingual? In that case I can name half a dozen elevator operators in the hotel across the way who ought to be made permanent under-secretaries." Bulstrode's eyes popped open. "Do you realize that statement of yours about a bilingual civil service has been picked up by every newspaper in Quebec? They're construing it as a promise binding on the government."

Ainslie breathed deeply and leaned back in his chair. So his gamble had been right after all. He did have some power here, if only the power of leverage to make the government do something it did not want to do. He realized also that Bulstrode could not demand his resignation without taking an open stand against Quebec, and Bulstrode had been in Ottawa long enough to know that no party could do this on a basic issue and hope to survive.

Their eyes met and Bulstrode was waiting for him to say something. Ainslie kept absolutely quiet, meeting Bulstrode's eyes, and finally Bulstrode turned away.

"I suppose you know," he said, "that there's going to be an election soon?"

So that was it! Had the P.M. told Bulstrode over the weekend that he was going to retire?

"This country must have some leadership," Bulstrode said thoughtfully. "There must be an end to all this crosspulling. I was talking to Laframboise over the weekend and he tells us there's not the slightest doubt we can hold Quebec—or at least enough of it."

"Hasn't Laframboise been asking to be made a senator —while there's still time?"

Bulstrode jerked around with a scowl. "You know,

Ainslie, sometimes you're your own worst enemy. You talk as if you knew everything. You aren't French. Laframboise is, and that's what he said."

"You should hear what his own people say about him."

Bulstrode looked down again at the backs of his hands, which were flat on the table. "You know, Ainslie, you could be so wrong about Quebec it wouldn't be funny. These people who are setting up the howl there are all intellectuals. The P.M. is very popular in Quebec and he deserves the absolute support and loyalty of all of us. Do you think the average voter cares about intellectuals?" Bulstrode snorted. "Cater to them and see what happens to you. My principle is to cater to nobody but the welfare of the entire country. I learned that lesson a long time ago. There was a politician I used to know in northern Ontario who was a great fixer. He was always promising people jobs for the sake of votes and he never knew how stupid he was. It never crossed his mind that for every friend he made by giving a man a job, he lost four or five in the men who'd wanted it and hadn't got it. So I think if I say no to these talkers in Quebec I'll get a great deal of grass-roots support there. This country needs leadership. I must have a clear mandate and in a democracy the majority must rule."

So it's been decided! Ainslie thought. Or has it been?

"You mean you don't intend to do anything at all?" he asked him.

"I never said that. And why are you making it personal? It's not just me. *I'm* not the Prime Minister. Over the weekend I had a long talk with the P.M. and we both agreed to the ideal solution. It's perfectly simple—a Royal Commission to look into this whole question about the civil service."

Ainslie's shoulders sagged. A new world and the situation within the country on the very hinge of it, hidden forces screaming and scratching to get out, and Bulstrode so marinated in party politics that he could see nothing except through the haze of them.

"This government," he said, "has appointed so many of these commissions of inquiry that the whole country's laughing at us."

Bulstrode's eyes flickered and concentrated on Ainslie, but the usual uncanny power to penetrate his defenses was not working today. Instinctively Bulstrode seemed to realize this.

"This French business seems to you the main thing because it's your job, but I tell you the main thing is the rising cost of living. The ordinary man is being crushed out of his mind by it. What difference does it make what language a man speaks when he's being driven into debt to keep his family alive?" Bulstrode pointed a stubby finger at Ainslie. "That's why we must get a clear mandate, otherwise those obstructors with their dirty, old-fashioned party politics will ruin the country. You know who's behind them, don't you? Who's behind the whole gang of them on the other side of the House? Bay Street and St. James Street, that's who's behind them, that's where their campaign funds come from." Bulstrode's blood pressure seemed to be rising. "For years I've fought them and they kept me down. Now that they can't keep me down any more they make fun of me. I tell you, Thomas Jefferson never said a truer word than when he said the businessman knows no patriotism but his own profit." Bulstrode pounded the desk with a fist like a mallet. "One of the very biggest of them was up to see me only a fortnight ago—the great Herbert Tarnley himself. Very polite, Tarnley is, very polished. Do you know what his idea was? He came up with a slate of economic advisers to help the work of my departments! Can you beat it? Oh yes, he was far too suave to come right out and say he was trying to buy into our party like he's bought into the other, but I saw through him like glass. 'Mr. Tarnley,' I told him to his face, 'I want you to know that I understand why you're here. And I want you to understand something else—you're tainted, you all are.' "

Bulstrode stopped and Ainslie said nothing.

"Well?" Bulstrode said.

"How can we possibly stand up to that kind of pressure—to say nothing of the international corporations—unless we have a united country?"

"That's exactly what I mean—a united country. And how can you get that without a strong, dedicated leadership? That's the priority—a clear mandate to govern."

"To return to your question about a royal commission," Ainslie said, "it's completely unnecessary, Mr. Minister."

Bulstrode rubbed his bald head and suddenly he gave Ainslie a fatherly smile. "Don't you think the time has come for you to call me Moses?"

Ainslie thanked him but was not deflected. "My department has all the facts that any royal commission would ever turn up. All we need is a decision to take action on the facts." He spoke quietly, motionless in his chair. "If we insist on bilingualism on the recruitment level of the federal civil service, it will be taken as a touchstone in Quebec and everywhere else that we accept that Canada is the home of two cultures and that the majority wishes the minority culture to survive and prosper. If this happens, we will have one of the happiest and most stable nations in the world. It's that, or disintegration. If we give French Canada another run-around at this particular moment, bombs will soon be going off."

Looking at Bulstrode, he saw a puzzled grin appear on his heavy mouth.

"Alan, how long have you been up here?"

"Nine months, going on ten."

"And you expect to be listened to right away!" Bulstrode shook his heavy head. "I sat here more than thirty years, on the back benches, people I had believed were my own friends keeping me down, before anyone listened to me." The strange face of Bulstrode suddenly

214

looked sad, almost prehistorically sad, and he turned his eyes away. "I love this country so much, but I often wonder how I endured all that. It's been lonely. Very lonely."

Ainslie did not know what to say to this and there was a long silence. Finally he said, "Election or no election, we can't stall about French Canada any more."

Bulstrode pondered; he looked worried; he stared at the backs of his hands and finally he lifted his jaw. "There's a principle here," he said.

"There certainly is a principle here."

"I've staked my whole public life on it, Alan," Bulstrode said earnestly. "I have never deviated from it. You can scrutinize my record and see for yourself. In this country, no man—not if I have anything to do with it—is going to be given preference over any other man. No one section, no matter what the political temptations, is going to be favored at the expense of any other section. Oh, I know it might appear expedient but—let me tell you a little parable, Alan."

Ainslie gave up and listened, and Bulstrode finally relaxed.

"This story concerns a man I have reason to believe was an ancestor of mine—Bulstrode Whitelocke was his name, one of the greatest lawyers of England at the time of the English Civil War and greatly admired by the great John Selden." The Minister's head nodded to emphasize the point. "No man, I venture to say, had greater cause to fear the King if the King ever regained his throne. Charles I has always seemed a tragic figure to me—few sovereigns were finer characters—he was an outstanding family man—but—principle again! You know what *his* political principles were. Anyway, when Cromwell decided to bring the King to trial, he called on Bulstrode Whitelocke to help him. Whitelocke wouldn't touch it." Another oscillation of the head. "It was simply a matter of principle with him. There was no law—the historians have subsequently agreed with him on this—there was no law that made it legal to try a sovereign of England, and therefore to do so—no matter what the provocation—was an assault on the law itself." Bulstrode paused. "We all know what happened. Cromwell was so impatient he rigged the trial and cut off the King's head. Bulstrode Whitelocke lost all favor with him, and his services to the state were lost in consequence. But how much better it would have been for England, to say nothing of Cromwell's reputation, if that man of principle had been listened to!" Another head-shake. "History is a great teacher, Alan." Bulstrode swung around and stared out the window and muttered as though to himself, "A very great teacher."

There was a knock on the door and an attendant appeared with a tray holding sandwiches, milk and tomato juice. Bulstrode perked up at the sight of the sandwiches.

"Sardines!" he said, and rubbed his hands. "In the Yukon they were a treat, I can tell you. There's nourishment in them too, but it's the taste. Saturday night in the cabin was sardine night." Bulstrode swallowed some tomato juice and began munching with relish. "When I was a boy I used to dream of going into the sardine business myself so everyone could have sardines. Funny thing," he went on, still munching, "I was having a crack a few years ago with one of the richest men in the country and he told me that when he was a kid he'd had the same kind of idea I had. This man was born very poor in a city slum and on Saturday nights his mother used to send him to the corner store to buy the family treat of the week. Guess what it was? It was Fray Bentos— bully beef! He told me they used to eat it drowned in ketchup. Well, this man told me that when he was a kid it was his dream to make a product everyone in the world would want to consume, and finally he did make it and became so rich he needs a whole battery of accountants and corporation lawyers to keep his books for him and keep the government from getting all his money." Bulstrode grinned ruefully. "He makes whiskey, I'm afraid."

They finished their lunch and Bulstrode showed signs of getting back to business, but it was not the business Ainslie was expecting.

"I saw you in the hotel with Lacombe the other night," he said casually. "I suppose he told you about it?"

"Yes, he gave me his report on the riot."

"You know I wasn't talking about that. I mean about your son."

Ainslie felt himself turning pale.

"They all know about him in the R.C.M.P.," Bulstrode told him.

Ainslie's throat constricted. "My son is only a boy, Mr. Minister."

"I thought you were going to call me Moses." Bulstrode's face was kindly. "Don't take it too hard, Alan. You're not the first man in public life who's had to suffer a blow from his own family. Look at what happened to poor Leopold Amery in the last war with his son. I don't mean the good one, I mean the one they had to hang. That was one of the saddest things I ever heard of. But I don't have to tell you what this could mean if the papers got hold of it." Bulstrode's head was nodding in rhythm to his sentences. "They've got no mercy. They've declared an open season on everyone in public life. Instead of treating us like public servants, they treat us like public enemies. This is no fault of yours, but in a thing like this I wouldn't be able to protect you. You're way out of line with the English provinces anyway, but at least you're honest, everyone knows you're not in it for yourself and so far they've had to respect you. But if they found out your son was an active separatist . . ." Bulstrode lifted both hands in the air. "Even the government could be endangered by a thing like that." He gave Ainslie a penetrating glance. "Why didn't you tell me this yourself? It was your duty."

217

Ainslie had recovered his self-command. So the cabinet knew about it too. So all this conversation they had been having had been nothing more than a charade. But what else could government be but a charade when the ones in power were living in the past without even knowing it? He looked down at his hands and saw them folded placidly.

"I didn't tell you," he said quietly, "because I didn't know. When you saw me with Lacombe I'd just found out about Daniel. I was on my way to Montreal to speak with him."

"What did he have to say for himself?"

"I couldn't find him. He wasn't home. The next day I drove all the way north to our cottage on the lake. Daniel used to enjoy it so much at the lake and that weekend was insufferably humid in the city. But he wasn't there, either. Not even my daughter could tell me where he was. I left word for him to call me. Perhaps the call reached my office while I've been here with you."

Bulstrode was sitting so impassively that he made Ainslie think of a buffalo chewing his cud, but suddenly he broke the pose and said sharply, "I wish it clearly understood that we can draw no distinction between separatism and treason."

"I hope none of you are going to say that in public— not yet anyway."

"Why should I not say that in public? If Sir Edward Gray had come straight out about Belgium in 1914— if Chamberlain had come straight out about Czechoslovakia at the beginning of 1938—history is a great—"

"When in the course of human events . . ." Ainslie said.

He was quoting one of Bulstrode's favorites, but no words and knew it. Bulstrode's mouth opened wide, but no words came out of it.

"Do you wish me to resign?" Ainslie asked him.

Bulstrode rubbed his chin and pondered. "Now listen, Alan. Listen very carefully to this. There is to be no talk of resignations. This information is safe in the files of the R.C.M.P. and they're ordered to sit on it. Of course, if your boy does anything illegal—you take my advice and take that boy of yours out to the woodshed. He belongs to a spoiled generation. If you'd any sense, you'd never have bought him that car."

"What car are you talking about?"

"That sports car he's driving around in. I've seen a picture of it. If you didn't buy it for him, you must have given him too much spending money. That's one of the chief troubles today. A poor man's son, or even the son of a well-off man with a sense of responsibility—they're made to feel out of everything if they haven't a couple of hundred dollars a month to throw away. When I was your boy's age my pocket money never exceeded fifty cents a month."

Ainslie's nerves were quivering. "If Daniel bought a car he must have bought it on installment with his own money. He's never been a spendthrift. He worked last summer, and this summer he's got a job on television."

"I know about that TV show. I learned about it three days ago. Did Lacombe have to inform you about that too?"

Ainslie bit his lip. "Yes."

"This is bad, Alan, this is bad. I don't know what things are coming to if a son doesn't tell a father—particularly if he's the kind of man you are—about a thing like that. There's no disclipline in this young crowd these days." Bulstrode looked at his watch and came to his feet. "Well, it's time for you and me to go forth to fight the beast at Ephesus. When the questions come—no matter what some of them may say—you just stick to your seat and let me handle them. After all, I have to bear the ultimate responsibility for what goes on in your department. And if I—when I—announce the government's decision to appoint the royal commission"—Bulstrode looked at him with a canny smile—"I'll take it for granted that you will accept it."

"So the decision was definite all along? It had been made before you mentioned it to me?"

"I told you that. I told you the P.M. had—"

"It's a mistake," Ainslie said, "and I wish you'd reconsider it. A royal commission might easily last three years or more."

Bulstrode put a hand on Ainslie's shoulder. "Yes, so it might. A lot will depend on who is appointed to the commission. Some men, when they get on a commission like that, their self-importance makes them want to drag things on and on. But you don't build Rome in a day and you don't unify a country like this inside a few weeks."

"Certainly not the way we're going," Ainslie said.

When he left the House late that afternoon, Ainslie believed that such usefulness as he had ever had here had probably been destroyed, and for the second time that day he realized that a change had occurred in his character. In the past, his natural competitiveness would have brought him to his feet, but he sat quietly and let Bulstrode take over because he knew that nothing he could say could change things in any way he desired. Was he getting old, or had the death of Constance blunted his edge?

Politically, what Bulstrode had done—or had promised to do, for he might easily use the coming election as an excuse to do nothing at all—had been to turn the competence of an official department of the government, a department with portfolio, over to a group of neutral investigators as yet unnamed. It amounted to a public and implicit admission that the senior officers in the government considered Ainslie's department useless, and one of the Opposition members had risen to point this out; he had even expressed sympathy for Ainslie and stated that if he had any self-respect he ought to resign immediately.

220

Ainslie sat with a frozen face and listened without anger. Had his own circumstances been normal, he would have risen and said, without anger, that he was resigning from the cabinet and have taken a seat in the back of the House. To have done such a thing would have brought to a head a growing dissatisfaction with Bulstrode's methods within his own party, and of course Bulstrode had been aware of this. But Bulstrode had also guessed that owing to Ainslie's uncertainty about his son he would do nothing, at least not for a while. Was it turning out that his personal honor was being compromised by his son?

Yet in the eyes of the majority party he had not been made to look like a fool or a man publicly humiliated by a stronger colleague. He even noted several nods of approval from members who came from ridings where association with Ainslie's ideas would be a liability. Also there was Bulstrode's personal performance. His command of the House was so complete that he made it appear that this proposal of a royal commission was a great step toward developing a dialogue with Quebec and that it was Ainslie's own idea. Ainslie realized with a shock that it was only too true that most of the members of this House of Commons were still only half-conscious of the realities that kept him awake at night. Well, he thought, they'll soon be educated.

When he reached his office he was told by Miss Armstrong that no message had come from Daniel. He glanced at the latest accumulation of bumpf and pushed it aside. He told Miss Armstrong to give up for the day and go home, then he sat by himself and tried to think but could think of nothing but Daniel. Suddenly he remembered that he had colleagues and that they would soon know, if they did not know already, that he had let them down. He picked up the phone and dialed Laurent Saint-Just and learned immediately that Saint-Just had been in the gallery of the House that afternoon.

"I know," he said. "I know, Laurent. I couldn't stop him."

Saint-Just waited for more.

"I know you saw me sitting there saying nothing. He just sprang it on me at lunchtime and I found out it had been decided over the weekend. You want to know what I'm going to do? You'll have to give me a little time to think it over."

Another silence and then, as he had feared, "How much time, Alan?"

"So you feel about it like that?"

"I feel about it like that."

"Can you give me a week?" Ainslie's voice rose in frustrated impatience. "I couldn't help this. There's something involved here I simply can't mention to anyone. You must give me a week, Laurent."

"All right. But in Quebec I'll be in even a worse spot than you are after this gets around."

"You know me well enough—surely you know me well enough, Laurent—to understand that I'm not consenting to this run-around indefinitely."

He hung up, left his office and walked back to his room in the hotel. The air was fresh and it was still cool enough for tweeds, though the weather report said it was going to warm up again. The north wind still blew through that cerulean sky. Looking up at he sky he saw, right on the dot, the feathered vapor trail of a SAC plane flying out on its patrol. Its altitude was so great that the plane itself was invisible and the vapor trail seemed to be growing out of itself like a finger pointed from the west over the Great Circle to the east. That thing up there and us down here talking in the same old way about the little human problems bequeathed to us by careless gentlemen in the eighteenth century.

But the megaton bomb to the megadeath man
Replied in a voice of thunder:

"It's not the earth you've hit,
It's yourself, you shit!
Your computer has made a blunder."

So the Minister of Cultural Affairs has made up another doggerel! he said to himself as he passed the statue of Sir Wilfrid Laurier.

TWO

IN THE cold air of the Monday morning after the storm
Gabriel Fleury walked through streets thundering with
pneumatic drills and dusty from excavations and building
materials. These days central Montreal reminded him of
London after a blitz. Old buildings going down and new
ones going up and his own firm making a fortune out of
it. His firm was very proud of having gone totally modern,
but to him all they were doing was to standardize ideas
that had been formulated by *avant-garde* architects half
a century ago. A generation from now, he predicted, these
styles would be hated, but it would then be too late to
change what they had done to the city.

When he entered his office, the windows reaching from
floor to ceiling, he felt himself in a glass cage. The chrome
and glass of buildings similar to his own glittered in the
sun of a new weather that made the heat and humidity
of the weekend seem as remote as his memories of Indo-
China. He found it hard to be interested in his work that
morning and wondered if the time was not at hand when
computers could do it better than himself and then, his
mind roaming, he wondered whether computers and
social-science surveys had replaced God in the modern
superego.

He was happy but at the same time anxious and worried. He ached for Chantal; his tenderness for her filled
his soul, but the fatal arithmetic of their ages—or was it

so fatal after all?—troubled him profoundly. Of course she wanted children; no woman could have given herself as she had done without being deeply maternal. His conscience was troubled because what he had done ran contrary to his idea of the rightness of things. His chief objection to modern morality, including some of Chantal's, was that it was sentimental. They seemed to have forgotten that morality's only use is self-protection. In their blind way even his own exasperating family had understood that, at least apart from their attitude toward the military.

He looked out the window and saw a white ship moving slowly up the river to its dock and tried to think of his position coldly, particularly in relation to Alan Ainslie. Surely it was the priority that no matter what he did or wished to do, he should not betray his friend. But was he actually doing this? There were regions in Alan he had never penetrated. Did Alan suffer from a kind of unconscious egoism that comes more easily to the unsophisticated than to somebody like himself? If so, it was never an egoism that wished to dominate others; it was larger than that; it sought a more ambitious identity. Alan himself had said of his father, "He told me I must school myself to belong to civilization." In Alan's mind was the belief that neither he nor his country had as yet proved themselves worthy of civilization. A very odd point of view in a time when the usual question asked was, "Is society worthy of me?" But in a personal crisis with Chantal or Daniel involved, how would Alan behave? At this point Gabriel was puzzled by a curious secrecy in a man who in most other ways was recklessly frank, and then he remembered the time they were shot down over the German city. It had been a traumatic experience for both of them.

When the plane staggered, screamed and caught fire, Alan had instantly taken command and ordered the others to jump. Gabriel had lurched forward to him and been met by a slap in the face by the back of Alan's gloved hand. He was sitting there with the flames coming around him

226

holding the plane's head up. Gabriel had gone back and jumped and the plane had lurched off in flames above him.

Swinging in his harness Gabriel came down through the semi-darkness with the tracers spitting past him and underneath the fires of the city growing rapidly larger in his eyes. He tried to manipulate the chute away from them, but the turbulence caused by the heat of the fires made it impossible to do so. He hit the pavement in a public square beside the statue of a soldier on horseback and sprained an ankle, unharnessed himself and lay flat at the base of the statue while the earth heaved and the air roared with exploding bombs, and spent bullets and flak fragments rattled like hail. Soon it was over and he heard the planes going away and the rushing noise of the burning town. He tried to remember the map of the city he had studied before the raid, but it was an old city with crooked streets and a number of public squares and he had no idea which one of these he had fallen into. He hobbled across to the sidewalk and around the nearest corner and walked straight into the arms of a German patrol. They recognized his uniform and seized him, one soldier hit him under the eye and shouted obscenities. Gabriel answered in broken German and the *Feldwebel* in charge of the patrol shouted to shut up and then shouted, *"Marsch!"* He hobbled in the middle of the patrol back to the square and across it into a burning street where he saw for the first time what an allied bombing raid could do. *"Neunzig kinder getötet hier! Neunzig kinder!"* Apparently one of the buildings they had hit had been a children's hospital. He was marched through a swarm of men and women whose eyes were staring and horrified, whose faces were smoke-blackened, but no harm was done to him and within an hour he was in a guarded truck *en route* to a prison camp.

There he found Joe Lacombe and some of the others but he did not know for two months what had happened to Alan Ainslie and only then when Ainslie himself appeared in the camp. He walked on a crutch and his face was in bandages and he had only one eye. He had fallen into another part of the city, had been shot through the left thigh and thrown into the fire of a burning building. A German patrol had hauled him out and Alan said to Gabriel, "All this about the German discipline is absolutely true. One of the soldiers who hauled me out of that fire is still in the hospital himself." More than this Alan never mentioned to anyone about what happened to him after he came down in his parachute into the German city. . . .

Gabriel got up and looked out the window and saw, far below, the crawling lines of pedestrians and automobile tops moving like objects on an assembly line. He wondered how many of the people down there had been in the war and what each one remembered of it. Then he returned to his desk, picked up the phone and telephoned to the gallery where Chantal worked and felt a loosening behind his knees when he heard her voice. She wanted to see him again that night but he forced himself to refuse.

"Have you heard from your—from Alan?" he asked her.

She told him of her phone conversation with her father and that he had come down from Ottawa on Saturday night and found his home empty.

"I told him I'd spent the night at your flat."

Gabriel controlled his breathing with difficulty. "Yes?"

"He was so relieved. He'd been worried sick about me. Now of course it's Daniel he's worried about."

"So you told him about Daniel? I think you were right."

"I didn't have to tell him. He knew—and from the worst source possible. He was told about Daniel by your old friend, Joe Lacombe."

"You mean, the R.C.M.P. are onto him already?"

"Of course he hasn't committed any crime yet. It's just that they know about him. I hope to God the newspapers don't find out, or Dad will be crucified. Daniel came home finally—yesterday morning when I was still with you, as a

228

matter of fact. Then he drove up to the lake. It was a crazy wild-goose chase Sunday, for Dad had the same idea and got there first. Something happened to Daniel's car and he didn't arrive till late and by then Dad had left. They must have passed each other on the autoroute going in opposite directions. Daniel stayed the night at the camp and I haven't even seen him yet. I just talked to him over the phone. He promised to call Dad this evening— that's something anyway."

After a few more words Gabriel said he had to go back to work.

THREE

It WAS a dark, low-ceilinged *boîte* murky with breathed air and cigarette smoke and throbbing like the inside of a drum. Its name was *"Le Cachot"* and it had been designed to resemble the interior of a medieval dungeon, with barred windows and heavy iron grilles and walls faked to look like thick granite blocks. There was a patch of empty floor where girls and boys twisted to the hammering racket of a juke-box and here they called it *"Le Separatwist."* There was also a small bar and a folk-singer who sat on it with a guitar in the intermissions of the juke-box and sang nationalist folk-songs of his own composition.

When the *chanteur* had finished his first round of songs, Daniel looked around at the young men and girls, the men with long hair or with short hair brushed forward like his own, crouched over the tables with beer and their girls. Why do the English have to be so much bigger than us physically? But aren't the little brown men of Viet Nam doing better in the jungles than the big Americans?

Aimé Latendresse leaned across the table toward him. "Did you hear the news about your father tonight?"

Daniel nodded glumly.

"That royal commission is nothing but pinky stamps from a chain grocery store. It's worse than a deliberate insult."

"It was Bulstrode," Daniel said. "It wasn't my father, it was Bulstrode."

Latendresse eyed him. "Your father was present. He took his seat in the House. By saying nothing, he consented. He approved."

Daniel remembered the night and morning at the lake and how beautiful it had been. Were there two Quebecs now—the old Quebec of the country and the new Quebec of Montreal and places like this?

"They're saying he's sold out to Bulstrode," Latendresse said.

Suddenly, and for the first time, Daniel dared ask himself if he really liked this man he had admired so much.

"Whatever else he does or doesn't do," he said, "my father's not on sale to anyone."

"I wasn't talking about money." Latendresse's lips moved in a thin, intellectual smile. "At any rate, it's now more important than ever for you to arrange a debate on your television show between him and me."

"I told you last week he'd never accept that."

"I don't agree with you. Evidently you don't understand how impossible his position has become now."

"Why is it so impossible?"

Latendresse smiled contemptuously. "Not even the official press of Quebec—not even *La Presse*—will accept this. Unless your father repudiates Bulstrode, even the Quebec bourgeois establishment will reject him. Bulstrode is a living impertinence to all of us." The opaque eyes narrowed. "A man like your father would not be influenced by criticism coming from the English—he'd be too proud for that. But if our side attacks him it would provoke a different behavior. He has nothing else, nowhere else to go. So far as French Canada's concerned, he's already *parti-pris*. He'll want to justify himself to us some way or other."

"My father's not an ordinary politician," Daniel said shortly. "He's never even tried to think like one."

"Anyway, arrange a debate—no, 'discussion' would be a wiser word—between him and me. Call it a friendly discussion between the both of us on your show."

Daniel squinted through the smoke of the Gitane. "Supposing he agrees, what kind of line will you take, Aimé?"

"The important thing for us now is to obtain a forum with somebody in an official public position. That will signify that we are officially recognized."

Now what Daniel was feeling for Latendresse was hostility but, though his instinct knew it, his mind still refused to accept it.

"The technique of revolution can now be called a science," Latendresse went on in his emotionless voice. "It makes no difference what group you belong to or what your ideology is. The techniques are all similar. A political movement is like a car parked near the crest of a hill. First, the brakes must be released. Then the car must be put into neutral gear. Then she must be pushed. The first pushes are the hardest, but once the car is over the crest of the hill our task is to get it to that point."

Daniel looked away from Latendresse and around the room. The singer was seated at a table surrounded by little girls and, as Daniel felt Latendresse's cold eyes on him, he wondered if he had become suspect because he was only half-French.

"Where will it end?" he heard himself say.

"I don't understand your question."

"This car you speak about—after it is pushed over the crest of the hill, where will it go? Where will it end?"

Latendresse contemplated him without expression. Finally he said, "A number of people in Paris are with us now. De Gaulle has made a lot of difference. He knows as well as I do that the French language is in danger everywhere. He also understands that there is room for judo in politics. If a country is as strong as America, its strength can be used to defeat itself. And of course, the chief American iron-ore reserve is here, with us."

Does he think I don't know all that? Daniel thought.

He said, "I don't know what I can do. My father was in town last night looking for me. I wasn't home and I didn't find out about it till this morning when my sister told me. He wants to see me very much, she said. I was thinking of going up to Ottawa tomorrow or the day after."

"Could you make studio arrangements in Ottawa?"

"I don't know. I suppose so."

"Then I will go up with you. We could do the show there."

"No," Daniel said. "I must talk with him first. I don't know what he's thinking these days. It's months since I've seen him."

Latendresse looked away and Daniel realized that for himself as a human being this man not only had no feelings, he did not even have an ordinary consciousness of his existence.

"Do you believe," he said, avoiding the eyes of Latendresse, "that my father would be accepted into the movement if he wished to join it?"

Latendresse's smile was ironic. "That's an interesting idea, that one."

"He loves Quebec, he really does. Other people besides —besides us French can love Quebec. He was very fond of my mother's family and they were very fond of him. You must understand that, Aimé. After what Bulstrode's done to him—and Bulstrode's simply doing it on account of the rural Ontario and western voters—my father's very unselfish, you know. He's brave too. Did you know he won the D.F.C. in the war?"

Latendresse's eyebrows lifted. "What does that mean, the D.F.C.?"

Daniel was silent and stared ahead of his nose.

"Anyway," Latendresse said, "I'll be expecting to hear from you inside a few days. The interview between you and me is for Thursday night, isn't it?"

"I told you it was for Thursday night, didn't I?"

Latendresse nodded, left Daniel and joined a group at

another table at the far end of the room near the singer. Watching him go away, Daniel thought he looked as incongruous in this setting as a priest would be.

Daniel smoked, glanced at the untouched glass of Cinzano in front of him and relaxed a little. A friend in a group at another table beckoned to him and as he went over he noticed a single man of indeterminate age sitting by himself in a corner near the door. This man had a half-empty glass of beer in front of him. With leisurely movements the man got up and strolled out the door and Daniel noticed that he had left his beer unfinished on the table.

There were girls in the group he joined and he stayed with them for half an hour. During this time the singer rose with his guitar, seated himself on the bar and sang three more songs and the whole room joined in the chorus of one of them. Daniel realized for the first time in his life that girls had an interest in him. One of them slipped her hand under his arm and kissed him breathingly in his ear and whispered something in English in a European accent. When he looked into her eyes she answered his gaze bold and direct. Three more people entered the *boîte* and one of them was Clarisse. She saw Daniel, nodded without smiling and looked for a place to sit. When she found one, Daniel left the group he was with and joined her.

"Did you have a good time over the weekend?" he asked her.

"It was all right," Clarisse said with indifference.

He searched her face, half-guilty and half-triumphant, but saw in it no glimmer of any new understanding. She made a semi-contemptuous reference to his father and he made no comment on it. How could he ever have been so blind as to have wanted a breastless girl like this? She looked at him with much the same expression she had always showed, and now he knew that what it really signified was indifference. He soon gathered that she did

234

not care whether he remained with her or not, so he said good night and went out into the street.

The night air was delicious after the smoke and carbon dioxide of the *boîte*. A moon was in the sky over Montreal and he walked for several blocks, breathing deeply and feeling better with every step. He found a sidewalk telephone booth, entered and dialed the number he now knew by heart. Marielle's voice gave him a physical spasm as though she were naked before him.

"Daniel dearest, I'd love to see you and I miss you already, but surely you know that tonight's impossible."

"Why is it impossible, Marielle?"

"Dear boy, be sensible."

"Clarisse won't be home. I've just been talking to her. She's in the café with the crowd."

A pause. "But that would not be proper. That would not be decent."

He flushed, yet was grateful to her for having said this.

"Don't you want to see me ever again? Was it just once and gone?"

"Of course I do, darling." There was a smile in her voice. "There's music in you—didn't you know it?"

He drove home in a state of mind unknown to him before and thought of the wonderful things he would do before he died. He did not know what they were, they were just wonderful things. When he reached home he found Chantal there and she looked at him in surprise.

"You look different, Daniel. What's happened?"

"You look different too."

"Do I really? Does it show so soon?"

"Does what show?"

They were trembling on the edge of revealment, they both were, but the familial reserve stopped them.

"I just said you look different," he said. "You said I look different. All right—we both look different and so what?"

"Are you going to call Dad?"

"Don't you think it a little peculiar that he wants to see me after all this time when he hasn't cared whether I was dead or alive?"

"That's not fair, Daniel. This year has been awful for him."

"I'm willing to go up to Ottawa if he's willing to spare me a few minutes of his governmental time. I said so, didn't I? Did you see what happened to him in the House today? He just sat there while Bulstrode sold him out. Did you see that, or are the newspapers below your notice?"

"Why do you have to be so horrid? Why do you have to say things that are like a slap in the face?" Her eyes filled with tears. "Things like that—why do you have to say them all the time?"

"Things like what?"

"Daniel, don't play innocent with me. And when you talk to Dad, please remember that he's our father. And after that, remember that he loves us both and that he's in a horrible position now, and that you've probably made it worse than it would have been anyway. I'm not going to argue with you about politics no matter how juvenile *your* politics are. But the position you're putting yourself in, to say nothing of Dad, could be a great deal more serious for both of you than you seem to have any idea of."

He looked at her and flushed. Then he laughed. "So my politics are juvenile, are they? You—who was so busy living a gay little social life you never even knew what was happening before I told you a few nights ago—*you* say my politics are juvenile! Well, well, well! However, if you're willing to stop talking, I'm certainly willing to telephone our father."

"You might have done it long ago. It's nearly midnight and the poor man's probably asleep."

Daniel went back to the extension in his father's study and made the call to the hotel in Ottawa. He did not break

236

his father's sleep; he heard his father's voice wide awake, grateful and kind, gentle in the way he remembered it, and he was surprised and troubled. He agreed to dine with his father in Ottawa the following night, and then he went rushing on.

"We're both home, Chantal and I. She looks very well. Indeed, with a little effort, she might even look beautiful."

After a few more minutes he heard his father say, "Good night, Daniel. I can't tell you how nice it will be to see you again."

"*Bon soir, P'pa.*"

Daniel hung up and stared at the silent phone.

What have I been doing? he thought.

What have I been saying?

What have I been feeling?

FOUR

THE NEXT evening was much warmer; it was windless and clear and after dinner Daniel and his father strolled together along the banks of the canal. To Daniel his father looked much older than he had remembered him, his face more noticeably divided between the injured side and the other one. To Alan his son also looked older and he recognized from a new expression in his face that he had crossed a frontier of some sort in his life. In their mutual recognitions was a deeper recognition that made them both afraid and self-conscious. Ainslie thought, That truck that broke Constance's skull broke the life of our whole family.

"Let's sit down here," he said, and they sat on the bank beside the canal and felt the coolness of grass that soon would be wet with dew. A short distance off was a young mother with three very young children, the oldest about six, the youngest barely able to walk. Her face was happy in her absorption with them, and as Ainslie made small talk with Daniel, he watched a man join the group and sit down with them. He was the husband. He was a poor man and his face indicated no signs that he would ever have any future importance, but he had great dignity because of his pride in being the bread-winner of the woman and the children.

As Alan felt the silence grow between himself and his son, he felt hurt and guilty because it was there. He began speaking in French, a little nervously, but after a minute Daniel interrupted him in English.

"You don't have to talk French with me, Dad. That makes no difference now."

"We seem to be far apart."

Daniel made no comment, but his father saw the muscular shoulders of the boy tighten.

"I'm pretty much alone these days," he said. "It can't be helped, but it's not good. I'm going to tell you something that may surprise you. When men grow older, it often happens that their imaginations become much stronger than when they were young." He smiled shyly. "That may be why some men my age feel younger—only in a certain way, of course—than they did twenty years earlier. They often feel much less sure of themselves. I was awfully sure of myself when I was thirty."

Daniel winced slightly and said, "Dad, please don't. You don't have to any more."

"Have to what?"

"Go on talking like that."

"I see."

A long, hurt silence brooded between them, the kind that comes when the souls of two people inextricably meshed peep out at one another and are not acknowledged.

"Dad?"

"Yes?"

"This means everything to me—can't you understand that?"

"I believe I can try to. But 'everything'—that's a very big word that can last a very long time."

"Why can't you see it?"

"Perhaps I can see it if you will help me."

"Dad?"

"Yes?"

"You're such an able man—why have you been so ineffectual?"

Ainslie felt himself swallowing air; also swallowing a

240

bitterness of disappointment the like of which he had never known in his life. He said nothing.

"It's not your fault, Dad. That's all I'm trying to tell you—it's not your fault. I'm not trying to insult you, I'm only telling you it's not your fault."

"What isn't my fault, Daniel? I honestly don't understand."

The boy made a violent gesture. "You don't understand what they've done to you. What they and their damned System have done to you."

"What do you mean, their System? The capitalist system, or something else?"

"Just everything. Why don't you get out of it? Why can't you go along with us?"

Ainslie looked at him in incredulity. "Do you mean that?"

"I do, Dad. I do. You just don't know what it is. You close your eyes to it because you think it's against what you want."

Ainslie continued to look at him. "Do you seriously believe this movement of yours is something new? Do you think there's never been anything like it before?"

Far over to the left the Peace Tower was visible in a gap in the trees. Ainslie glanced at it, then back to his son.

"If this year has taught me anything," he began, but stopped when it came to him that he did not know exactly what it had taught him except a little more about his own vulnerability. He was ashamed of himself for sounding stuffy when he next spoke. It was unnatural to be speaking to his own son as though he were a student or some half-stranger he was doing official business with.

"The last thing I want to do is give you orders. I'm sure they wouldn't be obeyed if I did. But it's my duty to warn you of some things you don't seem to have thought of. Quite a few of you are marked men. I'm afraid you're a marked man too, Daniel." He paused, and

241

saw a startled expression on the boy's face. "Several weeks ago my own investigators heard about a secret organization that calls itself *'Le Ralliement à Mort.'* The very title is so theatrical that no man of experience can possibly take it seriously. However, nobody knew who was in it until that riot." He held up his hand to forestall an interruption. "I'm not saying, or even implying, that you or any of your friends are in it. I'm merely saying what I'm saying. And I want to tell you something else—the R.C.M.P. aren't stupid or irresponsible and they're not unkind. But they're competent men with a job to do."

"They certainly have a job to do, all right."

"They have photographs of every face that was visible in that riot. Now don't get the idea that this means they believe that everyone who was out in the street that day belonged to some conspiracy. I'm not for a moment suggesting that you belong to one yourself. I don't think you do. But if this organization ever becomes militant, the police will quickly be able to narrow down the field. It won't be difficult for them to infiltrate."

He searched Daniel's face for a reaction, but this time none came. He said no more and was conscious that daylight was failing. Soon it would be dark. At least five minutes passed before either of them spoke again and it was Ainslie who broke the spell.

"Do you know what brought you into this movement, Daniel? If so, I wish you'd tell me."

"Of course I know. Do you think everyone who disagrees with your way of looking at things is crazy?"

Ainslie looked at him steadily. "You won't tell me?"

A wild exasperation entered Daniel's eyes and he cried out at his father, "Why do you have to be like all the rest of them? We scream it from the housetops and not even you can understand. Even *you* ask me what we want and what we mean. Don't you understand words?"

"Words can be disguises, Daniel. I learned that in the 1930s."

"The 1930s!"

"You still haven't told me why you've joined this movement."

Daniel looked away. "What's the use? How can anyone like you understand what it feels like to be an orphan?"

Tears filled Ainslie's eyes; he reached out and put his hand over Daniel's wrist.

"I certainly know what it feels like to be a widower," he said quietly.

Daniel wrenched his wrist from his father's grip and made an impatient sweep. "I wasn't talking about *that!* I was talking about the whole French-Canadian race. You grew up a part of the British Empire with the United States beside you and talking your language, with the whole huge, insensitive, crass, clumsy, conceited, interfering, hypocritical Anglo-Saxon System behind you. But we're orphans and at last we've found the courage to admit it. We don't want to spend the rest of our lives in an orphanage—and that's all the Province of Quebec will ever be unless it becomes an independent state and regains the pride that was milked and crushed out of it." He stared at his father. "Oh, what's the use? You'll never understand. Not in a thousand years would you be able to understand a thing like this."

Insects were making tracks on the surface of the canal and in the near distance the Peace Tower struck nine resonant notes. The mother and father on the grass near them rose and gathered in their children, the father carrying the smallest one, and Alan watched the young family move off together. He imagined the children being tucked into bed and the parents looking at each other at the end of another day in their lives together.

Ainslie turned and said, "I've decided to tell you something I perhaps should have told you long ago. It's strange, your comparison of French Canadians to orphans. I happen to have grown up an orphan myself. I dare say it's had a bigger effect on me than I've been willing to admit."

Daniel started; he looked at his father to see if he really meant this.

Ainslie went on quietly, "My real father wasn't Dr. Ainslie. He was someone very different. Your mother was the only person I ever told this to. I remember my mother very well. I wasn't illegitimate. We were poor, but I was very happy with her. When my memory begins we were living alone, just she and I, in a miner's cottage in Nova Scotia. Dr. Ainslie was the colliery doctor at that time. He befriended us and after my mother was killed he adopted me. We didn't stay in Nova Scotia long after that. The doctor and Mrs. Ainslie took me away, and I did my best to think of them as my parents. Dr. Ainslie was a difficult man, but in his own way he was rather a great one."

Daniel was watching an expression in his father's face he had seen several times before and had never understood.

"Did you say your mother was *killed?*"

"Yes."

"Murdered?"

"Not deliberately."

"Was it your father who killed her?"

"He—he came home very suddenly one night."

"Came home? Had he deserted you?"

Ainslie smiled as though he had discovered a memory that was very tender to him.

"She taught me a little story about him. She was a very simple woman and it was almost like a prayer. She used to say that Father had gone out into the world and then she'd ask me why he had gone out into the world and I'd answer, 'He has gone away to do things for us. And when he comes back everything will be good. We will go into the store and get whatever we want and people will be proud of us and we will live in a fine house and be different.' "

A fascinated embarrassment had come over Daniel as he listened to this. He stole a glance at his father, saw him as a stranger and looked away.

"What was your real father doing when he was away?" he said.

"I never knew till afterwards because my mother hated what he was doing. His life was a tragedy of poverty. He was a prize-fighter because he was too independent to work like a slave in the mines." Ainslie smiled wryly. "It's as strange for me to know this as I expect it is for you to hear it. That must be where you got the cut of your shoulders from. You remember meeting Joe Lacombe, don't you? My old friend from the Air Force? He was talking about you only a few days ago and he told me that the first time he saw you, the slope of your shoulders made him think of a middleweight fighter. You're very strong, you know. Much stronger than I ever was."

Daniel looked at the ground. "So you're telling me that my grandfather—on your side—was a prize-fighter who killed my grandmother?" He laughed soundlessly. "What was his name?"

"Archie MacNell. Just before the First War he was a contender for the world's championship."

"Did they hang him for what he did?"

"No, he died. I don't think they'd have hanged him anyway."

"Did you see this happen?"

"Yes."

There was a long silence and Ainslie broke it finally. "He just went insane for a moment. Men do, sometimes. I saw it happen more than once in the war. I think it might easily happen to me." He concluded lamely; "Anyway, Daniel, I thought the time had come for you to know this."

Daniel was frozen with a mixture of sensations he could not understand.

"Why didn't you tell me this long ago?" he muttered.

"I couldn't bring myself to do it."

Daniel muttered again, "There's no sense in anything."

He got to his feet and Ainslie saw his son's stubborn profile against the lingering light in the west.

"Above everything else," he said, "I've wanted you and Chantal to feel sure of yourselves—to feel that you belong to something permanent. You see, when I first met your mother, I was like a man from nowhere. As a matter of fact, your Uncle Jacques once called me *'Le Survenant.'* Both of my foster-parents had died by that time, you see. Your mother's family was very kind to me. Anyway, I hoped that belonging to them would give you and Chantal something I never had. That may be why I never told you this before."

"Did you tell Maman?"

"Of course. I just said I did."

"What did she say?"

"She was sorry for me." Ainslie gestured slightly. "I've been very lucky, you know. Dr. Ainslie was childless and he treated me like his own son. I suppose he drove me pretty hard, but he gave me every chance. Sometimes I've thought that if this had happened earlier—I mean when I was too young to remember it—it wouldn't have made any difference to me at all. It need not make any to you and I'm sure it won't. After all, what are our grandparents? Sometimes, what are even our parents?. Dr. Ainslie believed that education could cure everything. He was a Victorian, of course, and all the Victorians believed that."

He hoped that his son would say something, but Daniel stayed mute.

"How would you like to go abroad next fall?" he suggested. "I'm not a rich man, but your mother was a wonderful manager and she had a small legacy when we married. We had just enough capital after the war to make investments at a time when even a fool couldn't help gaining. Of course, I lost a good deal of that with the

246

magazine, but I've had a pretty good salary ever since the war. Chantal is practically self-supporting now and you"—he smiled—"you're practically self-supporting too, aren't you? I could easily manage a few years abroad for you. I was thinking you might like a university in France. It would be fun to talk about some of them together. As a matter of fact, I've already talked a little about them with Uncle Gabriel. Even though he went to the Sorbonne himself, he thinks someone from here might do better at Aix or Grenoble or Bordeaux."

Still Daniel kept silent.

Ainslie smiled wistfully, "I hope you're not thinking I'm offering you a bribe to get you out of the way."

"If you had to pay for that," Daniel said, "you'd have to hang onto your job in the government."

"No, that wouldn't have anything to do with it."

Daniel gave a slight shrug. "Anyway, as you just said, I'm earning my living now."

"That's splendid and I'm proud of you. But that can't be a permanent thing at your age. You must complete your education."

Daniel swung around, his voice suddenly high-pitched. "Dad?"

"Yes?"

"There's a man I want you to meet. His name's Aimé Latendresse. He's older than me and he's going to become one of the great men of Quebec. He wants to meet you very much. He wants a discussion with you on my show."

"What does he want to discuss?"

"The only thing any of us wants to discuss."

Ainslie smiled. "Separatism?"

"No. Independence."

Ainslie shook his head. "Daniel boy, you know I can't do that."

"Do you think it will fold up and die just because you put your head under the blankets?"

Ainslie smiled faintly again. "As they're so fond of

saying here, I'm by way of being a minister of the Crown."

Daniel looked away. "I thought you'd say that."

Ainslie rose and they began walking together in the twilight toward the hotel.

"My show with Aimé comes on the French channel next Thursday night," Daniel said.

"I know it does and no matter who you're interviewing I intend to look at it. The only thing that could stop me looking at it would be an unexpected cabinet meeting."

They walked in silence for several minutes before Daniel asked, "Why did you call that book of yours *Death of a Victorian?*"

"Have you read it yet?"

"Some of it. The early part doesn't mention what you've just told me, though. But why did you call it *Death of a Victorian?*"

"If you read to the end you'll find out for yourself."

Feeling the resistance in his son, Ainslie wondered if they would ever be able to understand one another again.

"Tell me something, Daniel—do you talk much with Chantal these days?"

"Why do you ask me that, Dad?"

"I just wondered."

"No."

"Why not?"

Daniel shrugged. "She wouldn't even try to understand what I was talking about. She likes older men anyway. A lot of the girls her age do."

"It was all that time in New York," Ainslie said. "Almost the only people she had a chance of meeting there were solemn bureaucrats from the U.N. She didn't meet enough people her own age. That's one of the things these days, Daniel. The way families are shunted from place to place in government and the corporations—it never used to be like that. No wonder everyone's so restless."

248

They had reached the square now. It was practically dusk and very little life was showing in the streets. After dark the murmurings of the bureaucrats ceased with the murmurings of the pigeons.

"So I take it you intend to stay on with Bulstrode?" Daniel said.

"I never said that."

"Well, just what are you going to do, Dad? I wish you'd tell me. You aren't Minister of Trade or Transport or in one of those purely executive departments that stay the same no matter what the government's policy is. Your department is mixed up in the very same thing I'm mixed up in. So that's why I asked if you're intending to continue letting Bulstrode push you around. I think I have a right to know whether it's your department or whether you're just his henchman."

Ainslie looked at the blunt profile and thought, Is this my own son? Is this really my son speaking to me that way? He winced, and then anger came to him.

"You're talking like a fool," he said, "and like a very young one. You're my son whether you like it or not, and I'm your father whether you like it or not. As I respect you, I expect you to respect me."

"That would seem to be obvious."

"You haven't the slightest idea of what you're getting yourself mixed up in. Hasn't it crossed your mind that these new friends of yours may be interested in you for one reason only—that you're my son?"

Daniel turned on him in fury and Ainslie's anger answered his.

"You can take this or leave this, Daniel—the first wave of every revolution there ever was, especially if it takes to violence, is used and destroyed by the second wave, and the second wave's used and destroyed by the one that comes after that. Movements like this one of yours are so full of sell-outs and betrayals that their enemies just lean back and let them ruin themselves. All history is there to prove it."

"History—that's the excuse you use for everything you fail in."

In angry silence they reached the portico of the hotel and Ainslie was wounded by his son's deliberate avoidance of his eyes.

"I'm sorry, Daniel," he said gently. "I shouldn't have lost my temper. Why not spend the night with me here? There's a spare bed in my room."

"And listen to more of this?"

"I apologize for talking too much. It's always been my weakness. Will you shake hands with me?"

"Why not?"

They shook hands and their eyes met. "There always has to be a government, Daniel, just as there always have to be older men."

The boy laughed bitterly. "Poor old Dad! There you go again. You just can't help it, can you? Well, in the States they're tearing up government draft cards and pretty soon this old man's government of yours is going to find itself with nobody left to govern. And what will the robin do then, poor thing?"

Daniel turned and left his father and Ainslie watched the thick, fighter's shoulders move away in the dim lights and disappear around the corner to the parking lot. Then he went in and up to his room and panic came on him and he reached for the whiskey bottle. The whiskey was hot and raw and when he lay down on the bed he immediately had to sit up for fear of being sick. He knew the impulse to vomit had not come from the drink, though the drink had triggered it. His legs felt dead, but nevertheless he knew he must go outside and walk in the fresh air. He locked his door and went down to ground-level by the staircase for fear there would be strangers in the elevator who might examine his expression or even smell whiskey on his breath. He left the hotel by a side exit and began to walk about the city, and while he walked a jumble of ideas and insights kept flashing on and off in his mind like signal lights contradicting each other. If he had had to tell anyone what he had just told Daniel, why had it not been Chantal? Why had he become so shy with Chantal since Constance died? Why was he sometimes half-afraid even to look at her?

It was an hour before he returned to his room, and though now he was clear-headed and wished to speak to Chantal, he was afraid to call her up. . . . *Run, run, run till you die! Fox at your heels and crow in the sky!*

FIVE

THE NEXT day in Montreal on his way to the studio to prepare the next program, Daniel met one of the young men who had interviewed his father in Ottawa the week previous. He was a shy youth, a student of philosophy with a pure and troubled expression. He was very fragile, and there was a desperate eagerness for justice in him.

"He's one of the nicest and finest men I've ever met," he told Daniel. "He's the only *Anglais* I've ever known who really understands how we feel."

"Well, I'm glad he made such a good impression on you," Daniel said. "But what difference does it make, after all? What can he do up there?"

"He's enormously cultured, Daniel."

"So are quite a few of them. Too many of you have the idea that all the *Anglais* care about is business and engineering. Not all of them do."

"I wouldn't feel right if I was opposed to a man like your father."

Daniel made an impatient gesture. "Listen, Jean-Claude —you'd never understand a man like him in a thousand years. I know—*I* know—if all the other *Anglais* were like him there'd never have been this situation in the country." Looking at his friend, he thought with wonder what a change had taken place in himself during the last week. Only a week ago he and Jean-Claude had been equals; now Jean-Claude seemed like a child to him. "I'd do anything to get him out of that government, but he won't budge. Bulstrode's using him for bait. But he's not sold out." Daniel added fiercely, "That's something he'll never do."

They parted, and as Daniel walked on he felt gas on his stomach. At the studio he was met by the producer of the show, who handed him a packet of letters. The producer had counted them at just under two hundred and was delighted. They had come from every part of Quebec and there were even some from Ontario and northern New Brunswick.

Daniel took the letters into a cubicle where he had a desk, a phone, a typewriter and a filing cabinet and began reading them. As he read on, he felt an incandescence growing inside of himself. If a response as tremendous as this had come from only two programs in which he had barely skirted the main subject, he must have touched something as deep as an ocean. He would be famous and financially independent inside of a month.

Reluctantly he put the unread letters aside and concentrated on the list of questions for his next program. He worked until one o'clock before he went out for lunch, and on the street he noticed a few passers-by looking at him with recognition. At the lunch counter a stranger addressed him by name and asked to shake his hand.

People were listening. In the warrens of shabby apartment blocks, in company towns where they worked for the unseen bosses of another race, people were listening to what was said on his show. Men and women in debt to the loan companies were listening. Young men who had not been able to learn perfect English but who wanted to succeed in an English-dominated world were listening. People who had felt inferior for years, not because of any native inferiority but because they were born into a minority with the weight and pressure on them—these people were listening and saying, "No, it doesn't have to be that way forever. We must have something better than that."

253

On Thursday morning Latendresse telephoned to ask whether his father had agreed to debate with him and when Daniel said he had refused, Latendresse said, "Don't give up. After tonight he may change his mind."

Daniel told him about the letters he had received.

"There'll be five times more letters after tonight."

Eagerly Daniel kept him on the phone. "Listen, Aimé, I wish you'd forget about my father. He's harmless. He's just a good, old-fashioned *Anglais* liberal who's lived too long and doesn't know the kind of world he's living in any more. You can't expect anything more from a man of his age."

"Men of his age happen to be the ones who are ruling the country."

"I'm thinking of bigger game than him. Listen, Aimé— these letters make it perfectly clear to me how this show's got to develop. What people are hungry for—what they're famished for—is just to hear things said out loud in public that have been taboo here for centuries. That's how I see this show developing—one taboo killed after the other—boom, boom, boom! The next show's lined up already, but right after that I want to start in on the Church."

There was a silence on the line so cold that Daniel could almost feel it.

"Have you lost your senses?" Latendresse said.

"What's so crazy about that?"

"The clergy are our own people. Later, we can deal with them if they make it necessary, but they're still our own people and always will be. What is necessary now is to concentrate on one single point—independence. There must be no fighting among ourselves. The English are as dumb and slow as oxen. They're so arrogant and self-confident they'd go on eating their dinners even if somebody told them there was a bomb in their cellars. They're not reacting the way I want them to. They and our own bourgeois swine will patch things up if they have the smallest chance. The English will learn just enough French and become just polite enough to us to make our own bourgeois believe they've won a great victory. Men like your father aren't unintelligent. Some other *Anglais* like him—not many but a few very influential ones—are working overtime on their own people to make them willing to accept enough of our demands to soften the rest of us up. We've got to make the English so enraged they'll go crazy and want to fight us. Otherwise we'll be sold out again. There's got to be an open split—one there'll be no chance of healing—and I know exactly what you can do to start it."

Daniel felt fear. "Tell me what it is."

"The Queen," said Latendresse. "She's practically their Pope. She must be publicly insulted."

Daniel sucked in his breath.

"I want you to get some woman," Latendresse went on, "some woman with prominent front teeth to impersonate the Queen on your show. Get her to lisp and speak French that will make everybody laugh."

"But the Queen speaks very good French."

"Your Queen won't. *'Mon mari et moi, nous aimons très beaucoup nos braves sujets, les Canadiens français.'* When she says that, ask her why French Canadians should have to pay for all these royal visits she makes and then have her say, *'Mon mari et moi, nous sommes toujours très fiers des deux grandes races qui sont nos sujets ici.'* Ask her why, when the Seaway was opened here at our doors, the Queen of England and the President of the United States opened it without a single one of us being invited to the ceremony. Then have her say, *'Mon mari et moi, nous sommes toujours très heureux de penser que nos sujets canadiens sont si bons amis de nos très bons amis américains.'* After she says that, ask her if she and her husband still enjoy pillow-fighting. Reserve a spot for the Queen on show after show till the English get the point."

Daniel almost drew back from the telephone. "Aimé, you're wrong."

"I am not wrong."

"That would do not good at all. It would kill the show. Our people are polite."

"You weren't brought up as I was, *mon ami*. You never lived in an orphanage. You never saw what I see every day—poverty that makes children ashamed of their parents. You never woke up to the smell of boiling cabbage. You never saw your father dragged off to fight for foreigners. You never had to say 'Yes, sir' to an English boss. The politeness of a subject people has always been the trump card of a ruling class. Who have been the politest people in the United States? The Negroes."

After this conversation, Daniel could do no more work in the studio that afternoon. He roamed the streets for a while and toward the middle of the afternoon a new idea came to him. He walked down to the office of one of the two English-language dailies and asked to speak with the oldest writer on the sports page. He knew his name and thought he knew what he looked like from the photograph that always appeared with his column, but when he met the man he looked older than his photograph. This sports writer was a real veteran.

"Yes," he said, "as a matter of fact I do remember the name of Archie MacNeil. I remember him very well. What are you interested in him for?"

"Well, I'm interested in boxing and the records and all that, and I heard somebody talking about this Archie MacNeil. I was told he was the best middleweight the country ever had."

The old man seemed pleased. "I wouldn't go that far, but he might have been. When I was a kid he was certainly the best prospect we had for the middleweight championship of the world. He fought the best there was, and even a middling fighter of those days could take on this present crop of TV roundhouse sluggers with one hand tied behind his back. If Archie'd been better handled and laid off the bottle, I always thought he'd have made it all the way. He had a bigger punch than any of them."

"What did he look like?"

The old man chuckled. "I can see him now. When I was a kid we all used to collect cigarette cards and I had a big collection of them with the pictures of fighters. And let me tell you, those were *real* fighters. It wasn't like now. All the kids did a lot of fist-fighting in those days. It was a part of going to school, and out of all that playground fighting a crop of real champions was bound to emerge. Let's see—who was the middleweight title-holder in Archie MacNeil's day? That was a great division around then and there were so many good ones—The old man rubbed his bald head. "Christ, but I've been in this sports-writing game a long time! Let's see—yes, the big boys in the division in Archie's time were Billy Papke, Frank Klaus, George Chip and Timmy O'Leary. Oh yes, and Georges Carpentier from France was fighting in the States just before the war. Archie's best fight was when he knocked out Timmy O'Leary. He fought Chip too, but I seem to remember that Chip gave him a bad beating. You're really serious? You really want to find out about MacNeil's career?"

Daniel said that he did and the old man hunted around for an old record book and when he found it he thumbed it through, muttered, "I thought so," jotted down a number of dates on a slip of paper and handed it to Daniel.

"Take this and come downstairs with me and I'll let you into the room where we keep all the old newspapers."

Soon Daniel found himself alone in a large, dark room filled with the musty odor of dried newsprint. The old man had showed him where to begin among the bound volumes and Daniel took one of them to a large table under a light and opened it.

Instantly he was caught up in the news of a vanished time, so caught up that he promptly forgot what he was here for. He read about the sinking of the *Titanic,* he saw a picture of the launching of a new British dreadnaught and read about the desperate armaments race that was going on in Europe. There was a picture of the German emperor strutting like somebody out of a comic opera in tight breeches and a plumed helmet. There was a picture of King George V looking like a king in a pack of playing cards. There were stories about strikes and lockouts, about Irish Home Rule, about anarchists' bombs, about gun-running into Ulster, and the impact of all this gave him a very strange sensation. It was all dead news and the people looked ridiculous in the clothes they wore, but what was going on then seemed just the same as what was going on now. They all seemed crazy and most of them seemed wicked, and he thought of French Canada during those years when his father was a child, French Canada living quiet and eternal with her faith and her land exiled from all this insanity that had led to the war, the opening of which he also read about in the papers. He had been there an hour and a half before he began searching out the papers under the dates the old sports writer had given him.

He read the story of Archie MacNeil's greatest fight, the one in Providence when he stopped Timmy O'Leary in the third round. MacNeil's picture was beside the story of the fight. It was a bleak, flat newspaper photo of a powerful man with heavy shoulders, a wasp waist and a fighting scowl, hair stiff, its color impossible to determine. He stared at this apparition from fifty years ago and tried to realize that it was his own grandfather. With a sensation of unreality he recognized that he himself resembled him a little. His father did not resemble him at all. He reread the story of the fight. It was an A.P. dispatch in the ring jargon of the time—the jargon seemed to have changed very little since—and through it Daniel could almost smell the brutal excitement of the fight, the sweaty crowd of hard-faced men roaring support for the battlers. Archie's last fight sounded horrible. That was when he was knocked down seven times by a younger and stronger man before he was finally knocked out. That was when the referee had let him be butchered because the crowd wanted to see his blood.

The last reference to MacNeil was a C.P. dispatch from a town in Nova Scotia and its title read:

BOXER GOES BERSERK—KILLS WIFE, STRANGE MAN, SELF

Broughton, N.S.: Last night this mining community was the scene of a tragedy that stunned it. Archie MacNeil, famed native son, one-time contender for the world's middleweight championship, returning without warning after a five years' absence, found a strange man in his home with his wife. Going berserk, MacNeil, 31, killed them both with a poker and shortly afterwards expired himself.

The stranger was identified as Louis Camire, 33, a French citizen who had been a sailor on the ship *Napoleon III*, wrecked a few years ago on the coast of the island. The fighter's eight-year-old son, present in the house at the time, was unharmed.

Dr. Daniel Ainslie, colliery surgeon summoned by neighbors, forced entry into the MacNeil house but was too late to save the lives of the victims. MacNeil collapsed while being apprehended and was dead on his arrival at the hospital. After performing an autopsy, Dr. Ainslie stated that the fighter had died of a clot on the brain caused by excessive punishment sustained in the ring. "He was clearly not responsible for his actions on the night of the tragedy," Dr. Ainslie said. The doctor added that this ought to be a lesson to legislators to outlaw prizefighting. "Three people, two of them innocent, died as a result of MacNeil's occupation," said the doctor.

In Montreal, Raoul Picotte, well-known promoter, stated on questioning that MacNeil had visited him in

259

that city shortly before the tragedy occurred. "He wanted a match for the Canadian title held by Eugene Masson," said Mr. Picotte. He added that MacNeil was "a sick man who should have been compulsorily retired from the ring some time before. I advised him to hang up his gloves and go home. He was broke and I offered him fare-money home but he wouldn't take it. It's too bad. If he'd been properly handled, he might have become a great fighter."

The faded page swam before Daniel's eyes. He closed the volume and replaced it on the shelf. He left the building and strolled for half an hour before he sat on a bench in a little park. He thought of Marielle Jeannotte and of how Clarisse had been born. Looking at passers-by he wondered what some of their stories had been. This swarm of animated automatons—a female body with a white skin and breasts and hips and thighs that overwhelmed the senses, two strangers seizing one another, a few spasms and a new life was on its way to being born, on its way to becoming a personality hammered, twisted, torn and molded by accidents and pressures. How could a man like his father have been the son of that brutalized apparition whose picture he had seen in that dead newspaper? He himself was closer to that man than his father was.

SIX

THAT EVENING Daniel ate his supper alone in a small lunch-counter restaurant. In a few hours his interview with Latendresse would appear and be watched by perhaps a million people, including his father. After supper he strolled the streets nervously in a pleasant, cool evening and the people he saw seemed different from the ones he had seen in the heat wave the week before. They seemed quieter and so did the streets of the city. The girls he passed were less suggestive. But Daniel was frightened. Those old newspapers had shaken him and now at last he knew what Uncle Gabriel meant when he said he had such a sense of *déjà vu*. Two world wars, more revolutions than he had ever heard of, H-bombs and moon-shots and still people were saying, thinking and doing exactly the same things.

He went home hoping to find Chantal there but the apartment was empty. He grew more and more nervous as the hour of the show drew near and finally he was sitting alone in the living room watching himself and Latendresse, and now the personality of Latendresse, singularly isolated from any background on the screen, made him feel chilled and alarmed. Yet the things Latendresse was saying were things he was sure he believed in his soul: "I ask you—any of my language who is listening to me—am I not right? Our home is the French language, and here, in our own country, the Anglo-Saxon System makes it impossible for us to use it except in the privacy of our families. ... We must speak the conqueror's language if we are to earn our bread. ..."

Why had he allowed Latendresse to say that instead of saying it himself? But he never would have used that word "conqueror." His friends in the movement all used it; for years French-Canadian history teachers had rubbed it in. But who, besides themselves, cared any more about a battle fought two centuries ago? Endlessly the French Canadians talked of their deprived past and what did that do except weaken their purpose to make the future theirs?

"The English are always asking, what do we want? I will tell you what we want. Dignity is what we want. The right to be ourselves is what we want."

Was not this a universal cry ringing around the whole world today? Why had he not uttered it himself instead of offering his show to Latendresse to utter it?

From the screen Latendresse looked at him in cold determination. Then the images of both of them faded out.

The telephone rang almost immediately and when he answered it he heard the voice of the girl who had breathed into his ear that night in the *bistro* where the folk-singer was and he had talked with Latendresse. The girl told him he had been wonderful and asked when she could see him again. He asked her what she thought of Latendresse and was startled when she laughed and said in a Hungarian accent, "That creep!" He told her he was too busy to see anyone that night and she sounded disappointed. She gave him her phone number and automatically he jotted it down on the back of a package of Gitane cigarettes. He had been smoking Gitanes ever since Marielle Jeannotte had introduced him to them. Marielle—suddenly he craved her. More, he needed to be with her because she would understand how he felt now. She understood how everyone felt. She knew what he needed and incredulously he said aloud, "I think I've fallen in love with her. I don't think

I can live without her. She will love me and that will save me." But Clarisse would almost certainly be home tonight. Why did Clarisse have to exist?

Again the telephone rang. It was his father and the authority in his voice seemed to reverberate out of an anterior darkness:

"That was a terrible program. At the end of it this man Latendresse was deliberately inciting to civil war. So he's the one you tried to trap me into a discussion with! So he's the one who's given you these ideas!"

"And what's the matter with those ideas? They're the same as your own."

"They are not the same as my own. I'm on the side of this whole country and I love Quebec. Latendresse doesn't. His kind only cares about people as abstract ideas—as *collections* of abstract ideas. What difference does it make if I agree with nine-tenths of what he *said*? We're not saying those things for the same purpose and we're not saying them in the same way. He's using you, Daniel, and I tremble for you. Your show appeals to every paranoiac tendency in the human race. Don't you know that paranoia is the one mental disease that's catching?"

Daniel felt as though a scream were being bottled up inside of his throat, but his father went on relentlessly.

"How many times have you heard Uncle Gabriel say that people can talk themselves into anything? Listen, Daniel—this country's in trouble, and no part of it is in more serious trouble than Quebec. It would break my heart if Quebec separates. If Canada can hold together, she could become a pilot plant for a new kind of nation and a new kind of freedom and I'm not exaggerating the importance of that for the whole world. If two old cultures like the French and English can't work together within a single national home without destroying each other, what chance have all the others got in what has practically become a single world society? Well, perhaps Quebec *will* separate. But if she does, let it be done decently. Let it be done without hatred and murder and all this paranoia of you and your friends. Your kind of nationalism is fifty years out of date and wherever it appeared it has caused misery. Furthermore, it won't succeed. Don't you young intellectuals understand the decency and *bon sens* of your own people? Even Bulstrode understands that better than you do. The Nazi movement was filled with pathetic misfits like this Latendresse. In the '30s some of them were communists. Do you think people my age have forgotten what can result from this kind of thing? Now I'm going to tell you something else—the whole lot of you are certain to come under some kind of surveillance—and by men who belong to what Latendresse has the effrontery to call 'my people.' "

The scream came out of Daniel's throat in a choked whisper. "So you're turning us over to the secret police!"

"Stop talking nonsense. You know perfectly well the R.C.M.P. aren't a secret police in the way you're using the word. How dare you use a smear word like that to me! I don't have to speak to them about you people. It's their job to know about you and they're not stupid. This Latendresse is a fanatic and fanatics are all the same. Their way out is the only way out and anyone who disagrees with them is a traitor. If this movement of yours ever succeeded it would bankrupt Quebec and you'd have a kept dictator here like some of the kind you have in South America. I'm still a servant of this country, Daniel. I'm not going to consent to you and your friends giving the impression that I can't be that and at the same time be a servant of Quebec. The government of this country may not be a good one. It may be confused and fifty years behind reality and behaving badly because what's really happening underneath has come so quickly that more than half of them don't even know it's there or what it's doing to us. But it's the only government we have and you don't seem to have the vaguest idea of what would happen without it. The salesmen would take over,

Daniel. And behind the salesmen would be the international cynics with their computer machines calculating precisely how they can persuade ignorant and helpless people to sell out all sense of responsibility and—"

"And you pretend they haven't done it already?" Daniel screamed at him.

"What's the use in making the present worse by blaming it on the past? The only possible defense a country like this ever has is its government, can't you understand that?" Then the hard tone vanished from Ainslie's voice. "Oh Daniel, what's gone wrong between us? Help me, won't you? I'm so worried about you I can hardly sleep."

"That's very pleasant for me to know," Daniel said, and his father hung up without another word.

Daniel's teeth were nearly chattering. He rushed back to his father's study, sat down at the desk and began reading in a high, desperate voice some words he had scrawled on a pad the night before:

"Flatter you, smile at you, grin at you, tell you anything, promise you anything, Big Daddy you anything and lie to you, spy on you, number you, measure you, analyze you, find out your soul in a urine-specimen, poison you and all the time say they love you, serve you, help you, think of nothing else in the world but you . . ."

While he read this, there ran like an obbligato to the rhetoric a stream of thoughts through his mind: The moment you touch any of them the masks melt off. They offer you their own stinking world of cheating, corrupting, lying, selling-out and excusing themselves by telling you this is human nature and what can anyone do about it, and all the time they keep on making their bombs. They keep on making you pay five times what you need to pay and if you don't agree with them that this is the only way to live they send you to a psychiatrist. Latendresse was right. I was right when I told Marielle that men like my father are more dangerous than those who openly hate us. I want a woman. I've got to have a woman or I'll go mad!

Coldly calm, he took out the cigarette box with the phone number jotted down on it and dialed on the extension on his father's desk.

"Sandra?"

"But Daniel"—the voice was childishly petulant—"you just told me were busy tonight!"

"I'm not busy any more. May I come over?"

"Oh, why didn't you say that sooner? How was I to know you were going to be free in half an hour?"

"You mean you don't want to see me now?"

"How about tomorrow? I'd simply love to see you tomorrow."

"No," he said between clenched teeth and hung up.

He went out to his car, patted the hood, got in and drove it. He drove with a roar of open exhaust up the switchbacks of the mountain, reached the top and saw the lights of the city like a quivering jelly, drove down the other side with screaming tires, intending to go to Marielle's apartment whether Clarisse was there or not, but when he reached level ground he heard a scream different from a tire scream and there in his rearview mirror was the revolving red beacon of a pursuing police car with its siren going. An intersection was coming up on his right and when the police car was only ten yards away from him and moving out to the left to pass and hail him down, Daniel swerved into it. The big car shot past and he heard a screech from its brakes. Miraculously on his right appeared the gaping entrance to an empty private garage and in the house adjoining it no lights were visible. He twisted the wheel and shot his car into the garage, braked it to a violent stop, vaulted out and pulled down the garage door. Just as he did so the police car, its siren silent, shot by with a quiet whir of tires. There was a door in the rear of the garage and he unlatched it and stepped out into the darkness. He stood sighting along the side of the garage until the police car returned. He watched it make still another turn and cruise more slowly down the street again, its searchlight moving along the fronts of the houses. Daniel realized that this must be a dead-end street. After a time the car returned and went back to the main avenue.

Daniel let a few minutes pass before he emerged. He walked casually along the sidewalk to the open end of the street and noticed that the house on the corner had a high hedge to serve as a wall between itself and the avenue. He slipped along the hedge, carefully parted some of its thick branches and peered through. The police car was waiting by the curb with its lights out. He watched it for five minutes and then he heard one constable grunt something to the other. The lights came on and the car moved off. He saw its red tail-lights disappear around a corner several blocks away, but he waited a full ten minutes before he came out from behind the hedge, returned to the garage where he had hidden his car, backed it out and drove away.

It had been fairly easy and he was sure there was enough mud on his rear license-plate to have made it practically impossible for the police to have taken his number at high speed in the dark. He drove home by a circuitous route and when he let himself into the apartment he found Chantal in the living room with Gabriel Fleury.

"Hullo, Daniel."

"Hullo, Uncle Gabriel."

They shook hands and Daniel sat down and looked from his sister to the only man of his father's friends he had ever liked and admired, the quiet man from the wise old country.

"Chantal and I saw your show tonight, Daniel."

"You did?" A thought came to him. "Where did you see it?"

"At my place. We came up here afterwards hoping we'd find you here."

"I see."

"You have a natural talent for that medium, Daniel."

Chantal said, "Daniel—how could you have!"

"Could I have what?"

"Done a thing like that to Dad!"

"What are you talking about? We never even mentioned his name."

"You know perfectly well that inside a day or two every newspaper in the country will point out that you're his son."

"What if they do? I didn't say anything. I just asked the questions, that's all."

Her toe tapped the carpet. "It was a rigged show, and what kind of fools do you think people are?"

"He may be right, Chantal," Gabriel said. "He didn't say those things, it was the other man."

Daniel glanced at Gabriel's face and saw on it the look he hated, the older man's look that frustrated him to the point where it had come to seem like a wall. Then he saw something else in Gabriel's face, understood it in a flash and got to his feet with his face chalk-colored.

"My God!" he whispered. "My God!"

"My God what?" Chantal asked him.

"Isn't there a single older man alive that can be trusted?"

Chantal knew what he meant. She stepped toward him, her eyes blazing, and for an instant he thought she was going to slap him. But Gabriel was before her. He put his hand on Daniel's shoulder and looked him straight in the eye.

"I'm glad," he said quietly. "I'm glad you could tell from our faces that Chantal and I love one another."

Daniel felt he was going to be sick. "And you were supposed to be my father's best friend! How long has this been going on?"

"How can you be so disgusting?" Chantal said.

Gabriel said quietly, "Don't say things like that, Daniel.

I hope I'm still your father's friend. What's the matter, Daniel?"

"What's the matter? Did I just hear you say what's the matter?"

"Why this hate?"

Daniel stared at him in contempt. Gabriel turned to Chantal and it would have been hard for anyone to know whether his expression was a sign of victory or defeat.

"I think I'd better go now," he said.

"Are you taking Chantal with you, Uncle Gabriel?"

"Daniel, there has been no indecency here."

Daniel laughed shortly and turned away. Gabriel left.

When he reached home, Gabriel telephoned Alan Ainslie in Ottawa and after a time the hotel clerk informed him that the room did not answer. He had Alan's government number and telephoned to his office, but there was no reply there, either. He wanted to tell him that Daniel should be sent to a psychiatrist. He also wanted, if he had the courage and if Alan's mood would tolerate it, to tell him that he loved his daughter. As he thought of the chaos into which Alan's life had drifted, he wished Alan had another intimate friend, another deep friend, besides himself.

SEVEN

THE NEXT day in the House of Commons a member rose with a newspaper clipping in his hand. After identifying the paper from which it came, he read a few paragraphs reporting Aimé Latendresse's performance on Daniel's show and said that he had a question for the Honorable Member, the Minister for Cultural Affairs.

Q. Does the Honorable Member realize that these words I have just quoted constitute a deliberate incitement to civil war in this country?

Ainslie: I think that is a very extreme way of describing the broadcast, but I fail to see in any case how my department can be held responsible for what is uttered on a public broadcast.

Q. The Honorable Member's department is concerned— at least we all hope it is concerned—with the question of national unity. I think even the Honorable Member would agree, though sometimes I wonder if he really does, that the toleration of propaganda, to say nothing of the open encouragement of it, leading to civil war is not in the interests of national unity. So I repeat my question—does the Honorable Member believe, or does he not, that this utterance I have just quoted is an incitement to civil war?

Ainslie: I suppose it might be so interpreted in certain quarters.

Q. In that case what does your department intend to do

about it? Is it going to make a stand, or isn't it?

Ainslie: My department is doing the best it can, under very difficult circumstances, to help the regions of this country understand each other.

The questioner sat down with a laugh in which others joined. He was immediately followed by another.

Q. Would the Honorable Member, the Minister for Cultural Affairs, tell the House in plain words where he stands on this all-important question of national unity? Does he think, as some of us cannot help believing that he thinks, that national unity can only be purchased at the price of the majority yielding to every form of insult and intimidation thrown into its face by extremists—I repeat, extremists—among the minority?

Ainslie: The question, as phrased, is too insulting a question to be worth answering.

With a sarcastic smile the questioner resumed his seat and suddenly Ainslie realized that the House was scenting an election. Another member was recognized and had still another question for Ainslie.

Q. Has the Minister for Cultural Affairs ever defined what he means by "culture?" When this unusual department was originally announced, many people in the country believed it was intended to foster painting, music, literature and so on, but soon it turned out to be something entirely different. Soon it appeared to be trying to sell the public the idea that this country isn't one country, but two countries, that it hasn't got one single democratic culture, but two different ones. Is that correct?

Ainslie: It is only halfway correct. Of course this is, and must remain, a single country. But it is the view of myself and of my department that it can remain a single country only on this condition—that it be universally accepted that this single country is the home of two different cultures.

Q. Two cultures—I see. Since your department has, presumably, had a considerable amount of time to develop a certain expertise in this amorphous field of endeavor—since it has done nothing practical, we must at least assume that it has been acquainting itself with this new, distinctive culture which has suddenly emerged in our midst from nowhere— would the Honorable Member do this House the favor of explaining how it happens that the region where this priceless new culture is alleged to exist leads all other regions of the country in traffic accidents, armed robberies, fraudulent bankruptcies and incitements to sedition, culminating in the recent riot described in last night's broadcast as "only the beginning"?

The House broke into pandemonium with members shouting, "Shame!" "Withdraw!" and Mr. Speaker pounding for order. When he could be heard, Mr. Speaker ruled the question out of order. Ainslie hesitated an instant, then rose and faced the House with an expression on his wounded face that made it fall silent.

Ainslie: Mr. Speaker, I could not more thoroughly agree with your ruling that the last question, as phrased, was as improper a question as I have ever listened to in this House. I am not on my feet to answer it, but I am not going to ignore it, for behind the Honorable Member's words is an anxiety we all feel. [*Pause*.] Until very recently, this has been a sheltered country. It has been sheltered in its mind. It isn't so any more. It is in terrible danger, and the danger comes from what well may be a change in its personality.

He felt something like a physical force working on him and, turning slightly, he saw Bulstrode's eyes fixed on him as if to command him to go on—

The Honorable Member who has spoken with such reckless insults of the province where I live has only said in a public place what many ill-informed people are saying privately today. What is wrong here, what is dangerous here, is the implication that these happenings have some kind of local origin from which the rest of the country is free. This is simply untrue. The rest of the country is not free from these things —far from it. What the Honorable Member complains of is well nigh a universal disease today, and if we did not persist in seeing the present with the eyes of the past, we would understand that to make politics out of it is not only irresponsible, it is lethally wicked. [*Pause*.] It seems only yesterday that this was a country where nearly everyone knew what his duty was, what his faith was, what his morality at least ought to be. It is not so now. It is not so anywhere now. Not here, only, but everywhere experienced people are asking, "What has happened to us?" I know I ask myself that question every day.

Another pause, and he resumed, groping for words—

I repeat that we try to see the present with the eyes of the past. It is human nature to do it. In this House we make a ritual of doing it. We use outworn political techniques to deal with something so new it—it so terrifies us that we refuse to admit even to ourselves that it exists.

I believe that the real cause of the world crisis— for that is what it is—no more respects frontiers than an influenza epidemic respects them. I believe the crisis came when humanity lost its faith in man's ability to improve his own nature. If the symptoms of this disease at times seem startling in my own province, it is only because the crisis has come there so suddenly. [*Another pause*.] When people no longer can believe in personal immortality, when society at large has abandoned philosophy, many men grow desperate without knowing why. They crack up—and don't know they have. Some of them will do *anything* —no matter how hopeless, criminal or idiotic—merely to have people mention their names and recognize that they exist. To be hanged for some senseless crime, to disrupt the processes of society by a meaningless riot—though a man may know he will be destroyed for this, he at least gains a column in a newspaper or a paragraph in a legal book. It will be recorded in some kind of record—for our age exceeds all others in keeping record—that he existed. [*Pause.*] The kind of thing the Honorable Member tried to limit to my province exists everywhere in the world. A senseless crime can be one way of passing into the only kind of immortality this sick epoch understands, and so can the leadership of a senseless revolt—it can go onto the records and into the archives.

Ainslie sat down and there was a moment of embarrassed silence. There were some coughs from the back benches. Mr. Speaker sat immobile. Then McCartney, the man who had spoken harshly to Ainslie the day after the riot, got to his feet and Mr. Speaker recognized him.

Q. Now the sermon is over, perhaps the House may return to business. In putting another question to the Minister for Cultural Affairs, I do not forget that I am a member of the party to which he belongs. I trust I have been a member of that party long enough that my loyalty to it cannot be questioned. But there are some things above party. Therefore, Mr. Speaker, I am speaking now as a member of this House and as a citizen of this country and I seek some information that the country, and this House, has a right to know—and from the Minister's own lips. I note from the press that the moderator of this disgraceful television program bears the same name as the Minister. Will the Minister tell the House whether or not he is the Minister's son?

Ainslie: He is.

Q. Thank you. Then will you tell the House whether or not your son is an active member of the Quebec separatist movement, which boasts that its purpose is to destroy this nation?

Ainslie: I don't know whether he is or not.

Q. Do you expect the House to believe that?

McCartney sat down while shouts of "Objection!" came from the benches. Bulstrode glared at McCartney and shook his head, but Ainslie sat calmly in his seat. At last, after all these years, he was understanding how simple life really is. McCartney was a member of his own party; he was devoted to Bulstrode, who at that moment was supporting what he himself had just said. But McCartney hated him automatically, the same way that one species of animal hates another.

The hunt was up, and now another Opposition member was on his feet, was recognized, and announced that he had a question for the Honorable Member for Algonquin, who was Bulstrode.

Q. I would like to hear from the Honorable Member for Algonquin, who has gathered—if I may be allowed to put it this way—the public broadcasting media under his wing, where it has disappeared from sight along with all the other things he has gathered there —I would like to ask him whether it is a principle with him, along with all the other things that are principles with him—to permit the state-supported broadcasting network to be turned over to the expression of any opinions whatever, even if those opinions are in fact seditious propaganda?

Bulstrode took his time getting to his feet. He rose lumberingly, looking up to the cathedral-like roof of the chamber as he did so. He put his hands on his hips and stood akimbo and formidable, with his eyes looking his questioner up and down. Then he turned to the Speaker's chair.

Bulstrode: The Honorable Member's question—or was it a question?—well, what can I say of whatever it was? Give me time. Yes, I think this will do for an answer. The Honorable Member's question is so ridiculously incompetent that the best comment I can make on it is that he is the only Honorable Member of this House who could have dreamed it up.

Q. The Honorable Member for Algonquin is his usual courteous and evasive self. I will adjust my question to him. Why did a minister of your cabinet— I apologize, Mr. Speaker—why did a minister of the Crown appointed by the Prime Minister—we notice that the Prime Minister is not with us today, he so seldom is—why did a minister of the Crown a short while ago admit that this broadcast we have been discussing might be interpreted in certain quarters as an incitement to civil war? My question is directed to the responsible minister here, the Honorable Member for Algonquin.

Bulstrode: [*Looking at the man as though surprised to find he was still there.*] Because he knew that trouble-makers would use it to make all the trouble they could.

With a barking laugh Bulstrode sat down and again Mr. Speaker had to pound for order. The House finally proceeded to other business and Ainslie was left alone. He sat trying to read documents in which the words swam before his eyes. Meanwhile Bulstrode had made himself comfortable behind a newspaper and remained comfortable for at least thirty minutes before he rose abruptly and left the House. Ainslie rose half a minute later and, walking fast, overtook Bulstrode at his office door. When they were inside with the door closed they both sat down and Bulstrode rubbed his eyes wearily.

"Now you see what I mean, Alan. Without any leadership, Parliament behaves disgracefully. I didn't expect anything better from the other side, but Tom McCartney —he never did have any sense. He never should have left his hardware store. It takes ten years to get a new idea into his head and it's usually wrong when it gets there. Then it takes another ten years to get it out."

Ainslie lifted his hands and let them fall again. "I reached the end of the road today. I must resign."

Bulstrode surveyed him with a kindliness Ainslie had never seen in his face before. "Have you talked with your boy yet?"

"It did no good at all. He's going straight ahead. I can't stop him. I'm sorry to say that show of his is getting a very large following."

Bulstrode swivelled around in his chair and looked out the window, then he swivelled back again.

"No, it's not getting a following. This morning I ordered it cancelled. What did I care about that fool who tried to play the smart aleck with me? Let him read about it in the papers."

"It was the only thing you could have done."

Bulstrode's forehead wrinkled. "It wasn't an easy decision for me. You know where I've stood all my life on free speech. Now I suppose there'll be the usual roars about suppressing it. Do you think there will be?"

"I still want to resign," Ainslie said. "Any usefulness I ever hoped to have here is destroyed now."

Bulstrode shook his head. "What you said today was fine. It was the plain truth and nothing but the truth. If you offer your resignation to the P.M. I'm going to advise him not to accept it. I've been here more than thirty years and I've seen them come and go. You're too sensitive. They're like a pack of barking dogs. And there's another thing—if you resign over this it will mean that you

277

accept—and that *I* accept—this guilt-by-association stuff that's half-ruined democracy in the States. No, Alan—you stay where you are and hold your chin up."

Ainslie shook his head miserably. "I was a fool to think someone like me could do any good here. I've been out of joint with the time. Two or three years from now, if the country holds together that long—"

"Don't you worry, it will."

"Anyway, at the moment it's too sour to listen and it's looking around for scapegoats. There's something new in the country and I wish I understood what it is. Every newspaper and broadcasting station is going to carry the story that my son is a separatist, and in the West a lot of people will believe that I was in league with him. You know exactly what I'm talking about because you were talking about it yourself. I love the West. I love it for what the people have done and for what everyone knows it's bound to become. But when I was last out there I was frightened. I had the feeling that a handful of the operators wouldn't mind selling out. It would be a Jacob-Esau deal, but the mess of pottage would still be worth hundreds of millions of dollars. How else can anyone explain why every sample of bad news from Quebec is blown up to ten times its natural size out there? It's because some of them are looking for an excuse to opt out, isn't it?"

"You're wrong about that," Bulstrode said heavily.

"I hope I am. But I have the idea that I've done ten times more harm than good just because of what happened this afternoon. The papers are going to have a field day with it. I can see the headlines now."

Bulstrode growled, his bear-like torso bunched itself and the enormous muscles of his back strained his suit drumtight so that Ainslie wondered if its seams were going to burst.

"The press! They've twisted everything I've said and done for years. They'll say anything about people who try to govern this country just to sell their papers. I know who these operators are you're talking about. They won't get away with it. The rich English of Montreal tried to sell out more than a hundred years ago and did they get away with it? When I think of the future of this country —when I think of the challenge God has given us here— it's going to hold. It's going to hold if I have to hold it together with these two hands, and that includes Quebec too."

Bulstrode's face was flushed and the veins were swollen in his temple. He shook his head and rubbed his bald scalp and looked puzzled. "Do you ever have the sensation of an electric current inside your head? It's a very funny feeling. It's gone now. I expect it's nothing. But whenever I think of those—those"—he leaned forward—"now listen carefully, Alan. This is hard but it's got to be said. Your boy is expendable but you aren't. Maybe you don't understand politics from a hole in the ground, but you've got a clean character and that's more than—I could tell you a lot about some of them—listen, Alan, just about every clever man in this country thinks I'm a hick and maybe he's right, but if there's one thing I've always been able to see it's been something so obvious that clever people don't see it at all. I trust the common sense of the ordinary citizen. I trust his decency and I trust his, his—His wife bites his ear off, he has ungrateful kids, his car's always breaking down on him, the prices go up on him all the time, the boss is on his neck and what else can he do but grit his teeth and take it? Okay." Bulstrode scratched his ear. "Now do we see what I'm getting at? Anyone can see you don't know your way around here, but at the same time a lot of people are going to like you for that. They don't know their way around, either. So let the dogs bark and bite. If they do, they'll end up by having their own heads chewed off—and by whom? By the ordinary voters of this country." Bulstrode grinned. "You know this fellow Tarnley—Herbert Tarnley I was telling you about—the one who was at me to use a team of his own hand-picked econo-

279

mics experts—I happen to know he's the one who started this idea about getting a fund to pension me off." Bulstrode's grin broadened. "Well, I'm not *going* to be pensioned off. And so long as I stay right where I am, so long as I just *stay* here"—now the grin was as wide as a pumpkin's at Halloween—"just what can any of them do? I ask you—what can they do?"

But when Ainslie left Bulstrode, and fought his way through the flock of reporters waiting for him, telling them nothing, he felt numb. When he reached his room he was afraid to leave it, though it was only mid-afternoon. He picked up the phone and called Chantal in Montreal and tears entered his eyes when he heard the tenderness in her voice.

"Dad, was it very bad for you today? I just heard a little about it over the radio. Was it awful?"

"It was pretty bad. Do you know where Daniel is?"

"I haven't seen him all day."

"His show has been cancelled."

"Thank God for that! Did Bulstrode do it?"

"Yes." A pause. "I'm afraid it will only make him hate me worse than he seems to anyway."

Chantal nearly sobbed. "Don't say that, Dad. He doesn't. I know he doesn't hate you. He's so mixed up he doesn't know where he is or what he's doing. Can you get away from that awful place and come home?"

"There'll be a night session and I'll have to be in my place. I tried to resign but Bulstrode wouldn't hear of it. He was extraordinarily kind. I can't stay here much longer, but he's probably right that I shouldn't give up under pressure. If I go now, some people will be sure to take it as proof that I've been in league with the separatists all along and had been working a fifth column inside the government. Bulstrode never mentioned that, but politically he's uncannily astute and he understood it all right. Listen, dear—I'd like to think of something happy. Remember my suggestion that you get Gabriel to drive you

280

up to the cottage and weed the garden? Why don't you do it this weekend? I'd like to think of you there."

Chantal hesitated before she said, "As a matter of fact, that's what we'd planned to do anyway. I'm waiting for Gabriel now."

"That will be lovely," Ainslie said.

He lay down and tried to rest, and after a fashion he did so. He must have been dozing for nearly an hour before he was wakened by the telephone.

"You fink!" Daniel said to him.

"What?"

"I said, you fink."

Shocked and confused, Ainslie said, "It was Bulstrode who cancelled your show, not me. For your sake I'm sorry, but—"

"But what? But what?"

Ainslie pulled himself together. "Daniel, there was nothing else he could have done. In his position, I'd have had to do the same thing."

A wild laugh reached Ainslie from the other end of the line. "Isn't that just wonderful! So at last I know. I know exactly the truth. This is a wonderful day for me, Dad—a wonderful day. I'm going to remember it as long as I live and I'll celebrate it instead of my birthday."

"Daniel—Daniel boy, don't!"

"Good old Dad—always in there trying!"

"Daniel—this world is a hard place. For God's sake, listen to me. I beseech you to listen to me. You can't even begin to guess what the odds are against you. The only way a civilized man can survive and function is to live like Robin Hood. That's what you've been trying to do yourself—live like a civilized man and make a world that's civilized and not raw material for computers and exploiters. But you haven't learned how to fight yet. It's guerrilla warfare, don't you see? You've got to know every track in the forest, you've got to know every cave to lie up in, for you're outnumbered and outgunned a thousand to one. You haven't a chance the way you're going. For God's sake, get out of it before it's too late. No matter what you think of me, get out of it! If we can hang on in this country—if we can hang on a little longer—we'll at least be at the beginning of making it a country the whole world will look up to. We'll give ourselves a chance to escape the unforgivable sin of throwing away the talent that is death to hide. But you've got to learn some more. Go abroad as I—"

Ainslie heard the receiver click and sat on the edge of the bed with his forehead in his hands. Then he drank some whiskey and, though it was very little, it affected him immediately and he looked half-dazed when the waiter from room-service knocked on the door and entered with a tray. He had forgotten that he had ordered dinner to be served in his room. The waiter looked at him shrewdly. He had worked in this city for years, but Ainslie failed to notice the experienced, almost the professional, assessment in his eyes.

After dinner Ainslie changed and returned to the House. He took his seat but nobody spoke to him or asked him any more questions from the floor.

EIGHT

SATURDAY WAS another beautiful day, warm and sunny with a mild breeze, and Alan Ainslie drove across the river into the Gatineau country and had lunch in the summer cottage of old friends from his civil-service days. They were Marion and Angus Sutherland and Marion's youngest sister Laura, who had been engaged when very young to an airman who had been killed in the war, and had never married afterwards. She had always been fond of Constance and himself and she was still an attractive woman with only a little gray in her hair. It occurred to him that it was not entirely an accident that Laura was there at the same time as himself. She told him she had flown up from Toronto early that morning.

The afternoon wore on. They swam in the lake and rested on the screened porch; they talked of the usual things people talk about when most of their working lives have been connected with government, but while the four of them were together no mention was made of Daniel or of what had happened in the House the day before. The whole country, of course, knew about it by this time; at least everybody who read a newspaper or listened to news reports on the networks.

About four o'clock Angus and Marion said they were sleepy and went upstairs to lie down, and Ainslie and Laura were left alone on the veranda. Cicadas were sirening in the woods and it was warm.

"Poor Alan—it's been hell, hasn't it?"

"I looked at myself in the glass this morning and said, 'Is that really you?'"

Her face was full of sympathy and admiration; her expression was an invitation to him to join her on the sofa where she was sitting.

"I hate to see you discouraged like this. You, of all people. It makes me terrified for the country if you're discouraged."

"Don't make anything out of that."

"It was never like this before Bulstrode appeared on the scene. When I think of all the hopes we had in the P.M. and look at what's happened to him! What *did* happen to him, do you know?"

"I'm not sure, but I think it's what the doctors call a depression. There's no obvious physiological cause. Or maybe it's something else. I don't know, really."

"Will Bulstrode ever become Prime Minister?"

"I doubt it, somehow."

"He's practically that anyway, isn't he?"

"The Opposition keeps pounding on that, but actually he isn't."

"It's his style I can't stand. He's ruining the country and he's made it impossible for intelligent people to do anything. Everyone I know thinks the same thing."

Ainslie shook his head and smiled quietly. "Everyone in the country is looking for a scapegoat, Laura. If the party loses the next election and a new government takes over, I doubt if you'll find as much change as you expect. Countries may move fast, but people move slow. At least Bulstrode's sincere."

"Sincere!"

"In his way. I always thought I was too. But sincerity may be irrelevant now."

Her lips pursed. "Does that infernal city ruin the self-confidence of every decent person who works in it?"

"It's only because it's where the problems come home to roost and because nobody really understands any more what the problems are. I don't myself."

She looked at him in disbelief. "I can't stand it—you, of all people, talking as though you'd given up!"

He smiled at her. "I've not given up for the country. Not at all. I know this sounds a queer thing to say, but I can't think of any other way of putting it, and I really believe it. I think God is still willing to give us a chance if we'll take it. I think we probably will take it, if time doesn't run out too fast. I'll be out of it, I suppose. For me, personally, the times just happened to be out of joint."

There was a long silence between them and with closed eyes he heard the sirening of the cicadas recede in the drowsy air.

"Lie down on the chaise longue, Alan," he heard her say, and did so.

Smiling up at her, he thought how fond of her he was. Or was it only because she was fond of him and he felt it in her? He closed his eyes and felt her hand gently stroke his forehead and he fell asleep immediately. When he woke, the shadows were long over the lake and he was cool and relaxed. The heat was less and she was still on the veranda. When he stirred, she looked up from a book and smiled.

"You've slept for two and a half hours without moving," she said. "Haven't I been good? I longed to talk to you, but I just sat and read my book like a good little girl."

"Why are you so kind to me, Laura?"

She glanced away. "Kind to you!"

He heard the others stirring and the clink of glasses and the clucking sound of shaken ice cubes. Soon Angus and Marion appeared with a tray of drinks and a plate of hors d'oeuvres. Ainslie had no desire to drink anything, but to keep them company he accepted a Cinzano and sat still, speaking occasionally, and afterwards at dinner he was abstracted. When they had finished their coffee he left them with thanks, kissing Marion on the forehead before he stepped into his car. It was only after he had recrossed

285

the river and saw before him the pile of Parliament almost golden in the last rays of the level sun that he decided to drive to Montreal.

Two and a half hours later he was driving up the familiar road winding up the side of the mountain and saw the city undulating in cascades of light like a vast Montmorency down to the river with the new skyscrapers standing up dark and austere out of the light-wash. He ached for Constance. He saw her beside him speaking, but he could not hear what she said. He parked his car and went up to the apartment that had been one of their homes.

NINE

A FAINT light was burning in the living room but nobody was there.

"Chantal!" he called.

There was no answer and he supposed that Chantal was still at the lake with Gabriel.

"Daniel—are you here?"

Again there was silence. He dropped his briefcase on the floor and walked along the corridor to the back of the apartment. Chantal's door was open, he flicked on the light and saw the room was empty. He flicked it off again, knocked on Daniel's door, which was closed, opened it when there was no answer and it was empty too. Then he went into his study at the end of the corridor, sat down at his desk and picked up the telephone. He had always been able to remember Gabriel Fleury's number, but now it eluded him and he had to rummage through two columns of Fleurys in the phone book before he found it. After three rings he heard his old friend's voice for the first time in months and a feeling of relief and comfort came to him.

"How good to hear you again, Gabriel! When did you get back from the lake? Is Chantal with you?"

"She's here now, Alan. Do you want to speak to her?"

"In a moment." He laughed. "Well, did you weed the garden?"

"Indeed we weeded it. My fingers are so stiff I can

hardly close them. We were intending to stay another night, but we heard so much jabbering about you on Chantal's transistor that we decided not to. Where are you now, in Ottawa?"

"No, I'm here. It's so good to be home after all that."

"Then you did resign? We heard on the news that you did."

"I don't understand why they said that on the news. I haven't looked at a paper or listened to a broadcast all day. No, I haven't resigned yet. I came home because I wanted to see Chantal. I wanted to see you too. Is it too late for you to come around? It's pretty late, but it's a while to midnight yet."

"You must be awfully tired, Alan. Why don't I just drive Chantal home and leave her? I can always see you tomorrow."

"I'm not tired at all. I slept for two and a half hours on Angus Sutherland's veranda this afternoon. It was the best sleep I've had in months and I feel as fresh as a daisy. Do come over, Gabriel."

There was a pause, then Gabriel said, "All right, I will. There's something I want to tell you anyway. Can you give us three-quarters of an hour? The reason being that we're in the middle of a very late supper."

With a lift of happiness Ainslie put up the receiver. As he had drunk nothing all day but a small Cinzano, he poured himself a mild scotch and water and returned with it to his study. He took out of his briefcase a few letters marked "personal" which he had thrust into it before leaving his office that morning for the Sutherlands and now he opened them. To his astonishment the first one he opened was from Herbert Tarnley:

Dear Ainslie:

You may recall meeting me several times in the early days of the war when you were with External. Since then I have followed your career—if you will forgive me putting it this way—with a certain wonder at its apparent disinterestedness. I am also one of the few men who know of the role you played in those negotiations with the Russians, and I may have done you a minor service once by persuading an eminent American that you were not what he called "soft on communism."

I am not going to refer to your experience in the House today beyond expressing my respect for your dignity and my agreement with your diagnosis of what is chiefly wrong with modern society. I was greatly impressed by your statement that nearly everyone sees the present with the eyes of the past. These were my own words exactly. That is of course the trouble with politics and I see no cure for it.

As Mr. Bulstrode may still be your chief, I will not say more on this subject than that the world he sees is not the world I see, at the same time admitting that I, too, see the world with the eyes of the past. If the Opposition regains power, their so-called left wing will of course seek to promote policies they were taught to think of as advanced when they were students thirty or forty years ago. They will seek to treat the beri-beri by intensifying the diet which produced it in the first place—in fact, they will make no other diet possible.

As I own several newspapers, I do not take as necessarily authentic the press statement I just read that you intend to resign over the weekend. But if you do so intend, and are at loose ends, I want very much to see you because I have something in mind.

I have never been one for uplift because experience has taught me that it is futile to cajole people into being better or more intelligent than their natures and abilities permit them to be. Our educators—they long ago ceased calling themselves teachers—think otherwise, and our present educational system is their monument.

289

A tragic experience within my own family—the death of my son four days ago by his own hand—convinces me that the chief cause of the blind revolt and unparalleled frustration among today's young is a mass education which robs them of all initiative, teaches the incompetent just enough to make them discontented, and so frustrates the competent that they seethe and hate the world. This leads to the very outrages you referred to in your speech today in the House, to which our legislators, according to the newspapers, listened in embarrassed silence, as well they might.

I have therefore decided to do something. I wish to found and endow a small college with ample scholarships and the best teachers I can obtain. I think I can pay enough to afford the best, though it is always possible that inflation will subsequently wreck the enterprise. It will make no difference to me what class of society a student comes from so long as he is capable of proving himself in tough subjects. I wish him also to associate with experienced men who love their subjects and who, I believe, find themselves increasingly useless in our so-called major universities where they must deal with the swarms of ungraded students processed in and out of them by the modern educational bureaucracy. Once the universities went to the state for money, it was inevitable that this would happen. I would be the first to admit, however, that our present educational system is the best training ground for consumers that any society has contrived to create. I admit, in short, that I have indirectly profited by it enormously.

My experiment, as I well know, may turn out to be nothing more than a modern monastery, and may actually be immoral. I mean, it might easily make its students unfit to compete in modern society. But the ancient monasteries did, after all, afford a refuge to dedicated men, and preserved at least the seeds of civilization in an earlier age of gullibility.

I have you in mind as warden of my college, because I not only want a scholarly man, but one who has spent a lifetime in various fields of government and knows at first hand what it is really like. The matter is not pressing immediately, but I would like to hear from you within the next few weeks.

Sincerely yours,
Herbert Tarnley

Ainslie stared at the signature and suddenly laughed aloud. "Good God! And they call me *naïve*! Can he possibly believe it's as simple as that?"

He glanced at his watch and realized that Gabriel and Chantal would be here within half an hour. Deciding to wash and put on a fresh shirt and dressing gown, he pressed the light-switch beside the closed door leading into the master bedroom which adjoined the study. When he opened the door the room was dark; its only illumination was the single shaft of light coming from the gooseneck lamp on his study desk.

"What's this?" he muttered. "I just turned on the light in this room."

He heard a stealthy movement, saw a shadow move, stepped back and again touched the light-switch outside the door. Into his eyes jumped the wide double bed, the coverlet laid over it but badly rumpled as though it had been replaced in a hurry. In the far corner, fully dressed, with a white face, stood Daniel. Beside him was an older woman Ainslie had never seen before, also fully dressed but with untidy hair and a face expressing something between shame and resignation, a knowing about everything very suddenly and at the same time knowing it was too late.

Something snapped in Ainslie and he leaped at Daniel with his fists clenched and raised. Daniel, hands at his sides, frozen, eyes horrified, awaited him motionless. Ainslie's fist moved and in his brain was a flash of light and a silent voice shouting, "Not you too—no, not you—for God's sake not you too!" and his fist stopped in mid-air as the muscle refused to drive it. His hands loosened and fell to his sides like weights. His shoulders sagged and he turned to go back to his study.

"Get out," he said quietly, "both of you."

He sat at his desk and stared straight at the wall in front of him. Ice had formed over his skin, but inside of him was the static tension that exists when a pair of hand-wrestlers are locked palm-to-palm with their elbows on a table. Through the drumming in his head came a woman's voice speaking French.

"Monsieur Ainslie, I respect you so much I would rather have died than this."

Ainslie neither moved nor spoke and the drumming continued in his head.

"Monsieur, I am not a woman entirely without dignity or decency."

Slowly he turned, and when he looked at her it was a recognition—Europe, the occupations and liberations, the gentle, the civilized who had lived through them.

"I recognize that, Mademoiselle. Or is it Madame?"

"I am a widow," she said.

"Then, Madame, perhaps you might leave us now?"

Ainslie again faced the wall and heard her going away. He heard the outer door close quietly and he remained motionless until the drumming inside of his head died out. Then he turned slowly around and lifted his eyes to Daniel and saw in his son's face the expression of a person who does not know whether he is awake or asleep or alive or on the point of death. He looked at him with a wonder which—it occurred to him only afterwards in recall—was actually a wonder at himself. He breathed deeply several times and when at last he spoke his voice was level and quiet.

"Daniel, I think all I have been really trying to do with

my life was to make the meaning of your mother's life and mine a reality in the country we live in. So far as I am concerned, I mean in my own work, you have destroyed any meaning my work might have had. When I was all alone and my back was to the wall, you struck at me. When I offered you again the love I always tried to offer you, you threw it into my face. You called me ineffectual. You have certainly helped to make me so." Ainslie's face seemed totally divided between its good and bad side and his artificial eye looked like the glass it was made of. "God knows why you set out to do this to me. But why did you set out to destroy yourself at the same time? You should at least give me some respect, if only for your own sake, for having tried to warn you against what you were doing to yourself."

Daniel's mouth opened and his throat muscles quivered but no sound came. It was as if his saliva had dried up.

"Chantal and Gabriel are on their way here at this very moment," Ainslie said. "I don't want you here when they arrive. So leave now, Daniel. You are on your own now. Go wherever you like. Do whatever you like. You will do it anyway."

He looked at Daniel steadily and the boy's eyes were filled with tears and terror.

"I'm not going to say another word to you now about this. I can't. Perhaps I never can."

Ainslie turned to the wall again. He heard a rush of feet, a stumbling of feet, and the crash of a slammed door.

"He's gone off with the terror in him," Ainslie said to the wall.

He was still staring at the wall when Chantal and Gabriel came in and found him there.

TEN

Now IN the night, hardly seeing, Daniel was driving his car, feeling nothing but a constriction in his chest his hands not tactile on the wheel in the labyrinth of streets in the old part of the city near the canal and the river in and out and back and forth, the car darting like a snake into one street after another with tires screaming and the exhaust roaring and then a great rushing swoosh into the tunnel underneath the canal and up and out again and still that car with the three men in it was behind him. He went twisting up the ramp and charged with a whining engine and a hammering exhaust onto the bridge, lights reflected in the St. Lawrence, the toll gates ahead, and he aimed at an empty one and shot straight through it, the clang of a bell announcing that he had not paid his toll and still the car with the three men was behind him. Off the bridge and faster and faster up to ninety-five miles an hour and he was on the autoroute leading east into the valley of the Richelieu and still the headlights of the car with the three men in it were behind him. The little triangular red shields marking the miles flicked past him and the shaking of his car was like the shaking in his brain, was the prelude to the obliteration that would come when the bomb exploded and he himself would cease to exist in the final flash. Then directly in front of him, leaping into his eyes in front of him, was a low wall and just as he wondered what it was he saw it was three police cars parked horizontally across the autoroute in a road block with policemen waving flashlights in front of them. "They're not my target, they're not my—"

His reflexes took over. The tires screamed under the brakes, the car twisted and swerved back and forth and nearly turned over, the wall of cars leaped at him and the policemen jumped clear, but when he hit the outside car his speed was down to ten miles an hour. There was a wrenching crash, the steering post struck his chest, there was a crack on his forehead but the light he saw was not the final flash. . . .

"All right, he's not hurt."

"I thought he was going straight through us," one of the patrolmen said. "What is it—a bank?"

"No, it's not a bank."

A quick hand reached into the sports car for the little suitcase. A flashlight played on it and a pair of quick hands snapped it open.

"He had it all right. I was pretty sure he had it. Take a look at it, Gaston, and tell me what you think of it."

The man called Gaston, working fast under the powerful flashlight, made a few movements and stood back and wiped his forehead.

"It can't do any harm now," he said.

"What kind of a job was it anyhow?"

"I've seen worse, but not many worse. Whoever rigged this one learned it out of a book, that's for sure. But what a load! Fifteen sticks."

Another of the road police came up and said to the wiry little man in plain clothes, "This bastard's wrecked the side of my car. I can't drive it."

"I guess you can't, at that."

Looking at the dismantled bomb, the patrolman whistled. *"Tabernacle!* If that punk had hit us full speed, what would have happened?"

"What *would* have happened, Gaston?" the wiry man said.

"Full speed with this in his car and we wouldn't be talking to any of you now."

295

The patrolman drew back. "If it wasn't a bank, what was it? Is this type one of the crazy ones?"

"For the time being I guess he was." The wiry man turned to Daniel who was sitting so still he seemed to be unconscious. "Can you move now, Daniel?"

The boy made no answer and the man again turned to the autoroute patrolmen.

"If you want to go back on the job now it's all right. Thanks once more." To the one whose car was damaged he said, "I'm sorry about your car, but without you men we'd never have caught him unless he ran out of gas before we did." Seeing a question-mark in the man's expression, he continued. "It's like this. I had the speed, but if I'd run up beside him I was afraid he'd turn into me and we'd all buy it. But nobody's going to crash a wall if it's suddenly in front of him and he doesn't expect it. His reflexes won't let him."

The patrolmen attached a chain to the damaged car and towed it to the side of the road and left it there with its parking lights on. Then they got into the other two cars and drove off, one of them taking the first turn-off and heading back toward Montreal, the other continuing east. Some fifteen private cars were stationary behind them, and with a few flicks of his flashlight the wiry man waved them on through. Then he turned back to the sports car.

"Well, Daniel," Joe Lacombe said, "you and I've met before." He turned the flashlight full onto his own face. "Don't you recognize me?"

Daniel nodded and Lacombe put his hand on his shoulder. "Get into my car now, Daniel." To the other two men who had been with him in the pursuit he said, "Georges, will you come along with me? Gaston, will you drive that sports car back to town? You can have the bomb too, Gaston. It's all yours."

On their return home, Lacombe driving and Daniel beside him, the man called Georges in the back seat leaning forward and keeping an eye on Daniel, nobody spoke until they reached the bridge. Lacombe drove very slow and relaxed, at least ten miles an hour below the minimum speed allowed on the autoroute, and car after car swished past them on the left. The lights of Montreal were spectacular when they drove in over the bridge, and finally Lacombe began to talk.

"Did you ever know that your father saved my life once, Daniel? He saved Mr. Fleury's life too. He saved the lives of all of us in the plane that night. What made you do this to him?"

Daniel was shivering and Lacombe could hear his teeth chatter.

"What's going to happen to me?" he whispered.

"I guess that's going to depend on the judge, Daniel."

"Do you hate me, Mr. Lacombe?"

The lights on the river were ripples of gold interspersed with the reflected crimson of neon signs.

"What difference does it make whether I do or not? But there's one thing I'd sure as hell like to know from you. You've been to college and that's more than I ever was, but what gave you and the rest of you kids the idea you could get away with a crazy thing like this? As for the guy who gave you the bomb—"

They left the bridge and, as soon as Lacombe found a place in a lower street where he could park, he stopped the car. He lit a cigarette and switched on the light in the car's roof and turned and studied Daniel, his trained eyes scrutinizing the scared young face. Then slowly he shook his head.

"You know, Daniel, in my line of work I've met all kinds of them by this time. Most of them I can tell from their eyes and mouths and sometimes by their ears, but the ones I always move first on I don't even have to look at." He put both hands on his stomach. "I don't have to look at them because I feel them right in here." Again he shook his head. "You know, Daniel, underneath you aren't any crazier than anyone else." And he added thoughtfully, "That's what really scares me."

With a wondering laugh, Lacombe set the car in motion again.

Epilogue

For a period of several days Alan Ainslie went through the mechanisms of a man in a state of partial amnesia. He did certain things he understood were necessary, but he observed the results of them as though he were in a sound-proof room looking through a window at people moving outside, seeing their hands make silent gestures and their mouths open and close without sounds.

After learning from Joe Lacombe that Daniel had been arrested with a bomb and had admitted his intention of planting it in a public building, Ainslie sent a telegram to the Prime Minister submitting his resignation to the government. Later in the same day he read a newspaper despatch from Ottawa stating that his resignation had been received. In the same paper, under a huge headline, a despatch from Montreal announced that his son had been arrested with a bomb.

The next morning he learned from the paper that the Prime Minister, after consultation with Bulstrode and other members of the cabinet, had reluctantly accepted his resignation and had offered the vacant portfolio to Laurent Saint-Just. He presumed that the Prime Minister had tried to reach him by telephone before making this announcement public, but he would never know for sure because he had gone into hiding. He was living anonymously in a rooming house; the arrangements for this had been made by Joe Lacombe so that no reporters could find him.

That afternoon he read in another newspaper an official statement from Ottawa denying the earlier report that the portfolio had been offered to Saint-Just. The active part of his mind recorded what must have happened: Bulstrode, unable to imagine anyone refusing a cabinet post if it were offered to him, had released the announcement to the press only to discover later that Saint-Just would not touch it. Ainslie wondered, with a distant affection for the man, how much longer it would be before Saint-Just left the government benches and took his seat as an independent member as a preliminary to leaving the federal government entirely and enlisting in the politics of his own province.

The next day Ainslie read that the Prime Minister had dissolved the Ministry for Cultural Affairs and that Bulstrode, who announced the decision to the House, had used it as an occasion for mounting a furious attack on the Opposition, accusing them of having deliberately wrecked, for cheap political purposes, "a bold and unique experiment in the continuing battle for national unity, a battle which would be won despite all waverings and failures in faith ... etc. Seldom in the history of this parliament has a more vicious, irresponsible or cynical display of wrecking for wrecking's sake been ... etc. Let them understand that their records will be scrutinized, and that by their deeds shall they be ... etc. History is a great teacher and history will ... etc., etc., etc."

During this period Ainslie saw Chantal and Gabriel, but only for a few minutes. Haltingly they told him—he had already sensed it in their looks and faces—that they loved one another. Though he loved them both, the walls of his life and meaning dissolved around him. He did not return to Ottawa. He wrote Chantal a note telling her that he wished to be alone for a time, and then he quietly disappeared.

"He's gone away from us all," Chantal said. "He's never done anything like this before. He must be trying to bury himself inside of himself. Oh, Gabriel—if he dies, it's Daniel who's responsible! The pathetic little fool!" She stopped and looked at Gabriel. "Is it really my brother who's done this to him?"

Gabriel looked at her with pity but did not speak.

"Daniel in prison and he's still a child! What will they do to him?"

"His bomb never exploded"—Gabriel shrugged—"in the present mood they'll let him off as lightly as they can."

"Nobody could ever tell that boy anything. What was the use of me even trying to?" Her eyes filled with tears. "If I thought it was us who'd done this to Dad I think I'd die. Why were we unable to help him? To love a person and be unable to help him—that's the most terrible thing in the world."

"I suppose that's why so many people these days are afraid to love anyone at all." He looked away. "Sex without love—it's been tried often enough before, God knows."

"What was Dad's real trouble?"

Gabriel lifted his hands and dropped them. "Too many things happened to him all at once, I suppose. There's a limit to what anyone can take."

"It's more than that," she said.

He went to the open door and looked out at the garden. The air was cool; the first flowers had gone over and the ones of late summer were in bud.

"When a man tries to do something positive in the world," he said slowly, "he's safe so long as he can believe the shadows are real. Until this year I always thought that Alan could."

"What's the use of talking any more about anything? Words, words—trillions of them every day. Everybody fighting with his mouth everywhere."

He turned back to her. "Alan understands better than

303

any of us what has arrived. That feeling he always had about this country—at the moment it may come close to being the psychic center of the world. This city, anyway. He even said a little of it in the House. Not all of it, of course. Not there of all places. But I think he suddenly realized that what's happening here is happening everywhere. If it could come to a country as innocent as this one was, you can be sure it's everywhere. The disguises may be different, but whatever it is, it's the same."

Youth seemed to fade out of her face. "I can't bear it. Dad gone into nowhere and Daniel locked up like an insect in one of those dreadful prisons we have in this country! I'm still only twenty-five, but when I think of Daniel and those friends of his I feel like seventy. What's going to happen, Gabriel?"

"I don't know," he said.

For weeks Alan Ainslie drove around the country alone. He went down to the Atlantic Coast and to the island where he was born. He smelled the alders beside the trout streams and the clover beside the roads and the seaweed along the shores and looked at the ruddy faces of people who did not know what was happening and would not understand it if they did. He spent his nights in motels and tourist homes and on each occasion he registered under the name of Alan MacNeil. Often he left his car to stroll in the woods or sit on empty beaches looking out over the sea as he had done as a boy when he had tried to imagine the famous cities beyond the ocean his unknown forbears had crossed, and had dreamed that if he studied and worked enough, if he became sufficiently intelligent and honorable, one day he might earn the right to sit, if only below the salt, at the same table with their excellent men.

After a time he drove back into the interior, never sure at the end of one day where he would go the next, but the main road led westerly and he followed it. Bypassing Montreal and Ottawa he followed the Trans-Canada Highway across the Shield and along the north shore of Lake Superior, then past Lake of the Woods until he emerged onto the black earth plain of Manitoba. The wheat was just beginning to turn golden and the wind ruffled it. Solitary grain elevators bisected the permanent line where sky and prairie met. He rolled westward across the open land into the Rockies and suddenly he found himself easing his car through a swarm of friendly, middle-aged Americans feeding popcorn to bears in a national park. He continued through the ranges to the Pacific Coast and after a day beside salt water he doubled back north-easterly and took the new highway all the way down to Great Slave Lake. It was early in September before he returned to his cottage in the Laurentians and found it empty.

The first morning there he walked to the hamlet for supplies and spoke with some of the local people he had known for years and they were all glad to see him. When they asked after Chantal, whom they had known since she was a little girl, he told them she was soon going to be married. Then old Monsieur Provencher, teeth very white in a wrinkled face the color of a hazel nut, broke into a smile.

"Now that's good, Monsieur Ainslie."

Ainslie smiled back at him. "Yes, I think it's good."

"Do you remember my seventh daughter? *Ma p'tite gosseline,* Stéphanie? Tomorrow she gets married to young Elzéor Laberge. Slow maybe, but a good boy. We did not know you were here. Will you come to the wedding, Monsieur Ainslie? It would give us all so much pleasure."

"It would give me more."

After leaving the church the next day, the wedding party continued into the evening with eating and drinking and dancing and songs, there was the happiness of people who knew all about one another and liked each other in spite of this, and it was quite late by the time Ainslie returned to his cottage. The first tang of autumn was in the air and his breath was visible in it; soon the leaves would change and fall, the woods would be bare, then the long snows would come.

The moon was nearly full over the lake and the white phlox in the garden were tall and fragrant. The garden had grown well after the weeding done by Gabriel, Chantal and himself early in the summer; they had got the weeds out at the crucial moment and nature had done the rest. Sitting on the veranda he watched the moon-path on the lake and the promontories emerging sharp out of the forest and the occasional cloud shadow shuddering over the water like a gigantic bird in flight. It was too cold to sit there long and he went inside and built a log fire and sat in his usual chair beside the hearth. Opposite was the chair where Constance had sat when the days were ended and the children had gone to bed.

The fire crackled and threw flickering lights along the pine boards of the walls and Constance seemed to be there again. How strange—was it wonderful or was it not? —he would never know what she would have looked like had she been permitted to grow old! The whiteness and litheness of her youth, the warmth and movement of her youth. Only occasionally in a dream a few of her realities returned: the actual sound of her curiously husky voice, her actual presence warm enough to touch as she came up the cottage steps with a basket of wildflowers. Each of them had lived together believing they had perfectly known one another and all the time both had been secrets even to themselves. Now thank we all our God! A coolness had entered his mind at last, a warmness had come back to his soul, a long sequence of images of the land he had crossed passed through him and a strange little smile appeared on his lips.

"One more step would have freed us all, but the sphinx returned."

Images of the land: the long wash of the decisive ocean against the granite; sunlight spangling the mist over the estuary the old navigator had mistaken for the Northwest Passage leading to the indispensable dream; the prairie wind almost as visible above the wheat as ruffling through it; the antlers of a bull elk cascading down the side of a Rocky Mountain; arrows of wild geese shooting off into the twilight over the delta of the Athabasca ...

"Chantal and Daniel, if I do not love you I don't know what it is that I feel now."

He went to the window and saw lake and forest married in perfect silence.

The vast land. Too vast even for fools to ruin all of it.

He went outside and walked in the cold air to the water and heard himself say in a normal voice, "The sphinx has returned to the world before, after all."

The silence was almost audible. Stars too remote to be visited shone down as they had shone on the poets and philosophers, on the generations who had loved them, on the mariners who had used them long before it was known that the stars, too, were trapped in equations.

"When I see you in prison, Daniel, will you mock me when I tell you that God Himself may have sent Joe Lacombe after you that night?"

Looking over the lake he at last accepted that he had merely happened into all this. Constance, Chantal, Daniel, Gabriel—they and all the others had merely happened into this loveliness that nobody could understand or possess, and that some tried to control or destroy just because they were unable to possess or understand it. Merely happened into this joy and pain and movement of limbs, of hope, fear, shame and the rest of it, the little chipmunk triumphs and defeats. He believed it would endure. He thanked God he had been of it, was of it.

Hugh MacLennan was born in Glace Bay, Nova Scotia, and educated in Canada and England. He lives in Montreal, where he teaches at McGill University. His novels have been published in many countries, and he has five times won the Governor General's Award. His books include *Barometer Rising* (1941), *Two Solitudes* (1945), *Each Man's Son* (1951), *The Watch That Ends the Night* (1959), *Scotchman's Return and Other Essays* (1960), and *Seven Rivers of Canada* (1961).

'The virtue of [Hugh MacLennan's] novel, as of all good literature, is that it brings the illusion of innocence, or moral idealism to the hard test of reality ... There are no easy answers; this is the Return of the Sphinx. A novel that few can afford to miss reading.'

Louis Dudek, Montreal Gazette

'A perceptive, balanced novel ... MacLennan, like any fine artist, universalizes what begins as local.'

Edmund Fuller, Wall Street Journal

'From the first sentence of this lucid, low-keyed book the reader is under Mr. MacLennan's spell ... How marvellous it is to read a literate book again, to hear a well-bred voice, and to be concerned with a problem that calls for no postures on the part of the reader!'

Dayton Rommel, Chicago Daily News

'Here is a novel as powerful and convincing as it is rich in character and colour ... It is a deeply Canadian book ... But it is a work of literature that goes beyond and farther. The tension is between generations, between parents and children, father and son — true for western civilization the world over. Here it is portrayed with humanity and compassion, with understanding intuitive as well as intellectual, by one of the foremost novelists now writing.'

A. L. Rowse

THE LAURENTIAN LIBRARY